To: Pam
Enjoy the story
Race Relations should
not be based on color
but the heart of the

Corporate Deceit

person.

Richard Taylor

Richard Carter

Corporate Deceit

Published by RSVP Elite Publishing
PO Box 210950
Dallas, Texas 75211

This novel is a work of fiction. Names, characters, places and incidents either are the product of the author's imagination or are used fictitiously. Any resemblance to actual persons, living or dead, events, or locales is entirely coincidental.

Book Jacket by MarionDesigns

Library of Congress Cataloging- 2005908293

ISBN 0-9776087-0-0 (Hardcover)
Copyright © 2005 RSVP Elite Publishing
All Rights Reserved
Printed in the United States of America
December 2005
First Edition

Dedication

This book is specially dedicated to my second daughter, LaTonya

and to

Reverend Bobby Ray Morgan
Reverend Carlos Jones
&
Emma Mae (Johnson) Abney

who delivered the message, "Richard, write a book."

Trust in the Lord with all thine heart
and lean not on thine own understanding
In all thy ways acknowledge Him
and He will direct thy paths

Proverbs 3:5-6

1

For Josh, this January morning started just like any other winter morning in Central Texas: cold, damp and with overcast skies. As he started to dress, his thoughts were centered on his meeting scheduled for that morning. This was the signing of the final proposal for an Identity Management System. Three hours from now, Josh's whole world as he knew it would be changed for the better.

As he started to his office, he was rehearsing his opening statement for the final presentation. While driving he noticed how unusually light the traffic was for a Tuesday morning, but immediately he refocused to his presentation.

After arriving into the office, he was elated to run into his division's President. Now he could share with Chuck the news of what his team was doing as well as highlight the meeting that he was preparing for today. All employees were aware that some folks had more favor than others in the corporation, but Josh felt there was no way upper management could not recognize his abilities and the impact of his labor when this deal was signed.

Chuck was very interested to fully understand what Josh's project entailed and insisted that Josh would call his admin and schedule time for them to meet. Walking on cloud nine as he entered the building, Josh in his usual manner greeted everyone he passed with his broad smile and positive attitude, bellowing, "Good Morning". After settling into his office, he checked his voice mail to make sure there were no last-minute cancellations.

He double-checked his to-do-list in his day-timer to make sure he had a clear grasp of his day. After verifying all he had to do, he hurried to the assigned conference room to make sure everything was in place. He checked with his assistant to see if she had any cancellations and if she had picked up the brochures and hand outs. She confirmed with him that everything was in place and told him to calm down. He heeded her advice and decided he would meditate privately in his office until it was time for the meeting to begin.

At seven forty-five an email notification popped up on his computer. So he opened the message, and it read:

To   : Josh Harrington
From : Alex Mann
Cc   : Paul Copeland
Subject :

Josh,

Please be available for a meeting at 9:15 in my office.

Alex

Corporate Deceit

"*Strange,*" he thought. "*What in the world does Alex want to talk about this morning? We met last night and discussed the whole plan for today and I really don't have the time for anything else until I gets this deal signed.*" But a strange feeling came over him that left him feeling somewhat perplexed due to the wording in the email. Hell, he would just call Alex on his cell phone and maybe whatever he wants can be handled over the phone. Alex is not the best time management person. He had a reputation of turning a fifteen or twenty-minute meeting into forty-five minutes if he got off track and Josh felt his meeting today was too important.

Ring………… Ring……………….. Ring………… Ring………………,
"You have reached the voice mailbox for Alex Mann. Please leave a detailed message including a phone number and I will get back to you shortly."
Beep…………………………….

Josh pondered for a minute of how odd it was for Alex not to answer his cell phone, but then maybe he is on another call. He would just call his office, and leave a message concerning this impromptu meeting.

Josh tried very hard to dismiss the thoughts that were running through his head concerning Alex and what was so important that he needed to speak with him before his meeting. He reopened the meeting request and at that moment noticed that Paul Copeland was copied. Why would Alex need to meet with both Paul and him? True, Paul was his manager, but with the exception of his monthly staff meeting he didn't have a clue about what he was doing. Paul is also too busy kissing up to Alex that he has given all of his direct reports the freedom to do their jobs. In Josh's mind this was great because being micromanaged drove him crazy and Paul's management style allowed him to create his own destiny. Oh well, Alex will call in a moment and he can answer any last minute questions that he has, if that is what he wants.

Just as he began to refocus on the meeting, a thought popped into his head, "No damn way would Alex be trying to get me to share with Paul the recognition of putting this deal together!" If this is Alex's plan, he had done everything to put this deal together. No, he must be losing his mind, Alex has always been fair. He would get the credit so why was he worrying he told himself. Maybe what he needed was a cup of coffee or something to soothe his nerves. He was losing it, and in about an hour, he would have ten division managers from within the corporation, and vice-presidents from existing clients, all pledging a half million dollars a piece to fund this project, so he needed to gather himself.

What will this deal mean to him? By the end of the day, he should be a division manager in the corporation and a member of the technical advisory committee with all of the associated fringe benefits. Should he join a club close to his house or one closer to his office? Now, those are the types of problems Josh wanted to focus his attention to instead of pondering what Alex wanted to meet about. Now, with his bonus check, he would take Veronica on a long overdue vacation. He was in his own little world daydreaming about the possible changes of his life and the associated financial rewards when his cell phone began ringing and his thoughts were interrupted.

"Josh, are you in the office yet? And if so, have you had a chance to check your emails this morning?" Alex asked.

"I am in my office and I have read your email. What is so important that we need to meet about this morning?"

"Look, why don't you just come on down to my office at 9:15, and we can discuss it then. Paul and I will be there."

"Ok. Do I need anything, since there wasn't a subject in your email? I just don't like going to a meeting without knowing what it is about. Can't you give me a clue on the subject, so I can formulate some questions or answers in my head on my way down?"

"There's no need to do that; just get a cup of coffee and meet us in my office." With that, Alex hung-up the phone never acknowledging Josh's request.

Arriving a few minutes before 8:00 A.M., Alex Mann called Paul Copeland to be sure that Paul was in the office as well. As he dialed Paul's extension, he wondered what in the world they were about to do. He had known Josh for the past six or seven years and the information coming from Paul doesn't match the profile of the guy that Paul is talking about. However, he had to trust those who reported to him directly. There were just too many people to interact with daily one-on-one, so his managers must give him the vital information that he needed, so he could make the right decisions. He places the call to Paul and, as usual, he picks up Alex's call after the first ring.

"Good Morning, Paul. Are you ready?" Alex asked.

"Yes. I am on my way to your office because we are to meet with Human Resources at 8:30 in their area," Paul replied.

"Paul, are you sure you are right about this situation with Josh? Hell, in certain circles he is an icon and is loved by the numerous client contacts he has all over the country; if you are wrong this could get very ugly quickly."

"Yes, I have been watching his activities for the last several months and I am sure that I am right. Hell, so what if it is Josh Harrington, who cares? He was wrong and this time none of those get out of jail cards of his will save him. I am on my way. I will meet you in the main hallway."

Alex heard the phone being hung-up by Paul and he was still hearing Paul's tone in his head. Paul was so cocky in his answers concerning this matter. Alex had heard the allegations and saw the reports that Paul had prepared. The documentation supported the charges, but Alex had an uneasy feeling on why a person with this much tenure would take such a stupid chance with his career? It just didn't add up.

When he got to the main hallway, Paul was standing there waiting for him, looking like a hunter with a twelve-buck deer in his sights. "Ready, Alex? I talked to HR about our concerns and their position is that we have two choices, but I don't think the right message will be given if we try to play this down," Paul stated to his boss.

"What do you mean we have choices?" Alex asked.

"Well, we really don't. What I meant to say was HR is taking their usual stance and won't commit to policy. The representative in Human Resources is wavering on how we should proceed. My option is cut and dry; his ass is out of here today!"

"Did I hear you say his 'ass'?" Alex was very concerned that one of his top managers was showing a side that he didn't think was proper and to publicly say it alarmed him a great deal. Alex made a mental note to speak to Paul about that comment privately as soon as possible.

"You know how Josh can be. He is the first to tell you about who he knows, what he thinks, and does not pull any punches when it comes to not supporting management decisions if they are not to his liking," Paul quickly replied.

"So because Josh is his own man and since he doesn't kiss up to all decisions being made that makes him a bad person or a threat if he is correct?" questioned Alex.

"No, but sometimes you have to go with the majority for the good of the corporation."

"Well, my personal view is no, that isn't true. What you have as a manager is the responsibility to make the best decision available with the information on hand. If the information doesn't provide you with enough facts, then you should either ask for more data or research the subject for yourself."

Alex's brain was on over load because Paul was displaying qualities that concerned him even more. How could such a brilliant engineer such as Paul show so much immaturity concerning his responsibilities as a manager? Was the office talk correct that he had ignored the fact that Paul was immature? Others had felt that the only reason Paul was in the position that he had was because he was Alex's friend?

Another mental note to perform an informal review of Paul's management styles with all of Paul's direct reports was added to his list. The conversation ended abruptly because they had arrived in the HR area.

"Good Morning, gentlemen," Helen Sparks spoke as they entered the conference room that had been reserved for their meeting.

Alex spoke first, "Good Morning, I am Alex Mann and of course you already know Paul."

"Well, actually I have only spoken to Paul on the phone," replied Helen as she held out her hand.

"Well, now you have a face to put with the voice. I am Paul Copeland"

"Well guys, let's get down to business because Paul informed me this morning that you have a meeting with Mr. Harrington in about forty-five minutes. Here is all of the paper work, Paul, and the instructions that you should give Mr. Harrington informing him of his rights," Helen said.

"May I ask a question? Is it Human Resources' position, that we terminate

Josh Harrington?" Alex asked. This had taken him completely off guard, because termination was not an option that he and Paul had discussed.

"We have reviewed the documents and our recommendation is termination. HR and the guidelines from upper management supports that this is the correct resolution to the situation," Helen replied.

"Well, I am taken just a little and I am not defending his actions, but the guy has been here almost ten years. Is there any other recourse besides termination?" Alex asked.

Helen looked confused when she heard Alex's question and she was justified for being baffled. Quickly, she replayed her conversations with Paul. From the beginning of their conversations, she was led to believe that Alex wanted this guy fired. There were to be no written warnings, suspensions, change in job functionality or anything else. She had to gather her thoughts before she answered him because she really didn't know how this could impact her own future if she crossed the wrong people. "Well, because of the offense, I believe that this is the only option available for the corporation."

Helen explained to them the corporation's stance on such matters and that her recommendation was supported by her superiors. She then reviewed the guidelines and procedures concerning such infractions. She wanted them to understand that regardless of the severity of the offense, the penalty was the same.

Paul had to count to ten to keep from smiling because he knew Alex was always politically correct, so if HR said terminate then termination it was. Paul's mind told him to end this meeting quickly before Alex could ask any more questions and throw a monkey wrench in this. "Alex, we better start back toward your office because we have some calls to make prior to our meeting."

"Thanks for taking the time on such short notice, Helen," Alex said as they got up to leave; then he remembered something.

"Oh, by the way, how should we handle this with Josh?"

Again, Helen's brain searched for the correct response. "My thoughts are that you should state your concerns. Inform the gentleman that he will be allowed to ask questions only after you are finished. Explain to him that there is no appeal process and your decision is final. Also inform him of the severance agreement, take his badge and escort him off the grounds. I know I make it sound simple, and there are never any two situations alike, but don't get into a verbal argument with him either."

Leaving her area, Alex was still puzzled about how Helen only looked at one option for this matter. He also wondered why Paul had this look as if he had just landed the largest deal in his life. Strangely the guy was actually smiling, when in Alex's mind this was not something any manager should have been looking forward to doing.

2

As he walked to Alex's office, those same strange feelings began to enter his mind again. Josh could not explain his thoughts, but he was pretty sure that his feelings weren't too far off base. What had he done or not done for Alex not to acknowledge what this meeting was about? The closer he got to the main hallway, the more out of sync his brain felt with his body. To help calm his nerves he placed a call to Veronica.

"Good Morning! Chapman and Chapman! How may I direct your call?"

"May I speak to Veronica please, and how are you this morning, Stephanie?"

"Mr. Harrington? I really didn't catch your voice. Let me see if she is available."

Ring……Ring….

"This is Veronica."

"Hi! And how is your day going this morning?" Josh inquired.

"Oh, hi! My day is going just fine. What about yours?"

"Well, I am still too excited about this meeting in about forty-five minutes, and I am on my way to a last-minute meeting with Alex."

"Well, from the way you have been the last several days trying to make sure that your bases were covered, I think that you are very well prepared to knock socks off."

"Well, I hope your impression is just the prelude of what is to come. By the way, do me a big favor today and I won't take no as an answer."

Veronica could picture him smiling on the other end of the line, so how could she even consider saying no to the man that adored her.

"OK, what is this task that you want me to do? I have to know what I am saying yes to first."

"I want you to go online, and book two tickets to the Islands."

Laughing, she responds, "So for what date and for how long do I book this trip?"

"The date and the length are totally up to you. Now, I have to be back at work within a year. Seriously, if your schedule only permits a week, that is fine, but I am leaning more toward 10 days."

"Ok. And how am I to pay for this?" She asked

"Call my office, and my admin will give you or the travel agent my credit card information. Now, Veronica, do this today. I have been noticing the stress in your eyes, so you are in need of this get-a-way just as much or more than me."

"OK, I will do it."

"Should I call Stephanie this afternoon to see if she has gotten around to booking our flight?" Josh said, laughing.

"I do take care of some things myself, Mr. Smart Pants."

"I know you do, but I want to walk on the beach with you as the sun sets behind the water."

"Ok, I will take care of that if you will take me to lunch."

"Can't commit to that right now because I don't know how long my meeting is going to last. How about you having lunch with a girlfriend or Gayle and I will take you to dinner tonight?"

"Deal, did you read about…."

Cutting her off before she could finish her last statement. "Veronica, I am in front of Alex's office, so I will have to get back to you. Love you!"

"Love you back and good luck in your meeting!"

After Veronica hung-up the phone she quickly posted a note on her computer to call her travel agent later that day. For she knew if she didn't do that right then she would probably forget about it because her focus would be on the other twenty items on her desk. Veronica was in some way just opposite of Josh in both the way she handled her business affairs and in her personality. Strictly a no nonsense kind of person, very logical in thinking— black or white, either it is true or false— there was no gray area in her mental make-up. To her everything was either a debit or a credit— the best way to describe her since she was an accountant. That included her personal life as well; either you were an asset or a liability, and liabilities she quickly got rid of.

In some ways she weighed their relationship in that same manner. Josh was the asset side of the books when they entertained or had an outside engagement because of his personality, and she was the liability because she was more of an introvert. However, on an income statement, she was the asset or the debit column because she took her financial responsibilities seriously whereas Josh had a few too many liabilities for her comfort level she believed. But overall, she continued to see the strengths in him because he had a firm grip on his manhood and wasn't afraid to admit those areas in his life where he could improve.

Veronica thought for a moment that Josh said all of the right things in their brief conversation, but something was missing that she couldn't put her finger on. Oh well, maybe he is too uptight about his meeting, she said to herself. She had seen him over the last six months trying to put this deal together and she had repeatedly told him of the possible promotions that could happen if he could pull this off.

Enough of thinking about Josh; early on in their relationship she told him that she'd rather he did not call her at her office. Her reasoning was that she believed there are times for everything and since she was at work that is where her focus should be.

Just as she was getting her thoughts back to where she was in her client's financial, her assistant walked into her office. "Sorry, Ronnie, to disturb you again, but do you still want to send a plant to Josh, today?"

She looked up with a puzzled look, "What plant and why?" Then she remembered she was totally out of character on last Friday, and she had asked her assistant to remind her to send something to him today because he was signing the contracts for his project. Since he was normally the one to do those types of things, he would never suspect that she would send anything to his office. Hell, he was taken by surprise on his birthday when she had given him a card. Not saying she never did anything in the relationship, for often if she was out shopping, if she saw something that she liked for him, she would buy it. Her philosophy was why wait for some special occasion, any day could be made special if you want it to be.

"Sure, and keep it under seventy-five dollars please. He knows how I feel, so we don't have to get carried away. And besides, he is a man, so make sure it is a plant and not flowers."

Her assistant just smiled and thought, Ronnie, you better be careful and smell the coffee and see what you got. How many women would love to have a man that not only loves them, but adored the ground that they walked too? Girlfriend, somebody is watching and if you ever gave her the chance she would make sure that she would try to rock his world and take that man from you. Hell, I would if I wasn't already married.

Veronica did look up as her assistant was walking out of her office and she felt she knew what she was thinking. Yes, I know what I have, but I also know where I want to go, and if Josh is the one that would be great too. Her feelings were it is great to have someone that makes you happy, but her drive to be successful had some deeper roots beyond those of her love for Josh. Josh had only been in her life for three years, but her ambition had been with her a lot longer.

Enough of Josh, I have taken five minutes thinking and talking about personal things. I need to be prepared when I get to my client's office this afternoon. I have got to break the bad news that he needs to find another revenue stream for his business. His only other option is he needs to update his resume and post it on the Internet.

Corporate Deceit

Veronica and her sister Gayle were accountants and their company Chapman and Chapman wasn't the typical mom and pop business. Within five years they had grown their business to have offices in six major cities and it was their mindset that it was still a small company. Veronica had often told Josh how happy she would be when their company truly became a corporation. Josh would just look at her in amazement, thinking it is a corporation, but until Chapman's financial showed a net worth of twenty million or more, she and Gayle looked at it as a two-person operation with a few employees. She was always reading something to get them to the next level, when instead of reading books they should have been writing one to encourage others to follow their lead.

Of course to add to the equation, they were women who were totally focused on succeeding. In many ways, she and Gayle were the twenty-first century versions of Eleanor Roosevelt. Raised in rural Mississippi, their parents instilled in them that they were blessed with strong minds and that education was the key for them to be successful. Each sister had taken a different path to get where they were today, but together they believed there were no challenges in business that they could not conquer.

Gayle, the oldest sister had taken the traditional route to obtain her degree. After high school she enrolled in Alcorn State University and finished her under-graduate degree in three and a half years. Being in the top five percent of her class, she was recruited by one of the major eight accounting firms and relocated to Chicago. After moving to Chicago, she enrolled in night school, received her MBA within a year and passed the CPA examination on her first attempt.

Veronica, the rebellious personality fought tooth and nails with her parents about attending college after graduation. She felt strongly that she was smart enough already and if she was given the chance to prove herself, she too would be successful. She tried her theory for the first three years in Jackson and soon discovered that it took more than determination to get where she wanted to be. Enrolling into Mississippi State University night school, Veronica worked and obtained her degree in a little under five years. Sure, she had some setbacks, a broken marriage and a child to name a few, but overall she would not let those issues keep her from her goal.

Richard Carter

Her ex-husband tried on several occasions to come back into her life, but Veronica was stern in who she was, so if she ended anything, she burned the bridge behind her. She only looked forward so that way she could never be hurt by any situation again. It took her two attempts in passing the CPA exam, but she was so determined the second time that she had the top score for the exam.

Ten years after getting her degree and visiting home for the holidays, she and Gayle were sitting in their parents' den laughing about their children and their careers since the last time that they were all together. They were close and called each other weekly, but it seemed to them, talking face to face, there were so many other events that they had not discussed in their weekly phone conversations.

"You know, Ronnie, I have been with this firm for almost fifteen years, brought in a lot of new business and the discussion about making me a partner has never come up. Yes, my bonus checks have been great, but the real money comes from being a partner. Well it's like there is a ceiling and I just can't break it," Gayle stated with some frustration.

"I understand where you are because at times in the last several months I had those same feelings. And besides, I am tired of seeing some blonde, blue-eyed size four, twenty-five year old making more money than me, when often she has problems looking at a balance sheet let alone passing the CPA exam. Now don't let an Ole Miss' white boy grad come into my firm. Hell, before they can get him a desk, I will be reporting to his green-ass," Ronnie says laughing.

"You know, sometimes I wonder if we Chapman girls couldn't start our own firm? Hell, I got some money in the bank; my 401k isn't that bad, and of course, if I had to I could borrow some from a whole life policy that Dad made me buy the first year after I left Alcorn. What's your situation, or have you become part of the establishment after all of these years?" Gayle asked smiling.

"Look, not bragging, but I am in pretty good shape to take a chance." What Gayle didn't know was Veronica had already set the wheels into motion to leave her firm. Actually, if her plans worked out, not only could she leave, but her old firm could finance their first year of operation without her touching her savings.

Veronica had filed an EEOC suit against her firm for racial profiling and the settlement offer was in her lawyer's office being reviewed during the holidays.

Her expectations were when she returned to Jackson, the worst case in her mind was she would only be employed by her firm at the most for the next sixty days. Perfect timing! In her mind was Gayle's suggestion of starting a company.

Just when she felt that they should take this conversation to another level, their mother walked into the room asking them to get the grand children from outside because dinner was ready.

Ronnie told her sister, "Seriously, if this idea of starting our own firm is what you really want to do I am all ears to talk some more about it. But I don't want to live in Chicago and I know that you said when you left Mississippi you didn't mind coming home to visit, but you weren't going to live here ever."

Gayle smiled, "Ok, Chicago and Mississippi are not options, so either we got to go to Atlanta or the West Coast. Simple."

"Atlanta is a great city, but everyone is moving there. And being based in Atlanta… well it tends to send the message that you are only looking at other minority businesses. And I know of ten CPA firms there already. I am not saying I am afraid of competition, but could we find some place besides that and make an impact?"

"Look, where we are doesn't matter. It is the chance to be what we want to be that makes all the difference. Do me a favor and think about this as a real chance for us and not just dreaming about what we could do while we were home eating mom's cooking."

Gayle didn't know that Veronica had sixty percent of her business plan ready. She would send it tonight and it would be in Gayle's email inbox as soon as she could get home to her computer.

That was six years ago and the sisters have been running full strength since their first day of operation.

3

Paul was thinking as he and Alex walked back toward Alex's office of the events of the last several weeks and the other conversations that he was in on concerning Josh Harrington. Well, it all started about five months ago when Josh was doing a special project for one of the senior vice-presidents of the company. As usual Josh was the fair haired child and everyone who ever came into contact with him just adored his upbeat attitude and his willingness to do whatever for the company.

Josh was part of a special project team for Russell Smiley, assistant vice president of Human Relations. The team, the Associate Task Force, was to understand how to retain talented employees within the organization. You see, the company normally recruited the top graduates from all of the major universities, compensated them about 10 to 15% above the industry standard and had a remarkable training program. But usually, after five years with the company,

Corporate Deceit

other companies would steal the top producers away.

Russell's mission from the CEO was to develop a strategy that the company could put in place to reduce that trend. Russell was sharp and he knew that to accomplish this he needed input from both his line management and from the worker bees as well. He hoped the team knew that the company could not give the keys to the vault to its employees, but there should be someway to make more of them stay rather than search for greener pastures.

The actual team was mixed personalities and Josh was somewhat taken by some of the views from his fellow committee members. He thought in terms of his company as a book that he had once read where the inmates might be running the asylum. How someone with that much education could appear to have missed the boat on common sense, he often asked himself. And the worst of all was Lori Greenspan.

What Josh did not know was Lori had Russell's ear, and her views he listened to and were thought highly by him. Actually, Russell publicly stated in his own manager's meeting, an engineer is an engineer, so if one leaves just go hire another. Boy, was he in left field about that. He nor Lori were not technical, so their perception on matters should not have been counted, but each had a way of painting the prefect picture that those too far removed from the pits bought into their theories— hook, line and sinker.

During their first meeting Lori and Josh clashed and neither had the attitude of finding common ground. Lori was from South Carolina with a deep southern draw. Josh found offense whenever Lori opened her mouth not because of her accent, but because, to him, she didn't bring value to the table in his mind.

Several times someone else in the room would have to intercede as mediator to get those two back on track. If Josh said it was a beautiful day when he entered the room, Lori would come right back at him and ask how it could be with the pollen count about 80 percent. It didn't matter what the subject was; those two made it a point to take the opposite stance.

Often after every meeting, Lori would get back to her office to call Russell and complain how that arrogant SOB had been rude to her that day. Russell understood that Lori was a drama queen and on several occasions when Josh and he talked one on one, he would stress the point that Josh should take his leadership role to a new level. Josh thought he was doing just that with all of his team members, he knew he should be kinder to Lori, but she was an airhead and she hadn't done anything to change his opinion.

Josh's mindset was a little different because before he came to this company he had been employed by a corporation whose corporate culture encouraged conflicts as long as all parties kept it toward the subject and never took their disagreement to the personal level. Actually, except for the language at times, that attitude brought a lot of benefits because everyone could express his or her ideas very openly. It worked there, but within the organization that he was in right now, that dog didn't hunt. Actually, between the two organizations, this one supported political gamesmanship more than honesty. So to get further ahead within this company, the fewer enemies one has, the greater his or her advancement stock climbed in value.

Several weeks after the formation of the ATF, Russell had to figure out what to do about Lori and Josh. Not only was he hearing the same story on how the other one didn't have respect for his or her contribution, but other committee members had emailed him on how unproductive the meetings were when they both attended. Russell had made up in his mind that he was going to ask one of them to step down, but he really wasn't sure which should go. Actually, both painted a great story about their perception on what the company could do to decrease its attrition percentages.

He had received feedback from both of their immediate managers and they thought highly of each of them. Well, he thought why don't I just sit down with the both of them and level this playing field. Now, that was the best idea he had on the matter until Lori called him one night from home around midnight with a new allegation concerning Josh.

(Crying) "Russell, sorry for waking you up, but this couldn't wait until I got into the office in the morning."

"What is the matter Lori, this is Lori?" He asked still half asleep.

"Yes, it's me," She replied.

"Ok, is this some type of family issue? Should I get Employee Relations on the phone and or someone else?" He was totally puzzled why she needed to call him.

"Russell, what's the matter? Is that Kathy on the phone calling from school?" his wife asked.

"No, dear, go back to sleep; it is not Kathy; it's the job. I'm going down to the den and take this, ok. Go on back to sleep; everything is fine."

"Hold on for a moment, Lori, while I go downstairs. Don't hang-up, it will only take me a few seconds, ok?"

After he got to the bottom of the stairs he turned on some lights in the den, found his cigarettes, lit one and now he was ready to find out what in the world was causing this woman to wake him up, and beside all of that she is crying. Now that he was fully awake, maybe he could get a clear understanding on what was happening.

"Ok, Lori what is the matter?"

"Josh Harrington, the bastard!"

"Ok, what about Josh Harrington?"

"Josh Harrington attacked me!" She screamed.

"He what, attacked you how, when, where?"

What in the hell was he hearing from her? He thought he was dreaming. How in the world does he handle this? Better yet, what is she saying when she says he attacked her? His mind was racing, but before he could do anything he had to understand the situation.

"Ok Lori, calm down, first things first. Do you need medical attention? He was holding his breath waiting on her to respond."

"No."

"Alright how about Security?"

"I am at home."

"Ok, when did this happen?" Since she was already home this must have occurred several hours ago.

"He just left about ten minutes ago."

Her reply floored him. What in the world was Josh doing at Lori's house this time of night? And what does she mean he attacked her? He needed a drink but he also needed his mind clear to help her.

"Ok, Lori, explain to me, and you don't have to go into details; what do mean attacked you? Are you saying verbally, or physically?"

"Josh Harrington tried to rape me!"

"Let me slip on some clothes; you call the police and I will be right over."

"He didn't rape me, he tried to. And there's no evidence that it happened, but you got to believe me; he tried to rape me!" Lori began crying harder.

"Ok, I believe you, but I am still coming over. Give me about ten minutes and I should be there; you do still live on Robins Nest, right?"

"Yes, 5438 Robin's Nest. It is the only circled drive on the block," she replied.

"Ten minutes, ok."

As quietly as he could without waking up his wife, Russell found a jogging suit and his tennis shoes and dressed on the stairwell. He woke his wife briefly, telling her he had a situation, and would be back shortly. Getting into his car, he wished he had poured himself that drink because he needed one badly if this woman was telling him the truth.

How does one handle this type of situation? Two mid-level managers within the organization, one being accused of trying to rape the other at her house was a great ordeal. Nowhere in college, his post-graduate studies, and all of the employee relation seminars that he had attended had this subject been discussed. He was still trying to understand how those two got into this situation. What was Josh doing at Lori's house and what led him to try to attack her? This wasn't making any sense, but he was clear on one thing he had a very delicate matter on his hands. What is he to do? Well, if she's telling the truth, he should try to convince her to call the authorities and make this a criminal matter. Yes, that's what he should do. But then protecting the company is also his responsibility too. The papers would have a field day, he thought as he was envisioning the headlines in the morning edition of the paper. And don't let one of the wire services get wind of it.

Hell, their stock was taking a beating in the market right now and a scandal could have serious side effects with potential investors. What message from a corporate level would that send? He could see some good ole Baptist Bible-carrying investor with a $100,000 wanting to catch them at a bargain price turning away because he or she didn't want to invest with a company that had those kinds of people working for them. Even though Texas was not really in the South, that Southern mentality loomed heavily within the state.

He pictured the questions that his Public Relations Department would be asked by the media including what is our company policy toward an individual under indictment for a felony crime. I need to check with legal first thing in the morning about that too.

What is his recourse when he gets to the office in the morning? Who does he talk to and how does he make sure the gossip grapevine doesn't get word about this? Two people's reputations are at stake here for the moment.

When he arrived at Lori's, she offered him something to drink and, thank God, she had pulled herself together by the time he had arrived. He needed to understand the timetable for this entire event first.

"Ok, why was Josh here in the first place?" He knew when he finished his sentence what he meant and how it came out sent the wrong message.

"We had been in my office working on the final draft for you when we lost power on that side of the building." she explained.

"So, I thought Josh and I would schedule some time first thing on tomorrow and finish what we were doing. Since there was a power outage, my thinking was that you would grant us an extension and that would be it. But he insisted that we should pack up our laptops, go to Starbuck's, McDonald's or anywhere we could get Internet service and finish the proposal. He said we only had about an hour of work left so we should finish and give you your deliverables."

"Alright, so how did your house become one of those public places that he suggested?"

"Since I am so close to the office, I didn't see any reason for us to be disturbed; have you ever tried to concentrate in those places? It doesn't work. I also did not see any reason why coming to my home would be an issue, it was business not a social event."

"I understand that, but I've got to ask some hard questions too. Because to my knowledge Harrington has never been accused of any type of misconduct; so how did work turn into a possible attempted rape?"

"Well, when we arrived it was just that— all work. We finished the proposal around nine, and since we both thought it was good, I offered that bastard a glass of wine to celebrate our accomplishment."

"He is so damn slick; we sat here and since he said he had gained so much respect for me the last few days he wanted to clear the air around some matters. So, he goes into his sales pitch on how non-technical people should have a greater sense of understanding when dealing with technical people. Oh, the bastard is good. He gives the right compliment here and there so you buy into that song and dance of his. Then if you are not careful, he will be leaving your house in your car."

"Ok, so he is a salesman, I will agree with you on that point, but how did that lead up to your being nearly raped?"

"Of course you know he can talk a mile a minute, so I poured us another glass of wine. He then changed the subject and asked who decorated my house. His explanation was he had just purchased a new home so he was looking for ideas and if I didn't mind, could he have a tour? I agreed and showed him the house and he kept asking where did I get this item or that item and the compliments kept coming a hundred miles a minute.

Russell was getting a little angry; could she get to her point where this damn rape almost rape took place.

"Well after the tour, he walked over to my entertainment center and was looking at my CD collection, and inquired about my sound system. So, he handed me a CD and I played it. He asked to dance, and I didn't see any harm in it; I said it was ok."

Russell thinking, *"was she attacked, or after a couple of glasses of wine did she and Josh damn near have a sexual encounter and she decided to say no."*

"While we were dancing, he tried to kiss me and as politely as I could explain to him our friendship was not or would never be at that level. That is when he changed acting like a demon or something came over him. He called me a teasing bitch, pushed me down on my sofa, and ran his hands under my dress and between my legs." Lori began to cry again when she got to this point in her story.

"I slapped him as hard as I could and he had the strangest look on his face, but he got off top of me, picked up his laptop as if he was leaving his office and walked out the door." Crying louder she turned red with anger.

"What do you mean just walked out the door? Didn't he say anything, like I don't know, I guess the wine went to my head, hell my wife or girlfriend left me, the pressure of the job, *something*?" Russell asked.

"Not one damn word that cocky bastard said. He probably would have raped me if I hadn't fought back, he just got his belongings and casually strolled out my front door."

"Russell, you got to believe me; I did not do anything to encourage that bastard to do this to me. And since, there is no physical evidence that it occurred how could I call the police?" She asked.

"Lori, to be on the safe side, I think we still need to file a report with the authorities, but I do have a favor to ask before they get here. We will give them his name but since you aren't logged on we can't give his address and we will acknowledge him as an associate of yours. Sorry, you do understand my reason for stating it this way. I want to protect you and the company from any bad press. We don't want the papers to paint their own story of lovers within the same company having a fight and since you are white, you scream rape.

Ok, when they ask why you called me before them, we will explain that you were in shock from the events of tonight."

Lori gets up, goes to the phone and dials 911. About ten minutes later the police arrive, takes her statement and leaves. One of the officers appeared not to have bought into her story completely by his expression, but he never said a word. It would be almost a year later before they would find out that their report was never filed. If they had better hindsight, maybe Russell would also suggest that she tore her panties before the cops arrived.

Arriving home shortly after 3:00 am, Russell went straight to his liquor cabinet and poured himself a double shot of bourbon. What in the hell does he do when he gets into the office? Let's see. It didn't happen on campus so should he call and get Security involved? Bad idea, Russell, because the least number of people who know about this the better. Ok, does anyone at the office need to know? Well, if they had an employee who rape another employee and the company has knowledge of it, we could be opening Pandora's Box and the corporate coffins to every civil attorney in this state. So, he had a corporate responsibility to inform somebody; now who that was he was not sure. Does he speak to his direct management or should he just run this damnthing up the flagpole to his boss. This is too heavy for him to sort out, so he would just schedule a meeting with Michael and let him ponder this.

Getting into bed, he kisses his wife gently on her cheek before he tries to get some sleep since he has been up most of the night.

"Where in the hell did you go? I thought you said you had a business issue, but you smell like you have been out drinking."

"I had to go over to Lori Greenspan's house. She had an incident with another employee."

Rising up on her side of the bed, "So, you had to go over and have a nightcap with them?"

"No, it is too complicated to discuss right now, I made me a drink downstairs."

"Sure, tell me anything, and I better find a glass in the sink in the morning when I wake-up too. By the way, why does she have our home number? You know it has been almost twenty years for us, not counting college, so are you out now test driving some new models, thinking about trading this old Model-T in for a turbocharged version with a CD player?

"You know, regardless of the miles on my Model-T, I always try to make sure that the pistons never stick, that's why I keep it well lubricated."

"Well, since you put it that way, I think it is about a half quart low at the moment. Feel like checking it with your dip stick, young man?"

Even after twenty years of marriage, his wife was still the love of his life. It has been a while since they had made love at 3:00 in the morning. So, he kissed her, stating that he would be tired, but will have a smile on his face.

"Come here, let me lift the hood on this puppy and see if the oil is low."

"Good Morning and how is my Mr. Good Wrench this morning? I knew you needed a good breakfast this morning since it took almost two hours to change my oil. By the way, if you get away early today, want to rotate my tires?"

"Sweetheart, I would love to but can I rotate them tomorrow, because that oil change should keep me going the rest of today; besides, I don't want to only rotate the tires, but I really think I should drop the oil pan and clean it out too," laughing as he ran to get a quick shower.

After having a wonderful breakfast with his wife, Russell had to regroup his attention to that other event from last night. The only thing good that he saw from Lori's call was that he still loved his own wife and just for a moment they had turned back the clock to when they were twenty-three.

Seated behind his desk, he asked his admin to schedule a meeting today with his boss and to not take no for an answer.

Clara asked, "If he is busy, Norma is going to ask why, so Mike can make that call to reschedule someone else to see you."

"Just say I have a situation that could blow-up in our face, if I don't see him," he said angrily to Clara.

"Ok, Russell, you don't have to take my head off. I just wanted to be sure that Norma postures your request correctly to Mike, and he is aware that it's too important for later this week."

Just as she is about to leave his office, his phone rings. From the caller-id he sees that it is Lori. Damn, he thought; I didn't want to talk to her until I knew which way to take this. Knowing that she would continue to call him, he picks up the phone.

"Good morning, Ms. Greenspan," Clara was looking straight at him, and she would be the last person he could tell about last night.

"Russell, I won't keep you, but thanks for coming to my rescue last night. And, Russell, what should I do about this afternoon?"

Russell was totally clueless about what she was saying. "What is going on this afternoon?"

"The ATF is making its final presentation to the executive steering committee at 2:00 and I don't know if I can keep it together being in the same room with that bastard." Russell could hear her beginning to cry.

"Look, Lori, my suggestion is for you to take the rest of the week off. Hell, the steering committee knows your involvement; so being out of the office won't hurt you. Pack up your things and I will see you on Monday."

"But I also have a presentation with my client this week."

"Look, send your client and anyone else who would be looking for you an email stating that you have a family emergency and you will be out until Monday. Now, do as I say and go home."

Clara walks back into Russell's office and informs him that Mike is available for thirty minutes only at 11:00. He asks her to fix his calendar so he is available. As she agrees to do so, Clara is wondering what is so important that Russell has to meet with Mike today. At their level within the corporation, normally except quarterly when financial are due, most of the executives are killing time or playing golf.

At ten till eleven, Clara sticks her head into Russell's office to remind him of the time. Like all good administrative assistants, she does this just in case he has to go the bathroom.

Walking into Mike's office, the first thing Mike notices was that Russell closes his door.

Normally, there aren't any issues that his admin isn't aware of and only when he is visiting with clients does he close his door. This really is serious; is Russell leaving the company and here to give me his resignation?

"Mike, we may have a big problem that happened last night around midnight between two employees. Well, not only are they employees, but they are both mid-level managers."

"What kind of problems do two mid-level managers have at midnight, may I ask?"

"One manager is accusing the other manager of attempted rape."

"I beg your pardon. Are you telling me a manager within this organization tried to rape another manager? Am I hearing the gist of this story? Where in the hell was security? We have over a thousand cameras watching this place. Do we have the attempted rape on film?"

"That's where it gets sticky. The attempted assault took place off campus."

"Were these two individuals at a client's site or at a conference? Where were they?"

"At one of individual's home."

"Russell, was there a rape attempt, or are they a couple who had a fight and now one of them is accusing the other of rape?"

"The victim swears there was no romantic involvement with the other party."

"Ok, then how in the hell did you get involved in this situation?"

"I got a phone call around midnight, with the victim accusing the other party of rape. So, I got dressed, went over, heard her side, called the police and went back home."

Holding his head and rubbing his temple with his fingers, Mike tries to get a handle on what Russell is telling him. "What happened when the police arrived? Did the crime lab people show up? Was the victim taken to the hospital for a rape kit test? What in the hell did the police do?"

Russell knew then this meeting was about to go down hill quickly after he filled Mike in on the entire story line, as Lori told it. So he gave him the cliff notes' version of Lori's recount of last night's events.

"So, there is no physical evidence; only her side of the story and now you walk into my office asking for guidance. Who are the parties in this matter?"

"It is Lori Greenspan and Josh Harrington."

"Of all the people here, I would never put those two together with this. Ok. From what I have heard, you did the right thing, and, yes, you were correct in trying to protect the corporation."

"But, Mike, since it didn't happen here and we only have her word, how do we handle this?"

"I am suggesting that you get Security to initiate background checks on both of them beyond the norm. Get them to perform the one that we conduct for senior management including pictures, the families, girlfriend, and boyfriends—whatever they can get. Then we need to make sure that she feels safe. I'm thinking off the top of my head, but we got to protect her from him. Now, I don't know at the moment, but if she is telling the truth, then that is our obligation."

"Ok, I can do that."

"Russell, send me a confidential report to with all details by the close of business today. Russell, that is my job; I am here to support you."

"I will, and thanks for taking the time to see me."

As Russell was walking out of his office, Mike thought to himself, he should have had everything I asked already started, what an idiot? I guess the old saying is correct: *'What do people from the UT call A&M graduates--Boss!'*

4

Russell went straight back to his office, stopping briefly to ask Clara to pick up a sandwich and some fruit for him. But before she did that, he wanted her to schedule a meeting with Tim Eldridge, the head of corporate Security, as quickly as possible. Tim was in his office and told her that he would come right down to Russell's office.

Tim knocks on Russell's door as if he was a U.S. Marshall serving a warrant. Russell needed his help, so he was glad to know that Tim was responding so quickly.

"Tim, I am not going to tell you how to handle this, but I want the most in-depth background done on two people, and I need the results of those within ten days."

"Russell, you can have full screens including their drug test within three days,

Corporate Deceit

so what's with this ten days from now stuff?"

"No, Tim, I am not talking about Security's normal procedures. What I want is the kind that you perform when we bring on an executive, with pictures and the works."

"I wasn't aware that we were adding any new executives or bringing in some new level twelve people."

"We aren't; the two individuals are already employees within the company."

"Ok then. It is about time we began to live up to our values and styles and promote an executive from the ranks."

This actually may work in my favor, since he thinks we are considering promoting these two instead of looking for something to terminate one or both of them. Russell thought.

"That's right, Tim. The two candidates were hand selected. I need full reports on Josh Harrington and Lori Greenspan."

Tim almost jumped out of his chair. A woman and a man, internally being considered for an executive position! The old man himself must have spoken from the grave to get this started. Tim could tell you the criteria that he had seen to be considered for an executive position. The person first had to be a white male and normally a University of Texas or Texas A&M graduate. Then he had to have an MBA from SMU although there were one or two exceptions. If he met those qualifications, he was almost guaranteed a high six-figure income with this company.

"I will put my best guys on this today," Tim assured.

"Actually, Tim, why don't we use that outside firm? That way we can control all leaks before the big announcement. Don't you agree?"

"That is why your office is twice the size of mine, Russell. I will give the Stanfield Agency a call just as soon as we are finished. Is there anything else that you need?"

"No, and I know that I don't have to remind you that this is totally confidential. Heads will roll if word of this leaks out before time."

Tim called the Stanfield Agency and spared no expense in getting the process started. They asked him how many people did he wish to use and Tim answered them saying as many as needed to finish within seven days.

Several days later Tim walked into Russell's office with two brown sealed envelopes. Inside of each was the complete life story of Lori Greenspan and Josh Harrington. Strange enough when he finished reading both, he found their backgrounds were not that far apart, as he had imagined. However, it did omit some vital information that he would need in making his decision.

After he had a couple of days to do some soul searching, Russell scheduled an off-site meeting with Mike to discuss his solution. He decided to mix business with pleasure and play some golf. While they were playing they could decide what the next steps should be.

After the round they ordered drinks and steaks to discuss the future of Josh Harrington and Lori Greenspan. Handing Mike a copy of the security report, Russell began to explain that this wasn't going to be easy.

"Mike, both of those reports are so clean you could eat off of them," Russell was amazed that neither of the two had any known faults.

"How clean is clean? You mean there is nothing questionable in either of their past?"

"I mean he is from a single parent home, got his first job at sixteen, worked two jobs while in college, no outside children, not gay, nothing. And she is cleaner than he is. I would have thought somewhere early in either of their careers one of them would have done something stupid enough that they would want to hide it from the public. If Tim's investigators did their job, you could place either of their names on the Republican ticket for President right now."

"Ok, then why in the world would Mr. Clean attempt to rape Ms. Spotless. Can you explain that to me?"

"That's the part I don't get. This guy doesn't even have a speeding ticket on record, let alone any charges from an ex-lover accusing him with abuse. He is even dating a woman and from her picture she is beautiful. He is a Christian, church every Sunday, a member of the Boy's Club, on charity committees—too many to list. He just does not meet the profile for your neighborhood rapist."

"So, is Lori lying on this guy?"

"You should have seen her. I mean she was upset and very angry when I got to her house."

"So, did she offer herself to Mr. Clean, and he said no; so she's going to make him pay for it?"

"See, she didn't want me to call the police and she admitted he only ran his hands under her dress and fondled her. Even when the police came, she did not try to embellish her story to make herself sound more convincing. Her statement to them was almost verbatim to what she told me. Actually, I don't know what to think?"

"Ok, what are our options? Would either of them accept a transfer to one of our satellite offices, let's say Chicago? See, from my view we can't allow them both at corporate, not now or ever."

"I think they both know taking a non-staff job would be a death sentence for their careers. Besides, would you want a suspected rapist as a division manager with several hundred women reporting to him? Just think how many young women could be his victims if he could also use the power of his position to get what he wants, if this is true?"

"Well, there is also her story too. What if this is a lie and if some other guy smarter than her challenges her; she sets him up with bogus charges. She could ruin another guy's career just by implying moral misconduct?"

"Damn, this is a tough one but since I have known her she has always been truthful with me. So I am leaning toward that she is telling the truth now." Russell just happens to forget to tell Mike that he recruited Lori from her old company. To him, she was bright, articulate, top one third of her MBA class and she had great legs.

"Well, it looks like Mr. Harrington's days with the company are numbered. Now how in the hell do we get rid of him?"

"Sounds simple except the guy is liked by everyone and I mean everyone, from the mail room to the CEO office. This guy knows just about everybody and I have never heard anything questionable about him."

"Look Russell, I don't care. You need to find out if she is telling the truth or not. If her story is real, then Harrington needs to be gone. If she is lying about this whole mess then she needs to be gone. You've got choices, so decide what you believe and act on it. It's that simple."

Russell heard his boss loud and clear. So, he has choices: either Lori or Josh Harrington?

5

As Josh came into Alex's office area he saw Alex's administrative assistant Pauline Calhoun and greeted her as he had done for the last six years since she joined the company. "Good Morning,' the high Princess of Administrative Assistants'." And in return she smiled and, just as his greeting was standard for him, her reply was the exact same, "Josh Harrington, you are going to have every assistant in this company hating me."

Pauline was exactly one of the best admins in the company, always willing to stay late if necessary, and her work was well above approach. Her main attribute from the first day when she joined the company was, she had a network and there was nothing going on within the company that she did not know about. Josh had kept their relationship on the very best of terms because she not once, but many times had given him a heads-up on events. Some of her information had even given him time to clean up his own act before his manager could pull him on to the carpet. So if there were anything that would cause Alex to be that pissed at him, Pauline would know.

So as usual, Josh asked, "Ok, what is the deal this morning that Alex wants to see me and most of all with Paul Copeland?"

Pauline's response caught Josh off balance, "I don't have a clue."

"Right, Pauline; something is going on and you don't know what?"

"Really, Josh, I don't know. What are you worrying about anyway? What I do know is that seven of those Division Managers that you are meeting with at ten think your meeting is a waste of their time."

When Pauline said that, Josh's heart skipped a beat because he knew that his group Identity Management Solution was better than any solution already on the market; including the Big Boys, i.e. Microsoft and I.B.M. In his mind, what in the world could seven Division Managers be thinking. In the proof of concept document, there were forty pages showing how his group solution was superior and where those other products had gaps. So, how could they believe this was a wasted meeting?

"What in the hell do you mean they think this is a wasted meeting?"

Pauline saw the disbelief in his eyes and it was taking every muscle in her body to keep from laughing. She hadn't seen Josh so nervous about a meeting before. Normally, he wasn't concerned, but the possible impact of closing this deal had his nerves on the edge.

"Yes, seven of them believe that you should have canceled this meeting last week. Well, the exact words of my sources were this meeting should not have ever been scheduled. Well, one source said, they are betting that apparently you have a new suit that you want to display."

"What?" Pauline was seeing a very angry Josh Harrington, something seldom displayed.

"Josh, before you have a stroke, everybody loves your group's solution. Love it! But the first statement I made was true. They did say after they had read your documentation and sat in on the demonstration that the only thing left for you to do was send them a statement of work."

When he heard the whole explanation, a smile that could have lit up a room came across his face. Before he responded, he prayed silently "Thank You, Jesus!"

"Pauline, I am not as young as I used to be, so don't scare the hell out of me like that again. Now back to this Alex and Paul meeting. Just between the two of us, what is going on? I spoke to Alex and he is being really blunt and you know that is not him at all. I can't call Paul. Hell, I haven't talked to him in six months. Well, every time I speak to Alex, I guess I am talking to Paul. Alex has to be the only senior manager in this company sharing an office?" (Laughing)

The inside joke was Paul was brown nosing Alex so much that you didn't see one without the other. Not only Josh, but also several other managers felt the same way. The question they all used came from an old chili commercial.

"When was the last time you went to Alex Mann's office and did not find Paul Copeland there sitting like a trained beagle?"

Punch Line –

"Well, that is too long!"

"You guys are bad. Paul, just does a lot of stuff for Alex, like get him coffee, blow his nose, and wipes his …"

"Now, who is being bad, young lady?"

"Well, if Alex could get away with it, Paul would be drawing two salaries. One for being a manager and the other for being Alex's administrative assistant."

"Pauline, you shouldn't say things like that about Paul. Paul should be getting four checks: three from the company and a personal check from Alex."

"Four? I know of maybe the two, but what does he do for the other two checks?"

"The third check should be from the company for Paul doing Alex's financial. And the personal check is for yard work, pool services, baby-sitting and for during laundry on Thursdays. That is why on Thursdays, Paul doesn't schedule or accept any meetings before lunch. You know Alex and his wife have five kids, so Paul has got to sort, wash and dry for seven people. Remember, that takes a lot of time."

They were both laughing so loudly that several people walking through the area wanted to know what the big joke was about.

"So, you don't know anything about this meeting this morning, or you can't say anything about what it is about. Which one is it?"

"Josh, I don't have any idea but I can say this: watch your back and keep your enemies close to you. Don't you know how many people would sell their children to be in your shoes at this moment? Think about it; your team is about to be the biggest thing in this company."

Pauline's mood changed as Alex and Paul were walking up behind Josh. When Josh noticed Pauline's demeanor change, he turned and was almost nose-to-nose with Paul Copeland. Trying not to look like a gazelle when trapped by a lion, Josh acted as if this meeting was not causing him any concerns.

"Good morning, gentlemen. I see you two stepped out and got some coffee, so I was just killing some time with the Princess of Administrative Assistants"— Josh's opening statement to those two.

That shocked him; normally with an opening like that Alex would grin and admit that without Pauline he would be nothing. But this morning, Alex was all business and, of course, Paul was following his lead.

"Josh, why don't we go on into the conference room instead of my office and get started?" Alex responded.

Leading the way, the three entered the conference room, but the way they seated themselves caused Josh's stomach to begin a serious conversation. "This is not good; this is serious; be prepared, and don't show anger."

They had him pinned in like a deer on both sides and he didn't see any indications that this meeting was in his best interest. Paul took the lead by speaking first and by his opening statement, Josh's attitude and body language changed as well.

"Josh, Alex and I have been in HR all morning and the topic of discussion was you."

"Ok and what is HR saying that they needed to see my immediate manager and his manager so bright and early in the morning?"

"There have been a series of serious charges given to them that they have been investigating for the last several weeks. And based on their findings Josh

Harrington you are being terminated effective immediately for professional misconduct."

"I beg your pardon! Hold up! What damn charges! And there is something called due process."

"Because this corporation is in Texas, a right to work state, due process, as you think, is the right of the employer and because of the offenses, HR has recommended termination."

"Alex, what in the hell is going on here? How can you sit there and let this little prick tell me there's no such thing as due process and that I am being terminated. Hell, I have the right to know what the charges are and who took them to HR?"

Alex, not wanting to give Josh any eye-to-eye contact, glanced over to Paul.

"Josh, as I was saying, you...." Josh interrupts Paul in mid sentence.

"Paul, I wasn't talking to you; I was talking to Alex. What is this all about?"

Again, Paul begins his spill, and Josh interrupts him once again.

"Ok. Since you two SOB's don't have the balls to talk to me, where is this representative from Human Resources recommending termination with these so-called charges?"

"Human Resources felt that because of the course of action being taken, that any additional parties present would only create a hostile environment," Paul said.

"Wait, what I just heard, and correct me if I articulate incorrectly, you, *you* Paul Copeland are firing me. *You*, Paul, are firing me based on an investigation by Human Resources and a meeting that you and HR had. And *you*, Paul, have not told me what the charges are, and *you,* Paul Copeland, say there is no such thing as due process in this company. Now, have I stated this correctly because, I want to make sure that I am hearing you correctly?"

Paul was about to answer Josh but he first made eye contact with Alex. He begins again, "I have a severance agreement here for you to sign, and information concerning COBRA if you elect to continue your insurance coverage under the company's benefit plan. Effective immediately, all access to the building has been suspended and I will need your badge, credit cards, keys and personal computer that are in your possession."

Corporate Deceit

"Do you think we are about to walk out of this room without you giving me an explanation of what this is about? You know I have never said this to anyone but you have to be out of your mind thinking that I am just going to say oh well and walk into the sunset. Now, like it or not, get me someone from HR down here right now or Alex and you had better start talking, saying this is the biggest prank in the company's history or all hell is about to break loose. There is no way I am going to accept this vague answer from you and end my career. You must be on crack to believe that!"

Just before anyone else could speak, calmness came over Josh Harrington and the anger that he was feeling just a few seconds earlier was no longer there. Later on that day, he would try to explain it but he could not find the words to express it correctly. With this new found peace, Josh was the first to speak. To him there must have been a ten to fifteen- second delay in his brain and he still could not tell why he said this. "Gentlemen, better yet, you can have all of the company's property that is in my possession. My laptop is in my office; here is my badge, credit card and long-distance access card. Have a wonderful day."

As he was getting up, Alex spoke for the first time. "Josh, sit down please; there is some information that Paul must go over with you explaining your rights and what benefits are still in effect and those that will cease because of the actions being taken today. Please sit down."

"Alex, and until a few moments ago, I had a ton of respect for you, your organization and this company. And I would have taken my seat just as you had asked so nicely, but when you said to go over my rights, no thank you. Those words, "My rights," don't mean a thing to you or to this company because I am still out in left field regarding why I am being terminated. So since I can read, please give me either the envelope or those pieces of paper that are my copies and I am out of here. I do receive copies of all of this? Correct?"

Paul tries to start again. "As I was saying, there are some documents that I must go over with you."

"And I was saying, hand me either the envelope, give me my copies or you can mail them to me. As for me, this meeting is over!" And with that said, Josh Harrington got up and walked out of the building, never looking back, as Paul and Alex both called his name.

6

Walking to his car, he asked himself: was he in shock or was he just tired of the corporate lifestyle? For whatever reasons, the events of the last twenty minutes were not on his mind. That calmness that was surrounding him was like some invisible force that he could not explain. When he arrived at his car, he picked up his cell phone and located Marilyn's office number, placing a call to her.

When her phone rang, she quickly looked at the caller-id and saw it Josh calling her. This boy is so uptight about his meeting. They had just had lunch on yesterday and she had assured him everything was going to be fine. Checking her watch, noticing it was ten to the hour, she thought that he wanted to have one more of those "go get them conversations." He is probably calling me to invite me to lunch later so he can give me details of how well it had gone.

"Josh, your future is set and I have a ton of work to do, so bye."

"Marilyn, you are right. My future is set, but not with this company."

"What are talking about, boy; in ten minutes you will be able to set your future on your own terms and there won't be a soul in this company who will want to stop you."

"Not exactly, I just got fired."

"Josh, didn't I just tell you that I have a desk full of work, so I don't have time for any jokes from you this morning? Bye!"

"Marilyn, seriously, take me off speaker, please."

Marilyn picks up her phone and asks, "Josh, what are talking about? What do you mean that you were just fired?"

"Seriously, if you look out your window right now, you will be able to see me drive by. Paul Copeland just fired me."

"Paul Copeland fired you? You mean someone told Paul Copeland to fire you. Paul hasn't made a decision ,and how could he fire you? You don't report to him."

"Per the organization's chart, yes, I do, Paul was my immediate manager."

"So what is the reason for your termination?"

"HR did an investigation of some kind, and their recommendation was to terminate me."

"An investigation about what?" From Marilyn's tone, Josh knew that she was beginning to become angry.

"Don't know."

"What do you mean, you don't know? Who was in this termination meeting? Was Bryan Wright or somebody representing HR there?"

"I mean I don't know; neither Alex nor Paul would ever tell me the reason. Actually, Alex did not say ten words. Paul was being very... (He pauses) Call me on my cell."

Josh hung up his phone and before he could close the face, his phone rang and it was Marilyn.

"Why did you stop in mid-sentence and have me call you back?"

"Well, since I am now unemployed, I got to save money. I have told you that incoming calls are free. Where was I? Oh, I remember what I was about to say. Paul ran the meeting and since they were not going to tell why, I gave them my badge and left."

"Josh, you know for yourself, HR doesn't conduct themselves that way when we terminate an employee. Bryan had me write a book to support why I was firing Rosanne. They have to tell you why; it is the law."

"No, it is not the law; Texas is a 'right to work' state. So under the law, you can really walk in any day of the week and fire everybody who reports to you. Now, the corporation's image keeps that from happening usually. But if they did they would be within their rights."

"Josh, are you alright?"

Marilyn was becoming concerned because Josh wasn't acting like someone who has been fired under those conditions. Now, if it had been her, she would still be there demanding to hear the charges. Josh, from his tone, was sounding as if he was on his way to play golf.

"I'm ok, so thanks for the memories. Look, I have some thinking to do and try to sort through what has just happened, so can I call you later."

"Wait, Josh; where are you right now? Maybe you can find some place that I can meet you. Tell me where you are right now and I am on my way."

"I am on 291 and thanks for the offer but I need to think right now. Look, I told you that I will call you later; we may even do lunch. Well, since I am now unemployed, I can't buy yours, so if we do lunch, it has to be Dutch."

Since he wanted to lighten the mood, she followed his lead. "You know I don't do Dutch well, and you are still on the company's payroll. You just don't have a job to go to. Have you called Veronica and told her what happened?"

"No and I am not calling her upsetting her day either. We have dinner plans, so in the middle of ordering a meal or having dessert I might mention it. And for being on the payroll, I don't know at the moment if there is a severance." Josh explained.

"Look, you know they have to go over those things."

"Well they may have been trying to get to that point but the meeting ended." (Laughing again)

"How did the meeting end if they did not cover everything with you?"

"I told them since they could not give me a reason why HR was investigating me and the offense that I supposedly had done, then that meeting was over from my viewpoint."

"You can't stop a termination meeting."

"Yes, you can. I know that personally because I just did it. Look, get off your phone, go back to work, and stop worrying about me because I'm fine and I will talk to you later."

With that last statement, Josh hung up his phone and continued driving.

Marilyn called his home and cell numbers several times that morning, but each call went to voice mail. Her assumption was he wasn't home, and he had apparently turned off his cell. Since there had not been any type of announcement about his leaving the company, she assumed many people within the organization were trying to reach him on business issues and he didn't feel like explaining to any of them his situation at the moment. So if that is what he is doing, she understood. They were close friends; she was trying to sort out this mess in her own brain just like he was.

Several people during the day stopped by her office and asked if she had seen or spoken to Josh. The grapevine was trying to put its version of why or what would have caused Josh not to be in the most important meeting of his career? Several people said they knew he was in the office because they had seen him that morning. Their comments were that he was his typical self—upbeat, positive and dressed for success. So where was he and why would he miss his own meeting? The only logical answer was there had to be a family emergency and they hoped that he and his family were ok.

Later that afternoon, Marilyn's manager Alvin Burkhalter came into her office, closed the door and began to tell her what his manager was told.

"Marilyn, have you spoken to Josh today?" he inquired standing next to her white board in his usual manner.

Since one of Marilyn's qualities was not to lie to anyone, she would either ignore the person's question or answer him directly.

"Yeah, I talked to him, why?" she asked.

"Well, because I just came from Roger's office and he informed us that Josh was no longer with the company."

Since Marilyn knew he didn't have the details of what had happened, he wanted to know what she knew. Her mind pondered if she should put an expression of shock on her face or just acknowledge that she already knew and move on? Let me play shocked for the moment and see where that leads us, was her final decision.

"What? Alvin, what happened?"

"You must have spoken to him earlier because he would have told you that he was fired." Alvin says.

"Fired? I thought you meant he just upped and quit? Fired for what?"

"That is the strange part; Roger either doesn't know or he can't tell. He just called all of his direct reports and told us that Josh was no longer here and an announcement would be coming out sometime today from Alex Mann to the division."

"Interesting?" Marilyn pondered.

"Yeah, that's what I thought as well. Since, he has only been talking about this new product that his group had developed and the impact it would have on the company, the last thing anyone could have imaged was his being fired. Actually, I don't even think he was given the choice to resign from the way Roger talked," Alvin stated.

"Well, who is going to lead his team?" She wanted to know because maybe that would put a piece of the bizarre puzzle together about what was really going on. Besides that, whenever she spoke to Josh again, this might also help him to understand the dynamics around this situation.

"Would you believe Paul Copeland? Now, if what Josh was telling you and me about the impact of his team's efforts is correct, and if Paul could make that happen, he will be one of our next directors? Talking about being in the right place at the right time," Alvin says; even he didn't believe that Paul had the people skills to pull that off.

That last statement from Alvin did not set well with Marilyn, but she could not let Alvin see that she was upset by his remarks.

"How? What had Paul done to be rewarded? " Marilyn asked.

"Now you know somebody, either Alex or Paul recognized the potential from this? If I were either of them, I would be changing all of the documents with my name so when Chuck saw them his only option would be to pay me. What was the amount of additional revenue that his FOP projected that Josh told us about?" Alvin asked.

"I think he said somewhere around $100 million and he said that was being conservative?" Marilyn responded.

"So, what is the potential bonus from $100 million in sales? Hell, if he gave Alex and Paul those projections, I would be looking for some way to share in on that windfall. Now that he is gone, well splitting that pie in half is a lot better than splitting it in thirds."

"Well, you do know that when you do something the wrong way or for the wrong reasons, somehow you don't get to enjoy the benefits. That is what I have seen." Marilyn tried to explain.

"I understand what you are saying, but that street runs both ways. Josh must have been doing something because they just don't fire a person without reason," retorted Alvin.

"Alvin, you know that in this company you only have to tick-off the wrong person and you can count your days. It may take them weeks, months or even years, but if it is the right person, they can find cause. To be totally honest, I have seen it happen before and I have even been in a manager's meeting where a person expressed his or her intentions of doing that. So being fired from this company or any company doesn't necessarily mean that the person was doing wrong and the firing was legit," Marilyn replied.

"Oh, I know that but those are the exceptions and not the norm, right?"

"I don't agree with you about that either. Even when you and I wanted to fire someone, we would paint the picture that we wanted. I just didn't think that Josh was under any type of PIP (Performance Improvement Plan) or had anything relating to a written notice in his personnel file? I can't remember him ever being angry or saying that he was being reprimanded for breaking any company policy?"

"Well, you know whatever the reason is; HR had to buy into it. And if he wasn't on any type of written notice, then it really must have been something serious."

"Anytime you lose your job for any reason, it's serious!" Marilyn shouts back.

"Look, I just stopped by to tell you if you didn't know."

"You are so full of it, Alvin. You stopped by to see if I knew more than you. Since, everyone knows how close Josh and I are, you figured he had called me and given me the details around it."

"You know I wasn't doing that?"

"Sure. And I guess that in your staff meeting when Roger told you guys about him, his very good friend Barbara just broke into tears, right?" (Laughing).

7

Watching Josh Harrington leave the campus without letting him have his one moment in the spotlight left an empty feeling in Paul Copeland. He had rehearsed his speech to himself over and over in his head and not getting to deliver it, really ticked Paul off. Not that his words were so elegant, but for the first time he was going to have the opportunity to take a huge notch out of Josh's belt of self-assurance.

Somewhere in Paul's mind, he desired to be more like Josh Harrington than he wanted to admit even to himself. He had heard the stories and seen this guy who could be the center of attraction in a room full of executives. What quality trait did Josh have that, no matter where he was, he felt that he was in control. Everyone else was dancing to music that Josh was supplying.

Paul admired and despised him for that very reason. Even when he attempted to take Josh's team from him, Paul was amazed at the sense of loyalty that his team had for him. Even his clients not only recognized his achievements, but also admired the number of people that he said he knew or met.

Once, when Paul was in Florida at one of the finest resorts, he played golf while he was there. The resort was surrounded by million dollar homes and had a championship golf course. Paul could only dream that he could live there and he thought of the type of money one had to earn to afford this lifestyle. During an afternoon off from the conference, he decided to play golf. Since he did not have this type of opportunity everyday he decided he was going to take the advantage of being there and play.

Arriving at the first tee, Paul was met by two members of the course and asked if he could join them. The introductions were only first names but after a couple of holes it dawned on him who he was playing with. One member of his group was a member of the New England Patriots and the other guy was from the St. Louis Rams. Both were not only members of their respected teams, but were also considered stars in the National Football League. Boy, thinking to himself, what a story he would have to tell when he got back to both the conference and to his office. Paul Copeland had played golf with these two football stars and he wondered would it be politically incorrect after the round to ask them for their autographs? After about five holes, he was playing way above his normal game; then one of them noticed the company's logo on his golf shirt.

"Paul, I have a question for you," said the guy from the Patriots as they were waiting for the group in front of them to hit their second shots.

"Sure, he said—thinking the guy was going to ask about his Driver or if he was hitting the latest ball from Nike—what do you want to know?"

"Is that the company that you work for?"

Proudly, Paul replied, "Yeah. I am a Technical Manager for them. What did you do buy some of our stock? The way the market is right now, it could be a great buy."

"My financial manager handles stuff like buying and selling stock, so I may have some, don't know. Nah, I was asking because we have a buddy that works for you guys in Dallas."

Paul was trying to think if he knew of any ex-professional athletes that worked for the company, and he was drawing a blank. Unless this guy they are asking about works in corporate sales and he was always on the road, he could not think of a name. "I am from Dallas, just here for the week for a conference.

What's your friend's name?"

"Then you might know him; his name is Josh Harrington."

Paul was floored. How in the world does Josh know these two NFL stars? So the suspense of wondering how in the world do these two not only know him, but also consider him as a friend was killing him on the inside. "Yes, I know Josh. He is a co-worker of mine. How do you know him?"

"Oh, that is a story in itself that would take too long to tell. But we met him through another friend of ours who plays for the Dolphins."

He knows someone on the Dolphins too? Paul had been thinking how he was going to tell his story in his manager's meeting on his return, but now he couldn't. He just couldn't stomach hearing Josh tell he not only knew them, but also every story that went along with their so-call friendship. Finally, the group ahead was out of danger, but for the next several holes, Paul's mind was no longer on golf. Just the effect of knowing that not even being there, Josh Harrington had up staged him. He went on to double bogey or worse the next four holes on the front nine. Until they called Josh's name, Paul was on pace to play the best front nine of his life. Now he was struggling just to keep from embarrassing himself.

That memory and several other incidents like that played on Paul's mind. See, Paul could not understand how an average working person could have or know those types of friends and associates. For a long time he had dismissed Josh's stories as a bunch of lies. How could an everyday person know this or that celebrity?

Once when they were in California eating dinner, an elderly couple on their way out of the restaurant stopped and talked to Josh. After the couple left, Paul had to asked, "What do you do to people that no matter where you are you run into somebody that you have met before? I have relatives in my own family who have to ask someone else what my name is and whose child I am."

Josh only would smile and say, "I don't do anything special in my mind. See, my mother doesn't meet a stranger, so that part of her personality, I guess, is a part of me."

Josh Harrington was liked by most that he came into contact with until 90 days ago. That's about the time Paul received a meeting request from Russell

Smiley, the Asst Vice President of Human Resources. The subject line of that email only read "Josh Harrington."

8

Veronica was just returning to her office and as she stopped at her assistant's desk to retrieve her messages, her assistant asked to speak to her privately. "Sure," she responded; and as the two of them walked into her office she sat behind her desk, her assistant closed the door.

"OK. Which client called this time and is so upset that you don't want the entire office to know about?" Veronica asked Stephanie.

"It is not about a client, Ronnie; it is about Mr. Harrington's flowers that you were sending him."

"OK. The florist could not deliver the plant today or did they make a mistake and send him two dozen of roses with a card reading congratulations on your new baby boy?" She responded smiling.

"No, they tried to deliver them to his old office and they were undeliverable. So I need his new company's name and address. The florist will deliver them tomorrow if I can get that information this afternoon. And the lady explained that delivery is still possible today, if his new office was in the same area.

"What new office? That is the only company Josh has worked for since he and I have been seeing each other. Stephanie, what company did they go to?" Veronica could easily become annoyed with incompetence.

"They went to the company and address that you gave me. When they called I verified the address on the phone. So I then double-checked your personal information for him in Outlook. They were at the right place, so I looked up their main number and called. When I asked for Josh Harrington the operator told me no one by that name was with that company."

"Stephanie, you must be mistaken. Don't you move! Wait!" She quickly logged on to her computer, looked up Josh's office number and dialed. To her amazement, there was a recorded message stating:

"The extension that you have dialed is invalid; please press the star key to be transferred to the operator." She pressed the star key, and an operator answered.

"Good afternoon. How may I assist your call?"

"Josh Harrington, please?"

"I'm sorry. Mr. Harrington is no longer an associate here."

"What? You must be mistaken... Joshua Harrington?"

"Miss, Mr. Harrington is no longer an associate here."

She reached into her purse, and found her cell phone and located his name.

"You have reached the voice mail box for Josh Harrington. Either I am not available, or I am on another call. Please leave your name and number at the beep and I will return your call shortly. Have a wonderful day."
Beep………….

Veronica did not know what to either say or think. She had just spoken to him earlier that morning and he was fine. What had happened in three hours that he wasn't available; better yet it appeared that he no longer worked for the company that he worked for this morning?

She forgot that Stephanie was still in her office, when she quickly called her sister's extension. "Gayle, by some strange chance, have you spoken to Josh today? I was trying to send him flowers today; the florist couldn't deliver them because he is no longer employed there. I even called his office, got a recording saying his extension is invalid, and he isn't answering his cell."

"What are talking about, Ronnie. When was this? Saturday morning. I spoke to him and he was so thrilled about some big deal that he was just going to be something just shy of CEO. So what has happened in seventy-two hours that he is not only whatever he thought he would be, but also unemployed?"

"That's what I am confused about. When I spoke to him this morning, he was on his way to another meeting before his big one, so whatever happened to him, I don't know and I haven't heard from him."

Normally in the office everyone thought that the stronger of the two sisters was Veronica, but little did they know. Actually, Veronica could cry at the drop of a dime and she had to work very hard to keep her emotions in check. Here she is worrying about a guy that she is crazy about and she cannot find him. She closed her eyes for a moment and said a prayer that there was a logical explanation around this.

Gayle, knowing how upset her sister was said, "Ronnie, maybe we are thinking the worst and there has to be a logical explanation to this. Did you leave a message on his cell?"

"No, but whenever he checks his messages, my number will show up in his call list."

"Well, then until you talk to Josh, take a moment to pray about the matter and everything will be ok. Remember, this is the guy who has a charmed life."

"Why would you say he has a charmed life?"

"He has you, doesn't he? That fact alone means that God is with him."

Stephanie had been standing there the entire conversation. Veronica blushed in embarrassment from her sister's statement, while a few tears ran down her face.

"Stephanie, I am so sorry that you are seeing me like this. And I don't know what is going on, but please do me a favor: please keep this to yourself."

"Ronnie, I understand; that's why I asked to speak to you privately. Look, I am going back to my desk, I am going to close your door and I won't let anyone disturb you for the next hour. Just say a prayer for Mr. Harrington, okay?"

After Stephanie left, Veronica tried to fit the pieces of this together in her head. No matter how hard she tried, she could not come up with a logical answer to it. She finally decided until she talked to Josh herself, she was trying to solve something that she did not have enough information on which to base his or her next move.

Josh was sitting in his den and looking at the caller-id on every call. He wasn't in a mood to talk to anyone because at the moment, he did not know what to say. His first reaction was to pour himself a drink but since he didn't really drink, 10:30 in the morning seemed a little too early regardless of the circumstances. He then decided he would just sit for a moment, gather his thoughts, and do what Veronica would do: map out a plan. Gathering his thoughts took too much energy and he could not find a logical place to begin.

Since Alex and Paul only told him that he was being terminated for professional misconduct and they only said it was because of the recommendation from HR, he didn't even have a clue on what grounds or why he was fired. He had the paperwork from HR, so he quickly opened the envelope that was lying on the floor in front of him.

In there was the normal separation paperwork, concerning insurance, a severance agreement and a few contact numbers for any additional questions that he may have. There was a letter dated today stating that his employment was being terminated effective immediately for professional misconduct, but there was not a reason given. That caught his attention. Reading the package over several times, he never found a reason for his termination. Something was really weird here, but first things first. What was he going to do or could he do about it?

Maybe he should just leave the house and just drive until he pulls his thoughts together. That didn't really appeal to him. How about going to the range and hitting some balls? Often, when he really needed to think about something or to get something off his mind, that's what he would do. Hitting balls fell in the same category as driving. Maybe he should go over to Veronica's office and ask her to help figure this mess out. Actually, that was the worst idea of them all.

Josh in his mind wanted Veronica to respect him and he didn't think she could respect a man who had just lost his job and career? To make matters worse, this was his problem to figure out, so why go cry on his woman's arm like some overgrown baby. Actually he remembered the calmness that he had experienced

Corporate Deceit

early that morning; so then he knew that God was involved somewhere in all of this. Since he knew that God doesn't get involved in man's messes unless He is there to fix them, he knew that sooner than later it would be all good from his standpoint.

So he finally decided that the best thing for him to do would be to pray.

Lord,

I am not understanding what is going on or the reasons that this is happening to me, but since You are the strength of my life, I know that Your will is being done. Lord, and I know that I should not ask, but why is this happening right now at this moment in my life.

I thought I had it going on; my career was at a point that it was taking off; I have a relationship that I think that you want me to be in and I even have some portion of my health and strength. But just a few hours ago, I believed that I was at my best, not trying to harm anyone; the world that I knew began to change right before my very eyes.

You see and know that I am trying very hard to understand, but this has really got me baffled, and only with You will I be able to make it. Lord, I need You right now to show me what I should do. For without You directing me I cannot make it by myself. Hide me behind Your cross; wrap Your arms around me, and take this anger from me.

Give me the wisdom to make the right decision; grant me both Your prefect peace and mercy. Keep my mind, my mouth and my heart focused on You. Not because of the events of this day, because just as quickly it was taken from me, I know that You cannot only restore it, but also give me so much more. What I thought I had is nothing compared to Your grace and mercy that I am seeking right now.

This is my prayer. In your Loving Son Jesus' name I pray, AMEN.

After Josh finished with his prayer, the calmness that he had felt earlier returned stronger than before. With that new peace, he had no problems answering his phone, discussing what he knew with whoever called. Shortly before seven, he showered and got dressed. He had promised Veronica that they were going to dinner and the events of today were not going to stop that.

When he picked her up, he told her just as much as he knew and she could not comprehend his explanation. She just could not fathom the story that he was telling her was the truth. She could not remember a time in their relationship that she believed that he had lied to her. What really shocked her was she was angrier than he was, and on face value, he seem to be ok with it. She never told him about the flowers that she had tried to send and that she had known since early afternoon that something was wrong.

She inquired what his plans were, and he wasn't sure at the moment, but he was going to take a day or two and sort out the cobwebs. She reminded him that whenever he decided to do whatever, he needed a Plan-A and a Plan-B just in case plan-A did not work out. He told her that he understood that, but right at that very moment, he had neither a Plan-A nor B and it might take him a couple of days before he could see the direction in which he was going.

Dinner was a little awkward, since Veronica still wanted clarity on who was in the meeting, why there wasn't an HR representative, and most of all no reason for the action. Several times he explained he didn't want to discuss it and could they find another topic to talk about. How did her client meeting go today with the guy she had told him about who needed additional revenue or he should update his resume and re-enter the workforce?

"Ronnie, what did he say when you told him to update his resume?"

"I couldn't tell him that, but I did point out he needed more options in generating cash."

"You better be careful when you tell people that they need to search for additional options. With the economy the way it is at the moment, legal means to boost your cash flow are pretty slim," trying to lighten up the conversation, (smiling).

"Speaking about cash flow, what about yours? And did they give you a good severance?" she inquired. One of the major differences between the two: she was financially solid, and had a very strong security need. Typically, in that regard she was like most women; whereas, Josh was on the other end.

Because he had always made money, he always felt that he would make money.

Now, he did do the normal things like invest in his company's 401k, but finance, or rather his financial future, was not high on his priority list. Since he had begun dating Veronica, his views were changing; but comparing the two, one was an adult and the other one was still being bottle-fed.

"I am OK, I think, for the moment. Now, was that your way of saying you wanted to buy me dinner?" (They both laugh).

Josh told her: "Seriously, Veronica, I don't understand this one bit. I don't know what I am going to do at the moment. I don't know how this is going to play out. I am only sure of two things in my life right now. God and you love me. That is it. Those are the only things that I do know."

She leaned across the table and of course there were a couple of tears in her eyes, and she kissed him.

9

The next several weeks were uneventful both for the company and for Josh. The rumors died down after several days and everything returned to some normality. As for Josh, he took the first week as an overdue vacation, deciding that the possible solution for him was to first clear his mind. So to accomplish that task, Josh played golf, redecorated a bedroom, and enjoyed some very romantic evenings with Veronica. But just like all vacations, after several days, he knew that life had to go on. Josh knew that he had to make some hard choices about his life.

Since he had so much anger, his first option was to forget that the company ever existed and start fresh within some other organization. Because of his extensive list of contacts within the industry, he felt landing another position should not be that difficult even in a soft economic market. After making numerous calls to friends, people who had the power to hire and head hunters who specialized in his field, his assumptions were not playing the same melody that he was singing.

Since he had a lucrative severance agreement, financially, he did not have to rush to the nearest Wal-Mart or Home Depot to subsidize his income. He did the usual and posted his resume on all of the Internet search engines and he checked the posted positions daily. Those that matched his background he would submit a resume for consideration. He even submitted resumes for other positions that he felt he was qualified for but no real-world experience such as sales or as a marketing representative.

Beginning the third week, it dawned on him that he had to file for unemployment, so he submitted the necessary forms online from his home office. Now with unemployment plus his severance he felt he could weather the storm until the right opportunity presented itself. To his surprise, just as he was about to leave his house to play golf, he received a telephone call from a Texas Employment Commission caseworker.

"Josh Harrington, please?" A very pleasant voice on the other end of the phone asked .

"This is Josh Harrington and to whom am I speaking with?" He inquired.

"This is the Texas Employment Commission. My name is Velma Peoples, badge number #4562910," the voice responded.

"I believe you said Peoples, and may I ask what is this about?" Since he had only filed to qualify, he was curious why TEC was doing a follow-up phone interview.

"The reason why I am calling, my office has been assigned your case, and I need to get some additional information. Is this a good time for you, Mr. Harrington? If not when would you be available to discuss your case?"

Golf was for fun but qualifying for his unemployment was business. So he made the time for her.

"What do you need, Ms. Peoples?" Josh asked.

"Well, first the reason for termination was stated "unknown." Was this an oversight when you filed your application for benefits? This is a required field that must be completed before your request can be processed," Ms. Peoples clarified the reason for the call.

"Well, it wasn't an oversight, Ms. Peoples. A reason wasn't given to me the day that I was terminated. So since my former employer didn't state a reason for the termination, then it is a little hard for me to give one. Now I could assume a reason and write that in if you wish?" Josh answered her.

"Since you did not provide that information, we did contact your former employer and was given a reason for your dismissal. The reason for future reference if you are asked was you were discharged for being unable to perform your assigned duties in a satisfactory manner."

When he heard that, Josh wanted to go through the phone. Actually, he had to hold his breath and tongue so he would not curse.

"What?" Josh asked angrily.

"The fax that we received stated that reason. 'Employee was unable to perform assigned duties.' Mr. Harrington, if that is not the reason that you remembered being told, I will insert your answer in your application."

"I can't believe this? Someone actually faxed you some document that says that I was terminated because I was unable to perform my job? Ms. Peoples, I was a manager that had twelve developers that were reporting to me directly. I was about to sign a statement of work on the day that I was fired that was worth $10 million. Now you are telling me that I was fired because I couldn't do my job. I was the only manager within my organization that generated additional revenue other than the revenue from my primary clients. And my profit margins exceeded thirty-five percent every month for the last eighteen months. I would put my cost center up against anyone else's in that corporation and I could hold my own."

"So, in your mind, this is incorrect?"

"Yeah, I would say that is incorrect! No, Ms. Peoples, it is more than just being incorrect; it is damn lie!"

"Mr. Harrington, then what you are telling me should be reflected in your personnel file. How often were you given performance appraisals, semi-annually, annually? And when was your last appraisal and do you remember the rating that you received?" She asked.

"My last formal appraisal was in December of last year. The company demanded that every employee should have a performance appraisal from his or her manager twice a year. The appraisal that is given at the end of the year is the one that is recorded and counts. The mid-year review is for corrective measures only if an employee is off track. As for my review, the rating that I received and should be in my personnel folder is 'Exceptional'."

"And the review before that?" Ms. Peoples inquired.

"Exceptional!"

"Do you remember the review before that one?"

"Look, Ms. Peoples, let me help you out. All of my reviews have been exceptional except one about four years ago and that one was just satisfactory. The reason for that rating was my team made a small half million dollar error that wasn't in our client's best interest."

"This is very strange? If your reviews have been exceptional, then I don't understand the information that they gave us. And your explanation today doesn't support the reason given by your company."

"That is my point. Why would anyone submit that to you if the documentation in my personnel records supports the opposite? If that's the reason listed in my personnel file, then there should also be supporting documentation showing areas in which I was unable to perform. Additionally, if I was on a PIP then there should be success criteria and deadlines for me to complete." Josh explained the process to her.

"Mr. Harrington, I am assuming that an employee must sign all of these documents: appraisals, written notices, performance plans and the reviews of those that were used for correction in performance, correct?"

"Yes, all of the documentation that I mentioned must be signed by both the employee and the manager giving the review."

"Mr. Harrington, what I am going to do is submit a request from your company for copies of your last five appraisals. I am also going to approve your claim for the moment while this is under investigation. I do recommend that you get some understanding concerning why you were released, but you too have to remember that Texas is a right to work state."

When he hung up the phone, Josh wondered why the company would say or take the posture that he was unable to perform. It also crossed his mind that since the company's official statement was that—and that was a lie—what else had they taken liberties with.

10

Paul Copeland had just finished his monthly staff meeting and was checking his calendar for today. His career was progressing on the fast track since the termination of Josh. Taking on Josh's old responsibilities, including the management of the Identity Management project, he was busier than ever. The signing of the proposal meant that his new team had both the funding and the support to take this project and market it as a true product.

Alex and upper management were giving them everything from outside consultants for marketing, an advertising budget and media support. The beta testing was to begin in about three months, so his daily workload was jammed packed.

Actually, except for a few informal inquiries from a few senior managers who had worked with Josh, the supporting documentation in HR was never needed, nor had anyone asked more than the usual casual questions around his firing. Paul was quite uneasy the first several days, but as time went on, he had placed that day in the back of his mind. What he did to Josh at first concerned him, and often when he was alone, he would question himself. Had he compromised his own beliefs or was what he had done best for the organization as a whole and for himself? Quickly each time he questioned himself he would try to validate his actions for his own peace of mind that Josh was the one who made the mistake, not him. He just used the instruments available to get that type of person out of the company.

Why was he thinking about Josh Harrington this morning he wondered? Get your mind on all of the stuff you need to accomplish today, for Pete's sake. Now, what is going to be the first task that he was going to tackle— mail? Just as he suspected as he was looking through the sack of stuff in his mailbox, all junk. What a wasted trip, thinking to himself, but then every once in a while it was a necessary evil to do. Then he saw an official looking piece of mail and that concerned him. Opening it up as he walked back to his office, the contents had his attention so fully that he did not respond when several of his co-workers spoke to him. As he got to the last sentence, he desperately needed to talk to Alex as soon as possible. It was Alex's idea in the first place to respond to the first inquiry, so this was their problem together, not just his alone. What he remembered the most was the final statement in the original letter. "Knowing and giving false information to this agency is punishable by fines not to exceed $10,000, imprisonment or both."

Calling Alex's office, he asked if he have time to speak to him. Alex informed him that his schedule was pretty busy that morning, but he would be available after lunch. Shaken by the letter, he tried to think what other words or phrases he could have used in his first response. Well, until he meets with Alex he had other things to think about, so he tried to get on with his day, but this letter was worrying him; the last thing he needed was inquiries about Josh Harrington.

Promptly after lunch, Paul was sitting in Alex's office when Alex returned. Taking off his jacket and hanging it behind his door, Alex asked, "OK, Paul, what's got you so rattled that we have to discuss today?"

You see Alex understood that Paul really didn't make any major decisions without first getting his input. To be truthful, even when Paul disagreed with Alex's thought, Alex's direction was what Paul would do. To him that was safer than following his own mind, because if something went wrong, Alex was always there to protect him and in some cases take the heat for the decision.

"We got another letter from TEC about Josh and why he was terminated."

"So, what is the point here? Why is that a problem?"

"This investigator, whose name is Peoples, is implying that our response and Josh's reason are not in agreement"

"Well, we knew that was a possibility from day one, Paul. Do you think he was going to agree with the company that fired him? That's my point; we answer their questions, and they pay him unemployment. Case closed. Simple."

"Not this time; she wants us to fax her copies of his last five performance appraisals. If we do that, then saying he was not doing his job is a problem."

"What did you put as grounds in the first letter?"

"Remember, when the first letter arrived, I came and talked to you about what I should reply. We agreed to save him the embarrassment of what he had done; we would put this generic unable to perform his duties reply and TEC would pay the claim and the case would be closed. Remember?"

"Yeah, I think I remember that conversation, but help me to understand something. If we actually put down what HR found, what would happen?"

"I am not sure, but I think, he would not qualify for it."

"So, we fax the documents to them and admit that those documents don't support us in terminating him, or we send them the documentation from HR that does support his firing; then they will deny his claim, right?"

"Yes, that is correct, I think. Then this woman might ask why we didn't do that in the first place?"

"Walk through this with me for a moment. Instead of sending her anything, could you call her, explain that the company does have supporting documentation justifying his termination, but those documents are confidential."

"But then she would……."

"Wait a minute, please, I wasn't finished. But because of the number of years of service he had, we gave a response that was very generic and one that would not send Red Flags to potential employers."

"But what if she says we can't."

"Since unemployment is paid using the company's dollars, we have every right to do as we wish. The other option is fight the damn claim. How much money are we talking about here anyway?"

"Just under ten grand, I think?"

"Call this lady; give her that story. Then let Josh and her get on with their lives. It has been sixty days since he left; he took his severance package, and the company can't be sued, so do whatever works best for you. Paul, this wasn't that hard that you needed my attention; that's one of the reasons I pay you to keep stuff like this out of my life. Now go earn your daily wages and put this behind us."

Paul understood Alex's message, but he didn't want to be left out on a limb by himself. He had one foot on a thin branch now by agreeing to help Russell Smiley and Alex didn't have a clue that he had done that. Now, to lie to a government agency—well he is beginning to take on more of this by himself, and no supporting documents that he has Alex or Russell's approval. Nowhere are their names on anything, and he wasn't comfortable with that.

Returning to his office, he called TEC and got Ms. Peoples on the second ring.

"Good Afternoon! Velma Peoples! May I help you?"

"Good afternoon, Ms. Peoples; this is in regards to case number reference 785-90-4567-352," Paul said.

"Just a moment, please. Did you say 4567-352?"

"Yes, that is correct."

"And to whom am I speaking with and what is your official title with the company?"

"Paul Copeland. And my title is Application Development Manager."

"How can I help you?"

"I received an inquiry from your office requesting documentation concerning this case."

"That's correct. The reason is the claimant's reason for his termination and the response from your company are not in agreement."

Trying to put a light spin on the matter and to see if he could get her into his corner, Paul responded with, "I don't know of anyone who was terminated that would ever agree that the company that fired them did it for the right reasons?"

Corporate Deceit

"True, they may not agree with the reasons or believe it is justified but this case is a little different."

Her answer concerned Paul a great deal. "How?"

"The claimant in his initial application left the reason for being terminated blank. I thought this was an oversight on his part, but Mr. Harrington stated that he was not given a reason for his termination."

"Every person fired from a company knows why they were let go. They may be in denial but they know."

"True, I must admit. Normally that is the case. When I gave him the reasons that….. could you please hold for just a moment?" Velma Peoples was pulling up the documentation of the response that Paul had sent her several weeks ago and she wanted to see who sent the response.

"Thank you for holding. I see here that you, Mr. Copeland, signed and returned the response from you organization. This is very helpful, since you and I should be able to clear up this misunderstanding quickly. Are you calling for a fax number to send the requested documents to my office?"

"Well, no, I wasn't calling about a fax number. The reason why I am calling is to find out why those documents are needed. Before I can release personal information about a current or former employee, I need to understand the need for that information."

"The need is very simple: you stated under oath that Mr. Harrington was released from your organization because of performance. Mr. Harrington claims that his performance while he was there was rated consistently "exceptional." Unable to perform and exceptional ratings are on opposite ends of the world; which one is correct?"

"Ms. Peoples, what if the company wanted to pay the claim regardless?"

"That is a company's right, but because of Federal regulations, I need supporting documentation to support your position."

Paul wasn't hearing what he wanted to hear. This woman was backing him into a corner and that was not good.

"What if, then, we were trying to give reasons to save Mr. Harrington the embarrassment of why he was really terminated and to assist him if financial assistance was needed until he was able to reenter the workforce?"

"Mr. Copeland, you can't do that. Because companies pay unemployment insurance they feel they have the right to state whatever reason they wish for a dismissal. Their only right is the obligation to pay the claim or the refusal not to pay it. The reason under Federal Statue 87802-1982 is that it is the responsibility of the employer to accurately disclose why the said party was dismissed."

"What? If we gave you the real reason for his dismissal, I have the right to still pay him if I choose?"

"That is correct; the law only wants to validate the termination."

"That is it?"

"That is the bottom line; we only want to know why. It is your right, then, to pay a claim or not; but reasons for the termination must be accurate and true."

"Thanks. I will send you that documentation either later this afternoon or no later than the close of business tomorrow. By the way, how long do I have to decide if I wish to challenge the claim?"

"You will receive a summary of status of the claim when a final decision has been made. From the date of that notification, you have twenty-one days to contest the claim," Ms. Peoples informed Paul.

"Twenty-one days? Then what is the process from that point on?" Paul wanted to know. He would need to know when he talked to Alex.

"If the claimant or you contest the findings of an investigation, there will be a hearing concerning the claim. This is normally a teleconference and all parties to the claim must be present. Each side has the right to submit evidence to support their case. The investigator will base his findings of the facts presented at the hearing. If you're submitting evidence, then you must provide the other party that information in a timely manner prior to the hearing."

"Ok, I think I got an understanding. Thanks for the information," Paul responded.

"Very well, Mr. Copeland, are there any other questions or matters you need to discuss at this time?"

"No, and thanks again."

Paul did forget to ask a very important question. Would the response fall under the Public Information Act, and that omission was critical for him to know.

His next call was to Helen Sparks in Human Resources. He asked her to place a copy of Josh's complete personnel file in an inter-office envelope and send it to him. Helen asked Paul what documents was he sending to TEC. Paul informed her that TEC wanted the specific reason why Josh was terminated. She informed him.

"Giving TEC that particular reason will automatically require a hearing," Helen informs Paul.

"Helen, why?" Paul asked.

"Because the official reason in his file states that he was terminated for financial misconduct. Under the rights of refusal section of TEC, that reason is not covered under eligible reasons to receive unemployment."

"So, when I send that, we are required to attend a hearing? Do we have to supply to TEC what the actual infraction was?"

"If you send supporting documentation, you will be required to send Harrington that same information. Paul, we are obligated to provide those documents under section.... I think it is 763 of the Commission Guidelines. You are required to attend the hearing. Failure to appear automatically dismisses your rights to contest. Remember, that on the date of the hearing to be sure you are on that call or you lose your challenge."

"So will I be send a notice of when I have to testify of why we are contesting the claim?" Paul asked.

"That's correct. The hearing is usually no more thirty minutes. Usually, the claimant has no supporting documentation to support his claim of why he should be granted benefits. If you appear, then there is 99% chance you will win."

'Thanks. Please get those documents sent as soon as you can. I really would like to put some closure on this as quickly as possible."

"I will try to get them by the close of business today, no later than tomorrow," Helen told him.

So, as soon as he received that information, he would fax the necessary document to TEC. Then the last step will be this hearing and Josh Harrington would then be just a memory.

After sending the supporting documentation to Velma Peoples the next morning, Paul went about his day with a broad smile upon his face. As he walked the halls, between meetings he even took on one of Josh's qualities, acknowledging everyone he met with a pleasant "Good Morning or Good Afternoon," depending on the time of day.

Two weeks later Josh received a notice for a hearing concerning his benefits. The notice indicated that his claim for unemployment had being challenged by his former employer. The grounds for his dismissal should disqualify his claims for benefits and the reason stated was financial impropriety.

When he read that, he became angry and wondered what was he supposedly guilty of? Apparently in his mind when his former company was asked to provide documentation showing his last five performance reviews, whoever submitted that first reply was changing the reason. The question that he couldn't answer was why? Now to claim financial misconduct, they are saying that I was inflating my financial.

The hearing was a teleconference and on the date of the hearing, he called but his former employer didn't. Because they were not on the call, the agent representing the TEC ruled in Josh's favor. Josh was informed that he would be eligible to receive his full unemployment benefits under the Texas statues.

Still puzzled about who was saying that he was unable to perform his job, and then saying he was financially irresponsible really had Josh confused. This was too weird to sort out; however, the company's actions toward him continued to make him wonder why was I fired?

Maybe, he should talk to EEOC or hire himself a lawyer and have a formal investigation done; at least he would know why.

11

A few days later Josh was having an early morning conversation with his ex-college roommate. Josh was bringing him up-to-date on his life and the possibilities of his future. His roommate, Keith Cash, was a professor at a small Baptist college in Florida, but through the years they had remained close.

"So, Josh, with all of this drama in your life, what do you plan to do with yourself?" Keith asked.

"Well, I have several options available, but the main thing—being fired— is not working for me, Keith, if you know what I mean?"

"It is not the idea of being fired; it is the not knowing what the problem was.

See, if you understood why, then you could get closure. But what you have been telling me is that you don't have a clue."

"Well, regardless of what the map says, this is still the South, so that alone is enough in some people's mind," Laughing. "No, seriously, what concerned me were the comments that they gave TEC about me: Joshua Alexander Harrington not being able to perform. Then saying it was professional misconduct for financial irresponsibility. That is like having a date with Jennifer Lopez for a night, and her replying to people that, 'He was not able to perform.'" They were both laughing.

"So are you going to go after them?"

"Me? Go up against a corporation with endless dollars, staff of lawyers, and no supporting documentation fighting for truth, justice and the American way? Who in the hell do you think I am—Superman?"

"No, I think you are one of countless millions in this country that are used, abused and discarded at the whims of the majority. See, Josh, that is what is wrong with the system and why it continues to operate even now the way it does. Man, there are ways to fight the GM's, IBM's and even Chase Bank if we want too. The problem is we see the size of the corporation first and not the real issues that corporations are made up with—people just like us. So, we go get our own corporation and fight them fair and square."

"And where do I find this mystical corporation that you are talking about? Could you hold for a moment, the CEO of my corporation is calling," making light of Keith's last statement.

In Josh's mind, Keith lived in a dream world of academia and not in corporate America, where the survival of the fitness is the law of the land.

"See, man, you do have at your disposal a corporation, with more money than your old company; it is called the Government's EEOC," Keith retorted.

"Oh, why didn't you say file an EEOC complaint, Keith? There you go talking as if you were in one of your classrooms, talking above my head about my own corporation."

This is how they had done from the first day that they met some twenty-five years ago.

"See, that is your problem: you never thought you were that important. Man, you are one of the smartest, sharpest individuals I have ever known, but you have always sold yourself short," Keith was not just saying words to his friend, but he truly believed in his friend's abilities.

"Don't you have copies of your reviews and stuff that support your case that you were better than most of your peers? Keith asked.

"Yeah, I have some of that junk in my folders."

"Then take those documents and what you got from TEC and go see what EEOC thinks? What's the worst thing that they could say?"

"They could tell me to get the hell out of their office and stop wasting their time, even though my tax dollars are paying their salaries."

"Right, but what are you doing about it right now but having your own pity party with me on the other end of the phone."

"Truthfully? Nothing, I just want to close that chapter in my life."

"So if they say you don't have a case then what do you? Lose? You are not doing anything about it right now. Stop crying how you have been hurt by the system and fight back!" Keith answers angrily.

"Keith, I hear what you are saying. I guess you are right that I have been having my own private pity party."

"My point exactly!"

"OK. But I have a small problem," Josh admits.

"Alright, we have a plan. So what is this small problem we have?"

"Well, I have the documentation to take them—— almost."

"Almost? Explain to me the almost! That sounds like being a little pregnant."

"I haven't gotten my personal belongings out of my old office, yet. All of those copies are in my desk."

"Why?"

"Since it's you that I am talking to about this…. I guess, I just couldn't bring myself to really close that chapter in my life. I just don't have the energy to go back there. Call it pride or whatever, I just can't face it."

"You can't cry over spilled milk, like my grandmother used to say, but you sure in Hell can get a damn mop and clean up the mess. Go get your stuff, today. It's still early, and the only thing you have been telling me is that you've been playing a lot of golf. You don't have any reasons not to get this done today—

not even talking to me—so hang up the phone and go get your stuff."

"Before you think I am a complete idiot, I have tried on several occasions to do that, but I can't seem to make that happen. Strange as it may sound, I have emailed both Paul and Alex about it, but they have never replied."

"Call them and demand that they either let you get your stuff or ship it to you. Tell them that it doesn't matter which one happens, but those are your belongings. Sounds to me like a cop-out on your part; the Harrington that I know has a customer's mentality. So, if they are not answering, somebody will if you holler loud enough."

Damn! He hated him when he was right. He knew himself that he would not let a couple of people stop him, if there was something that he really wanted. He was finding himself allowing other people to dictate his actions…. and reactions.

"Keith, you have my word; I will have it all by the end of the week. I'm going to contact the EEOC and fight this thing. Why am I allowing anyone to lie about me?"

"Josh, for the first time you are letting someone else control your life. Now, that is not the man I know. Do what you have to do."

With that, they promised to talk after Josh had gone to EEOC. Directly after he got off the phone, he sent another email to Paul Copeland and Alex Mann, inquiring about getting his personal belonging. He was thinking to himself that if he didn't hear from them by mid-morning, then they were not going to like his next move.

High noon rolled around and no response, so he sent another email, adding Alex's boss and the head of Human Resources.

Within an hour after sending his second email, his phone rang. The caller-id showed it was from the office. Boy, he thought that was fast, but he remembered they too knew how he was, but to his surprise, it was none of the people that he expected.

"Josh, how are you doing?" The voice on the other end of the line asked.

It was Brandon Harris, his former boss. You see not only had Josh worked for Brandon through the years; in Josh's mind they were friends. Actually, their career paths were almost identical, and Brandon had worked for Josh at one

Corporate Deceit

point in his career. Also, Josh had worked for Brandon as his assistant cost center manager handling Brandon's day-to-day operations and financial when Brandon's group was in trouble with a major project.

"Hi, Brandon. OK. What took you so long to call?" Josh wanted to know.

Since he did consider Brandon as a friend, he was somewhat surprised that he hadn't heard from him. He had heard from several of his peers but the call he had expected to be one of the first had never come until today.

"Man, you know we are like brothers, so when you left I just didn't know exactly what to do or to say. And I knew if you needed my help you would call me."

Since he really treated Brandon as a friend, he was upset that it took his friend sixty plus days before hearing a word from him.

"OK. So why this sudden change in heart?"

"First, because I care about you; and secondly, to give you some information off the record. Since, I know that you are home, I will call you back in a minute."

Within seconds, his phone, rang, and it is Brandon.

"What's this information, why off the record, and where are you?" Josh asked.

"I am on my cell and I didn't want to make this call from the office. I am driving to meet Edith for lunch. The "off the record" stuff is from Alex. He wanted to let you know that he and Paul can't talk to you or respond because of the directions that they have been given by HR."

"Brandon, are you smoking crack or are those two doing drugs at lunch? What do you mean HR won't let them to talk to me? Hell, I only emailed them to get my personal belonging, so what is the big deal behind that?"

"Look, Josh, don't kill the messenger. Alex wanted to let you know that he did receive your emails, but HR got him over a barrel."

"Brandon, that wouldn't make sense to a crazy person. All I have been emailing them about is scheduling a time that I could get my personal stuff. Actually, I talked to Security and they informed me that the only way for that to happen is that Alex or Paul has to okay it. So why are those two making this harder than it should be?"

"Look, you know Alex; if HR says don't talk or email you, then he won't. Let's change the subject. Is there anything I can do for you, and why don't you come out to house for dinner next week?"

Josh had not heard a word out of Brandon's mouth. He was fuming with anger and plotting in his head his next move.

"What? Sorry. My mind drifted off for a moment. I was thinking why would Human Resources advise them that way? It's not like I wanted to go into the system or anything, all I have ever written them about was picking up my belongings, not blowing up the building."

Brandon repeated his invitation, Josh promised to call.

Josh on the other hand, began round three and sent another email, adding the vice president and the President of his division to that email.

That afternoon he received another phone call; this time it was a person from Human Resources who wanted to talk to him.

"Josh Harrington, please?" the lady on the phone asked

"This is he; who am I speaking with?"

"My name is Helen Sparks and I am an associate relations specialist in Human Resources."

"Okay, Ms. Sparks, how may I help you?"

"I have tried on several occasions to reach you and have left countless messages that you haven't returned. The purpose of those calls was to schedule a time that you could retrieve your personal belonging that are still in your old office."

Josh knew at that moment that this conversation was being recorded and by law she was supposed to acknowledge that fact to him. So, because he had started to play their game, somebody decided they would turn up the heat on him. Okay, he said in his mind, let's see who can blink first?

"I beg your pardon, and what is your name again? I never heard from you or talked to anyone else concerning this matter? So your statement about countless messages—I haven't received any messages or emails from you. So this is the first call," Josh responded to her statement.

"As I stated before, my name is Helen Sparks, and this is just one of many times that I have tried to contact you, Mr. Harrington."

"First, and please hear me out. First, change your tone of voice; secondly, this is the first time that I have spoken to you; and third, I have never received any messages from you or anyone else. Now, those are the ground rules for this conversation; would you like to start over?"

"Mr. Harrington, as I stated previously, over the last sixty days I have left…"

"Look lady, first of all you will change your tone, or this conversation is going to be real short."

"About your personal belonging………"

Since she had decided that she was going to do it her way—as she was making her last statement— she heard a dial tone in her ear. Within minutes, he received this email from Helen Sparks.

To   : Josh Harrington
From   : Helen Sparks
Subject : Personal Belongings

Josh,

I apologize for the delay in scheduling a time for you to retrieve your personal belongings. I left several messages at the home number we have on record and did not receive a response. It appears that your contact information has changed and was not updated prior to your departure. I have also attempted to contact you on your cell phone twice since your email, and on both occasions, you refused to speak to me and hung up the telephone.

Please retrieve your personal belongings from the west lobby security officer during normal business hours (8am-5pm Monday-Friday). If you have not retrieved the items by COB Friday, we will make arrangements to dispose of the boxes. Please contact me if you have any additional questions or concerns.

Kind regards,
Helen

Well, since she wanted to play the nasty emails and document her version, Josh thought it was only fair to do the same. What she didn't know was that since he had nothing to lose, then the normal rules of engagement did not come into play. So, when he drafted his version, he was going for the kill and he didn't care who was in his line of fire.

To : Helen Sparks

CC : Alex Mann; Paul Copeland; Benjamin Clack; Braylen King; Garrett Parker; Wayne Schier; Anthony Singleton; Sebastian Robbins; Emily Simmons

Subject: Re: Personal Belongings

Helen,

It does appear that our accounts of events over the last several days and months are not the same. I have left messages previously for Paul Copeland and Alex Mann; no responses were ever received or calls ever returned. And then to have an associate to call me on behalf of Alex, was insulting! That person's involvement and knowledge of this matter was totally inappropriate from my viewpoint. So, I did not understand the logic or the reasoning for that decision from Human Resources.

I have done it by the book, and let us say, bad timing, too much spam mail, miscommunication from HR, whatever—this situation is out of control. I am really confused that something so simple has taken so long to even get to this point. Until I started to add names to this distribution list. Now we are having open communication around the subject. Without those additional names, I am assuming this matter would have continued.

Your statement below, "You pick it up or we will dispose of them," is an insult and the implication that it is now my responsibility for the way this has been handled by your department, is insane. HR took the posture and made the decision on how to handle this, so the responsibility of returning my personal items should be yours. I can't just walk into there? I have called and written so I think the attitude of Human Resources in this matter at this point is invalid and does not support the intent of the organization as a whole.

Even in Paul's last response, rather his first response, he was forwarding the handling of this matter to your department.

Josh

    Surprisingly, after that email, his personal belongings were delivered to him the following morning by special courier. Josh immediately found the documents in question that supported his stance that his work and reviews for the last several years was beyond reproach. Believing that all of his files were there, he didn't notice that one folder wasn't.

    He phoned Keith informing him that he had taken the lead, and was scheduling an appointment with EEOC. Keith wished him well, and said that he was glad that his former roommate had returned.

    After that conversation, he called Veronica and relayed the same news to her. She was glad that fire that she had admired in him was returning, and she told him that she was praying for him. They planned to have lunch for the following day.

12

Having his bi-weekly departmental meeting Russell Smiley heard from Emily Simmons, head of Human Resources, that a former employee named Josh Harrington was raising all kinds of hell with TEC and internally about his termination. Feeling his face becoming flushed, he quickly asked what she meant by "raising hell". Emily explained to him how this guy sent an email copying vice presidents, department heads and blasting one of her top assistants to shreds. This guy was totally out of control in her thinking, so she had spent $500 to have his personal belongings shipped to his house, which included getting a service to pack his old office after hours. Russell wanted to know exactly what was in the email, so he tabled the issue, and asked Emily to stay a few moments after the meeting to discuss in more details.

He really wanted to know if Josh Harrington had started to fight back. He had talked to Paul Copeland several times after hours about Harrington, and Paul kept assuring him that the company was out of danger. Quickly, he continued with his staff meeting, tabling a number of items for the following month. Several of his direct reports were puzzled, but if your vice president says it can wait, then it can wait.

When the meeting was over, Russell excused himself for a moment, walked out to his administrative assistant's desk and asked her to check Michael

Jefferson's calendar, and to pencil him to see him whenever it was possible.

"All right, Emily, sounds like you got a tiger by the tail. Why?"

"Well, Russell, I have talked to Helen Sparks about this, since this caught me totally off guard. You know we let countless people go, place others on performance plans daily, deal with state agencies across the country about unemployment benefits and claims; a termination is a termination in my book. Of course, unless it is a senior leader that requires special attention with contract settlement, Josh Harrington was just that—an everyday occurrence, nothing special."

"So, since it was routine, how did it become an issue to senior management?"

"Would you believe... well before I continue, could we close your door?"

Russell got up and closed his door. Waiting for him to be seated before she continued, Emily opened a bottle of water and took a sip.

"As I was saying, would you believe, his manager would not schedule a time for the guy to come and get his personal belongings? And since his manager didn't do his job correctly, this guy Harrington began firing off emails copying whomever"

"What was the logic there?" Russell was really curious of why this happened.

"That is the part that is confusing to me. What did he think the guy was going to do: blow up the building or something?" Emily continued.

"So they just could not connect or find a time that was satisfactory to everybody? Security is on duty twenty-four seven, so there had to be a perfect time somewhere?" Russell asked. "So you are saying that Harrington has been writing this dumb-ass asking him for some type of relief or a phone call so he could pick up his things?"

"That was Harrington's thinking too. This dumb-ass, excuse me, I better start using his name, because I got a meeting with him today; and as furious I am at this moment, that is what I will say to him face to face. Harrington's manager, Paul Copeland, would not even respond to his emails. Now, if I was in Harrington's shoes and it had been me, I would have taken the same approach and copied everyone that I could think of, including Serif."

Serif Wali was the CEO of the company.

"Emily, you wouldn't go to that level would you?" (Smiling)

"Sure, I would; the guy's request was very simple. Nowhere did he ask to talk about his termination; he only wanted what was legally his."

"So why didn't we get him access and be rid of this matter?"

"That is were I get lost. Per Copeland's emails, he is saying that my department told him not to do this. I told the person that is handling this that she and I are going to have a meeting about this as soon as I returned this morning. I have to give an account to several senior leaders today explaining why they were included on a very nasty email that Harrington sent."

"Just tell them the guy is a mad former employee. Case closed."

"That would normally take care of the matter, if he had simply written a hot email. This guy was smart. He included the entire email trail with his. Helen sent one that would cover her and the department stating how she had tried to contact him. You know, in his response he even stated that he hung up the phone on her because her tone was rude. He didn't deny a damn thing—just laid it out there so everyone reading could read his response and draw their own conclusions."

"So, after you respond, is it now over?"

He was holding his breath waiting on her reply.

"Personally, I don't think so. What I am suspecting.... the next piece of correspondence that we receive about Josh Harrington will either be from the EEOC or some big shot law firm."

"Did he take a severance package, so he can't sue?"

"Russell, any good attorney can say that our severance agreement is given to an employee under duress. And if EEOC comes in, then that is another animal all together. Well, that could be discrimination and you know how the Feds are about that."

"But there is a Republican in the White House, so set-a-side, Affirmative Action; the rest of those programs are not popular at the moment."

"It doesn't matter who is in the White House; if this thing goes that far, it is who is in the jury box that matters."

When their meeting was over Russell thanked her for bringing him up to date on this. He also asked her to copy him on all future emails. Just in case some VP asks him what is going on. His last request was for her to forward to him the email that was floating around and has everyone in an uproar."

After she left his office, he called Paul Copeland, asking him to meet him that afternoon for lunch at Wellington's, a Bar and Grille which was in the lower Greenville area of town. Though he was very concerned about Emily's observations, he could not bring closure without raising suspicion that there had been a conspiracy around the termination of Mr. Harrington? Something had to be done to end this mess. What Russell didn't want was an EEOC investigation. Then he began thinking to himself, what if he hires an attorney?

His attorney could just show up one morning with a subpoena asking for documents trying proves that his termination was a fabrication of lies.

Even if the trial could not be directly connect him and his involvement, he didn't trust Paul Copeland to keep his mouth shut. For the first time since this started, he was beginning to feel the pressure that could result if this goes wrong.

Before the inception of Chapman and Chapman Veronica and Gayle sat down and did an in-depth business plan stating the objections from the beginning, but also they were going to try to define the responsibilities of both of them. Both recognized the strengths and the weaknesses of the other so to be successful they defined who would be responsible for a particular area. Veronica's strength was the detail accounting aspect of accounting: monthly financial, balance sheets and income statements.Gayle's expertise that she brought to the table centered on audit, tax law, and quasi-reorganization of a company.

Each took the lead in generating business for her particular area. Even running six offices nationwide, staffing was divided along those same lines. Looking from the outside, Chapman and Chapman would appear to be two separate companies sharing the same office space. Even when one of the sisters had an employee who was failing them; often the employee, when possible was transferred to the other sibling. This had worked great for them, because so often the person was a better fit in the other organization.

So when Gayle landed the audit with Josh's former company, Veronica was not aware that Gayle's team would be on-site. Actually, Gayle did not know that this was the company where Josh had worked. She only interacted with him at family gatherings. They were sisters, business partners and close friends, but their outside interests differed as much as night and day.

Actually, Gayle was envious of her younger sister and the relationship that she and Josh shared. For too many years, she had entered and exited several relationships, looking for the attention that Ronnie was now receiving.

"Ronnie, I just got a call for a big audit job," Gayle was so excited.

"Before I start jumping up and down— in town or out?" If the assignment was away, that meant Ronnie would have to take care of the kids while Gayle was away. Not saying she didn't love them, but each had their own styles and rules. Besides, she enjoyed not having to care for someone every day of the week.

"In town, and it is one of the largest…….."

"Hate to cut you off, but I am late to an appointment; call me later tonight and give me the details," as she rushed out the door.

Gayle just stood there thinking to herself. Sure, sis, I will. Now, if tonight had been like the last several months—first call her cell because nine out of ten she isn't home. Second, whatever I got to say, say it in thirty words or less, because she will cut you off, explaining that she and Josh are at such and such. Third, do not stay up late waiting on her to get back to you.

Well, this is too big of an accomplishment, and she wanted to share it with someone. Let's see…. Who? Maybe, she would call her new friend Bryon. No, that was a bad idea; too early for him to know how successful they are. OK. I will pick my ace in the hole.

So she goes into her office, picks up the phone: "Hello, Mom, are you busy?"

As Gayle was giving her mother the good news about her latest contract and the potential impact to the company, Josh Harrington was sitting on the third floor of the Federal Office Building filling out a questionnaire. As he answered each question, he was wondering if him telling the facts as he knew them would warrant an investigation by the EEOC. Finishing it, he returned the form to the guy at the front desk, returned to his seat and waited to be interviewed.

Corporate Deceit

While sitting there he wondered, do I really have a case; does the government care that people are losing their jobs across this country that a percentage of those individuals could be just like him: hard working, dedicated, strong, but for some unknown reason, terminated from their jobs without just cause. He would not have liked it, but if his company had told him it was because of job elimination, or just because of financial pressures to meet margins, then he could have accepted that. But to say unable to perform his assigned duties or financial irregularities— that he could not accept his personal pride had been wounded by that statements. In addition to following up the incident by not letting him get his personal items. Something had begun to smell, and he wanted someone to look into it. This wasn't his last hope for justice, but this was the biggest corporation that he could hire to fight his battle. Finally, he heard his name called, so he got up and was met at the door by an agent.

"Good afternoon, I am Stacy Taplin, badge number 297821; you are Joshua Harrington, correct?"

"Yes, but I go by Josh; only on legal documents do I use Joshua."

"So, do you prefer Mr. Harrington or Josh?"

"Josh is fine; that Mr. Harrington sounds so formal."

"Alright Josh, why do you think you need the assistance of the EEOC?"

13

"Well, it's slightly complicated, I believe I'm a victim of wrongful termination."

"So, could you tell me why you think this is true, and after that I will ask you some questions? So, in your own words, give me your version."

Josh then explained to her the events on that day when he was terminated. Then he explained his conversations with TEC, and most of all, how he wasn't allowed to get his belongings. After he had told her his version, she asked him questions surrounding his management.

"First, were you the only manager reporting to this Paul Copeland that was released and was this a downsizing by your company?"

"Yes, I was and no this wasn't based on a downsizing."

"Were you the only manager above the age of forty?"

"I can't answer that for sure, but I believe so."

"To the best of your knowledge around the events in question,, did you receive either a verbal or a written notice about any possible violations of company policy?

"None."

"In the previous three years, did you receive any performance appraisals that would be classified as unsatisfactory?

"No."

"Have you ever been placed on any type of Performance Improvement Plan?"

"No."

"In your last job assignment, if someone wasn't performing to the expectations of the company, would he or she be placed on a performance improvement plan?"

"Yes."

After she had asked her questions, she went over with Josh his rights as an employee. She also explained that the normal practice was for her office to send an inquiry to his employers so that they could have a chance to answer the charges.

"You have explained the steps to me, so may I ask you a question?"

"Sure."

"From what I told you, in your professional opinion, do I have a case?"

"Well as of right now, there are some blanks that need to be answered, but we've only heard one side; often there are bits and pieces that are forgotten. So it is hard to say at this moment."

"So, what if I am telling the truth and my facts are accurate?"

"Oh, what could happen? There could be mediation to resolve the issue. Also, there can be monetary fines imposed; and, of course, you could get your job back, with all back pay, any bonuses, and punitive damages."

The last part, punitive damages, was what he wanted to hear. Leaving EEOC, he was still unsure where this was heading, but for the first time in several months, he thought he was regaining control of his life. He knew the mentality of his former company and it did not bend to pressure on the norm. If anything, they would dig their heels in and fight to the death even if they were wrong.

In Josh's estimation that the company would not just rollover and give up easily was absolutely correct. Several days after his meeting with EEOC, Emily Simmons had a meeting with Helen Sparks and Paul Copeland to discuss not only Josh's email, but also to understand the evidence that had warranted his termination.

Emily Simmons was the department head for Associate Relations; however, her career in corporate America was in accounting for one of the large Big-Eight firms. So her mindset was similar to that of an accountant; either the information before her was an asset or it was a liability. Since she too understood the good ole boy system, she also knew non-whites and women were typically the sacrificial lambs if anything went wrong. So her goal was to attend the next bar-b-que as a guest for the meal and not be the hot entrée for the event.

Paul, Helen and Emily met in a conference room on the third floor of the administrative wing of the company. The agenda was very straightforward:

I). Why wasn't Josh Harrington able to retrieve his personal belonging from his office?
II) What was the logic not to return his calls or to answer his emails? Who instructed those decisions?
III) What evidence do we have to support his termination?
IV) Why is TEC inquiring about his termination reason, and what reason did we give Josh for being let go?
V) What measures are in place to put this issue to bed?

If Josh either hires an attorney or gets EEOC involved, are there any issues known that will support his claim?

Emily thanked them for being available, and acknowledged her tardiness to the meeting. Actually, being late is a standard practice for her. She always enters a meeting that she is leading five minutes past the start time. This allows the attendees the time to organize their thoughts, get any required documentation or layouts to be passed out without her involvement in the normal greet and meet exercise.

"Let's get started with item A, if that pleases everyone. Why wasn't Josh Harrington extended the common courtesy that is extended to everyone of coming back into the building after hours to get his personal belongings?" Emily asked.

The room was silent for several seconds. Then Paul Copeland attempted to answer Emily's question.

"Well, if my memory is serving me correctly, Alex Mann and I never finished the exit interview with Josh, and that is one of the last items on the check-off sheet from HR."

"Yes, I want to know what happened in the exit interview as well; but the question is what were your reasons for not letting him retrieve his belongings?" Emily reiterated her original question.

"I was following the directions from HR and not communicating with him on any subject. Our directions and the package suggest that all communications following termination should be done by your department, so we followed the guidelines. Any requests or calls from him were forwarded to Helen," Paul told her.

"Helen, then why didn't we ensure that Mr. Harrington was able to come back and pick up his things?"

"Emily, just as I told you this morning, I didn't know that his personal belongings were still here until his first email showed up," Helen replied.

"Do you recall receiving any of the emails that he included in his response to you before? You should have received those if they were forwarded as Paul said he did?"

"I don't remember seeing any of those emails," she answered.

"Well, I sent them and copied Alex Mann," Paul stated.

"Do you have copies of those with you today? Because if HR dropped the ball, then we will take the heat," Emily pointed out to everyone in the room.

"I didn't bring any of those with me. Sorry, I wasn't aware that I would have to prove that I did or did not do something," Paul shot back.

"Well, those emails are very important at this point. If you sent them as you said, then Helen is responsible for making sure that you made the arrangements for him to get back in. If she wasn't, then it is like he is saying he tried, we didn't, and it is our fault. After this meeting, please send me copies of the emails that you forwarded on to HR."

"That might be a problem, because I don't believe I kept them. I get so many emails because of my responsibilities and the limitations of available space on my PC, I only keep things that I must. Therefore if I forwarded an item on to someone else, normally that auto-trail would be deleted within a month or two."

"Well, if you can't locate them on your PC, please submit a request to the Mail team to retrieve those documents for you. After you have received them please forward them to me," Emily wanted the documentation as proof of who dropped the ball on this. She wasn't afraid to take the hit for her department if they had.

"I will submit that request, but the expense of finding them doesn't make sense, to me. What does it gain us? We should be one team, so placing blame on this department or that department is a waste of time in my mind. If you want in your explanation to say I dropped the ball, that's fine by me," Paul told her.

"No, that isn't the reason. I just want the truth. If you did what you said you did then Helen is accountable for that mistake. I really don't like saying it this way, but if you are lying about forwarding them, then that is another matter altogether that needs to addressed. So send the request and pass that information on to me."

Paul knew that he could not do that.

"What did you mean Paul when you said a moment ago that you didn't get a chance to finish the exit interview? That is the purpose of the check-off sheet that Human Resources gives to you."

"Josh stormed out of the building before we could finish," Paul was trying to explain.

"Stormed out? So where in the process did Mr. Harrington walk out?" Emily asked.

"Well, we had only begun the reason for the meeting and Josh began talking about what he would or would not do and he walked out."

"Are you telling me that, just as your meeting with him began, Mr. Harrington became upset and left the room? Is that what you are saying, Paul?"

"Basically, yes."

"So, was he ever told that he was being terminated and the reason for the decision?" Emily inquired.

"Yes, he was told that HR recommended that he should be terminated," Paul responded.

"And the reason for that decision?" Emily restated the second part of her original question to him.

"He became upset when we told him that he was being terminated, so he never allowed us to finish. From that point forward it was strictly damage control."

"So is this how it happened? Josh, effective immediately, your services with this company are no longer needed. Josh gets upset, storms out of the meeting and the building. Meeting is over. Is that how it happened?"

"It did not happen quite like that."

"If it did not happen like that, then give us an illustration on how it *did* happen."

"Well, we sat down, informed Josh that Human Resources had been investigating allegations about him. HR had come to the conclusions that the evidence presented to them was true. He asked what the charges were and wanted to speak to someone from HR. We informed him that based on those finding he was being terminated for professional misconduct. He got upset and the meeting is over. Let me explain something else. This happened almost 120 days ago, so what I just said is how I remember it."

"Mr. Harrington at some point asked to speak with someone from HR. True?"

"Yes, that is correct." Why did Paul feel that he was in court and instead of being a witness, he was the defendant in the case?

"Paul, are you aware that Mr. Harrington is over forty years of age?"

"Yes"

"Are you aware that Mr. Harrington is African-American?"

"Yes"

"Are you aware of the Federal Law, concerning age discrimination and the associated fines to individuals and corporations that practice that policy?"

"I am aware of the Law, and I figured there are some associated penalties for breaking that law."

"Did you know there are several similar laws concerning racial discrimination?"

"Yes, and I understand the point that you are trying to make. But Josh Harrington was not fired because or his age or his race; he was fired for professional misconduct, Ms. Simmons."

"But Mr. Copeland, in our country's legal system requires that a suspect cannot be asked questions without his or her attorney present, if he or she requests counsel; similar rules apply here too. When Mr. Harrington asked for, or where was Human Resources, that meeting should have halted until a representative from my department got there. In other words, Mr. Copeland, that is the first place you guys messed up," Emily was furious at that point. "Why wasn't an HR person there from the beginning? Was there no one from HR available?" Emily was sharpening her claws on Paul's backside.

"Alex and I felt that an HR person should not have been necessary since he was a manager in the company."

"Let me explain something about people. If by chance someone in this organization tried to fire me for whatever reason, they better have an HR person present. If they decided not to, my lawyer and I would own a huge portion of this company when we finished. Let me put it to you another way, Paul, and see if you can relate to what I just stated?

Paul, it has come to my attention that several individuals informed HR of misconduct on your part. HR has investigated, and talked to all of the individuals; so, Mr. Copeland, your services at this company are no longer needed. Please give me your badge, any corporate items that you have, and security will escort off the premises."

When Paul heard Emily's words a chill went up his spine; he became flushed and because of her tone this wasn't role-playing; she was firing him. His mind thought about what he had actually done, so her words had a deeper effect on him than he could ever have known.

The other question that entered his thoughts was what evidence had she reviewed, and why isn't she giving me a chance to face my accusers? He understood then what she was saying, and how that may have affected Josh, but with Josh he couldn't change his words.

Emily asked Paul: "Tell me, Paul, at that brief moment, how did those words make you feel?"

"Well, to be honest, I wanted to know why; but if that is how the company feels, so be it. I can always get another job," His reply affirmed in Emily's eyes: this man is dumber than a bag of rocks.

"You mean to tell me, with your salary, your obligations…. losing it without knowing really why didn't bother you? I personally would not walk away from a minimum paying job if that is my only source of income, without a fight?"

"That's why each of us is different. I never want to be anywhere that I am not wanted."

Emily almost lost her tack, but then she thought, what is the use? So, she decided to move on because apparently this person was not worth the effort of her energy. Besides, there were other issues on her agenda for which she needed answers.

Since they had been going at this for about an hour and a half, Emily suggested that they take a break and meet back in about fifteen minutes. As the ladies walked out together, Paul remained seated at the conference table, sipping a diet Coke. As soon as the conference door closed, he picked up his phone and called Alex Mann.

"Alex, this Emily Simmons is a tough woman. She is asking for me to get with the mail team and locate emails where I replied to Josh. She even was implying that we handled his termination wrong. She is sounding more like his lawyer."

"Paul, calm down; it is her job to ask hard questions. I bet her only concern is that she knows we got our act together. She is also trying to protect her department and staff from being seen as the ones who screwed up in giving us advice on this as well."

"Whatever she is trying to do, I am really tired of being slaughtered in here!

Hell, we haven't gotten to the real issues and she is building a case to tell Russell Smiley, and other senior managers, that her department did it correctly, and we blew it."

"Don't jump to conclusions so fast. It also in her best interest that we all stick together in this matter. Sure, after the smoke has cleared, we will get beat up a little because of this, but I am betting she will too."

"All right, I guess, but her tone and actions lead me to think she is positioning her department as angels, and we are the devil in this."

"That is her job, just like it is mine when there is a difference of opinions of who blew a project with a client— them or us? Just don't let her rattle you; the facts will support our decision. They will support our decision, right?"

"Sure they will, but remember it was Helen Sparks who said to fire him."

"Tell her that. That should take the heat off us, and put that monkey on the back of her department."

"Right. I got to go. I will stop by after this and bring you up up-to-date, so you won't be surprised if anyone calls you."

"That's why I trust you, Paul. You've always got my back."

Paul hung-up his phone as they were coming back into the conference room and took another sip of his drink. With all of the tough questions that Emily had asked before the break, the three ladies were talking about an upcoming baby shower for someone and were laughing. Their mood was light, but that changed as soon as they took their respective seats. Court was back in session and Emily started back with the same tone when she asked her next question.

14

About ten days later as he got his mail out of the mailbox, Josh found a letter from EEOC. Opening it quickly he read that this was a request for him to schedule an appointment as soon as possible. Checking his watch— it was 3:30— maybe he could reach her. Finding Stacy Taplin's extension at the bottom of the letter, he dialed her number.

"Good afternoon, Stacy Taplin, badge number 297821, how may I assist you?"

"Good afternoon, Ms. Taplin; this is Josh Harrington. I received a letter from you today, asking that I schedule an appointment with you as soon as possible."

"Thanks for calling. Actually, let me check my calendar so that you may come in. Hum, I have initial interview duty tomorrow morning, but I think I am available early afternoon. Let me check one more thing before I give you a time, Mr. Harrington. Could you hold for a moment, please? All right I can see you on tomorrow, the 17th at 2:00 P.M.. Is that time okay with you?"

"Yes, that will work. Ms. Taplin, does this mean that EEOC thinks that my former employer did something illegal in letting me go?"

Why wait until tomorrow? Ask the hard questions now since he wanted to know right then and there.

"Let's say that we do have matters that we need to discuss."

"Ms. Taplin, come on now; did they screw up, yes or no?"

"Let me leave it this way: I am not a judge or a jury, but they could have handled your situation a lot better. I will explain all of your options tomorrow in detail, Mr. Harrington."

"That's fine. I will see you tomorrow promptly at 2:00."

The first thing he wanted to do was to call Veronica and share with her the news that he had another meeting with EEOC and see if her case worked the same way. But each case was different and until a few weeks ago she had never mentioned that she had filed a suit through them. When she told him about it, he did find it odd that she had never shared that with him or even given her opinion that he should speak to them.

Well, that was Veronica at her best. She often painted the picture that she wanted to believe of herself in her mind, so what she painted was her reality. Never —well that was too strong a word— but seldom did she expose anyone her weaknesses. Her thought process was if anyone knew, her true feelings, including him then she was vulnerable. Didn't she realize that he would never do anything consciously to harm her? Actually, he only wanted to protect her because of the way he felt about her.

Since leaving the company, his confidence concerning their relationship was hit harder than words could express. Why would she want to continue with him, for he did not have the means to even keep their relationship at the level that it had been when he was employed? Was she shallow? No, but she was a woman that was ambitious and wanted a relationship with someone equally yoked to her. The only problem she saw was that opportunities to find a man with the qualities, money, and drives equal to her were slim and none.

That was the realist Veronica, but not the woman that he fell in love with—one she kept locked away in the deepest portion of her emotions. The funny, charming, caring individual was that person. Too often when he spoke to her about that person, she understood what he meant, but her rebuttal was that person got hurt more than she ever wanted to experience again. On one occasion,

Josh told her that he loved both personalities, but the mentally tough person was destroying the warm sensitive, loving and caring person day by day.

In certain ways, she treated their relationship as a business relationship. In her mind it was a Limited Liability Partnership, with, of course, a buy-out clause. Why couldn't she see, that when it came to either loving a person for himself, nothing else should matter. She had thoughts of her own when they talked about that and she, as always, had a valid argument. At this stage in life she would say it's not all about love because we are not twenty-five, but it has to also deal with security and the quality of life that one wants.

Enough about their differences of opinions— about who's right or wrong— no matter what she says, he knows that she loves him, but as Tina Turner sings, 'What's Love Got to Do with It.' Love to some is just a secondary emotion.

Come on, Josh, put your mind back on the matters at hand, and think through the next steps and the possible questions for Ms. Taplin tomorrow. What will I do if she tells me that I have a case? Should I ask if EEOC files the suit or if I have to get outside counsel? Is my case strong enough in her opinion to win in Federal Court? Boy, getting to this point seems to have taken decades and the company's legal department isn't involved with this yet, I don't guess? Knowing how Alex's mind works, he has touched bases with someone in legal. I am willing to put even money on that.

The next afternoon sharply at 2:00 Josh met with Ms. Taplin.

"Mr. Harrington. Sorry I forgot you prefer Josh. Josh, our initial investigation does support that your termination may have been handled improperly."

"Could you define improperly, please?"

"Reviewing your former employer's policies and procedures, your personnel file, and all of the supporting documentation that they provided and the documentation from TEC, it seems that procedures were not followed."

"So they screwed up in terminating me, but do I have a case to retaliate or fight them over?"

"There is never a case where retaliation is an option, Josh. I think what you meant was this: was your firing justified?"

"Yes, you are correct; was I fired for a valid reason?"

"Yes, you were."

At that moment, all of the blood left his brain. Nowhere in his rehearsal was he prepared to hear those words come out of her mouth. What justification did they give her or whoever reviewed those documents a valid reason for firing him. This had to be some type of mistake; he had never in his mind done anything to be fired for. How and why should he risk his future? Josh understood that he was blessed to earn the type of living that he was earning and to do anything to jeopardize it was stupid.

"For what damn reason?"

"Misappropriation of company assets, and they have the documents to prove it."

"That is a bald face lie! I have never stolen anything from anybody. You got to believe me; that is a lie!"

"Josh, why would a company single you out to accuse you and plant evidence to support those claims if they weren't true? What motive would that accomplish? You are just one person in that company."

"Look Ms. Taplin, I am telling you the truth; whatever reason and regardless of this so call evidence, they are lying."

Seeing that this man really believed that he was part of some big scheme to plant evidence against him, she wanted to be sure he understood the charges that were given to her.

"Josh, your company has evidence that you misappropriated assets and that is fraud, to say the least."

"What assets?"

"Josh, I wasn't the actual investigator who visited or was in contact with your former employer. From the follow-up report, the agent states that your company does have documented proof to support their decision, and provided that documentation to them."

"How in the hell can I see this so-called evidence that says that I misappropriated assets?"

"Your employer has the right not to show you anything unless they are forced to by a court of law."

"Since, I know this is a lie. What can I do?"

"If what you are saying to me is the truth, you could file a lawsuit claiming defamation of character."

"Does your agency handle those?" He already felt he knew the answer, but he wanted to be sure.

"No, we don't; you would have to get outside counsel if that is the course of action you wish to pursue."

"Then would the suit be in state or Federal jurisdiction?"

"That would be your choice. Josh, you have to remember I am not a lawyer, so I am only giving you knowledge from my experiences here. I think you could file it in either, but to file in Federal court, the damages that you would have to be seeking have to be above $50,000."

Fifty grand! Oh, no! Fifty grand would not even pay the taxes on the amount he had in his mind. Accusing him of theft, firing him, plus the embarrassment of letting people think he was that type of person…. it was going to cost them a lot more than fifty thousand dollars.

"Ms. Taplin, thanks for your time in this matter. I guess the only thing that I have gotten out of this so far is the reason why. Now, I guess my next steps are to find me an attorney to take my case and fight those bastards. Somebody in that company really does hate me? What on earth did I ever do to someone for them to do this me?"

As he was leaving her office, he turned and apologized for losing his temper. She acknowledged that she understood. If he was telling the truth, then he was correct— somebody really did hate him and then they also had the power to plant that type of evidence against him. He had an uphill battle on his hands, she thought, as he walked out of her office.

15

After his grueling meeting with Emily Simmons, Paul Copeland needed reassurance. On his way to Alex's office, he placed two phone calls on his cell. The first was to Russell Smiley and the second to Monty Cooper who worked for him. Since, both had as much to lose if this thing fell apart, they needed to be updated on the events of today.

Calling Russell his thoughts were first Russell had to be kept in the loop and control Emily. Since Emily was fighting for the integrity of her department and since she was looking for a way out, her sights were on Alex's organization. What she should be doing instead of pointing the finger is finding a way to protect the company if this Harrington thing began to unravel. After several rings Russell did pick up.

"Russell, Paul Copeland speaking, sir. Do you have a moment to talk?"

"Paul, are you just finishing your meeting with Emily?"

Emily had sent Russell a brief email stating that she was having a meeting with Helen Sparks and Paul Copeland about this Harrington matter. Her memo stated that the purpose was to resolve, address, and brainstorm the best possible strategy around the Harrington case. She promised to send him a recap and a copy of the meeting's minutes by the close of business the next day. Reading that, Russell became concerned, because he knew a trail of any kind, paper or electronic if found could be used as evidence if the matter got that far.

"Yes, sir, just finished."

"How did it go?"

"That, sir, depends on whose eyes you are looking through. I personally felt that this was not just a fact-finding meeting, but part of the discovery process looking for a pigeon to blame this on."

"Why are you thinking that this was a witch hunt?"

"For example, she came off and she didn't hide her feelings and emotions that Alex and I fouled up the termination of Josh Harrington. She even made me role-play at the damn thing based on my brief memory of the events of that day. She focused her attention to our group, and never accepted any responsibility on her organization for giving us bad advice."

"You know the drill, Paul. Every manager in this company is not going to publicly acknowledge that his or her team screwed up. So she was protecting those who report to her, but I will bet you whoever was involved on her team cannot sit down at the moment."

"Sure, I have done the same for the loyalty aspect, but I still don't know what she will report to upper management. From how she ran that meeting, my career, even my job in this company— may be *over*."

"You are over reacting to a very tense meeting with someone with whom you have never interacted with. Since I know Emily…. I know her far better than even she imaged. True, she's honest as honest can be and everything on the surface is either black or white. But the good news is, she still hasn't achieved the respect or the job that she thinks she is entitled to, so she is team player. See, Paul, if you want something bad enough, you will dance with the devil to get it."

"From where I just came from, I have already danced with the devil's wife."

"Paul, I got to get back to you, but before I hang up I want to understand one thing. Regardless how bad you think that meeting was, don't worry about Emily. I am still her manager so she does what I allow her to do."

After his conversation with Russell, Paul tried to reach Monty with no luck. Checking his watch, he noticed it was a little past six, so at this time of the day most of the technical people had already gone home. When Monty's phone rolled over to voice mail, Paul left a brief message for him to call him first thing. Still a little flushed from his meeting with Emily, he decided he needed most was a cold beer, some good country music and maybe, if he could reach her in time, a pretty woman. Finding her number in his cell's, he called her.

"This is Lori."

"Hi, are you still in your office?"

"If you thought I was in my office, you would have called my office number. Since you called my cell, you were thinking I wasn't."

"For once, can we start a conversation without the word games, please?"

Laughing, the voice on the other end replied, "OK. I am sorry, but you always start our conversations with where am I. If I answered the phone it should tell you that I am not too busy to talk to you."

"Point taken. Do you have plans that you can change for the next couple of hours?"

"For what reasons?"

"I have had a tough day and I was thinking I really could use a cold beer and the company of a pretty woman."

"Yes, I am still in my office so give me about twenty minutes and I will be there."

"See you in twenty minutes."

Well before he tackled the traffic to Murphy, at least he will be in a better mood. He called Alex's office explaining that he had to leave, so he would catch him up on the meeting first thing in the morning.

Stopping by his office, he looked at his laptop, decided there wasn't a need to take it, he just picked up his keys and left. He almost made a right at the light but got over in time to head toward that cold beer.

16

Another late night in the office for me, she thought. How was she going to explain to her husband that he would have to cook and possibly put the kids to bed because she really needed to work? He had just told her a couple of weeks before Christmas, when he was doing all of the Christmas shopping, that he was beginning to feel like he had a roommate more than he had a wife. Men and their egos; he would just have to make a few sacrifices for her professional growth. If the shoes were reversed, it would be expected of her. Why are women placed on guilt trips because they want more out of life beside babies and a Volvo? Emily had known since the day she graduated, she wanted to run a corporation and just because she was a woman, so what.

"Steve, how is the hunk of my life?"

"Emily, what are you trying to tell me?"

"What are you talking about, honey. I called my husband; where is the crime, sweetheart."

"For starters, the caller-id says you are in your office, and not on your way home."

"Well sir, couldn't I be packing up my office wanted to talk to my husband as I was doing that?"

"Sorry, but you know we have had this evening planned for three weeks?"

Quickly, she was trying to think, *"What are we supposed to be doing on a Thursday night? Damn, the concert! Oh, he is going to kill me. I forgot. What am I going to do? I promised Russell this damn report first thing in the morning, but those tickets were $200, and she and Steve hadn't been out in over two years."*

"I am walking out the door! I had a meeting that ran late. I just came in to get my purse and keys. I will be home in thirty minutes. Do me a favor; in twenty-five minutes, turn the shower on. I will start undressing in the garage. I should be totally naked by the time I reach the stairs." (Laughing)

"Were you serious about the shower?"

"Yes"

"Well, on tomorrow night, could you do the same thing? I can get Meagan down the street to watch the twins."

"Bye! See you in a few."

As she was driving home, she planned their evening. Concert. No problem. That was a given— then straight home. She would change into something comfortable and be back at the office by midnight. A couple of hours of work and send Russell his report. That way she could sleep in tomorrow morning, make love to the man she loves, and be in the office late. Boy, will her staff wonder what came over here when she strolls in around 9:30.

Paul arrived at his destination, pulled his car to the back and waited. After waiting only a couple a minutes, he was surprised when he heard Lori's Lexus SUV coming up the driveway and saw the garage door opening. Getting out of his car he walked on into the garage looking over his shoulder as if she had been followed.

While she was pulling into the garage, his mind wandered to when they first met about three years earlier at a conference in Atlanta. Sitting at the bar on the third night, she walked in looking drop-dead gorgeous and sat next to him. After a couple of drinks at the bar, they moved to a table and continued their conversation.

Their conversation centered on how each got into this field; then the topic changed to heir personal lives. She was married— no children—and her husband was an attorney who worked ninety hours every week and she played the clarinet. They had met during his third year in law school, and they had gotten married three months after he had passed the Bar exams.

His wasn't similar to her. He had married to his high-school prom date. What he didn't mention was he didn't love his wife and never had, but because she got pregnant on their prom date, he married her. Paul came from a strong Baptist family, so having a baby out of wedlock was out of the question.

As they continued to drink, they found that they had a strong physical attraction to one another. They began to flirt with each other, and before they knew what or how it had happened, they were in her hotel room making love.

That was three years ago, and now they worked for the same corporation. Their areas of responsibility are so totally different and because of their individual drives to climb the corporate ladder, their relationship was a total secret. No one in the company had ever seen them having lunch or a cup of coffee together; and if either called the other during the day it was always on their cell phones.

"OK. What is the reason for this mid-week need for a cold beer?"

"Well, let me say, it has been one of those days. Have you ever been in a meeting with Emily Simmons?"

His question answered her question, she thought to herself. Yes, and if she considered you friend or foe, you may need something stronger than a beer.

"Yes, I have been in several meetings with her. Were you friend or foe?"

"Oh, why couldn't I have been just a neutral observer?"

"Because….with Emily there is no such thing as neutral, so which one were you? I am placing my bet on foe since you need a cold beer, some music and most of all me." (This amused Lori because, except for the scheduled Saturday mornings together, this was totally out of character for them.)

"I was the foe. I was her entrée for dinner. That woman tried to eat me alive, and then she wanted to pick her teeth with my bones."

"Actually, she is a nice lady and one of the smartest women I have ever met. Now, you can't BS her, and never tell her a lie that you could get crossed up on; then you are dead meat."

"Well, it was like this: four people in the room including her assistant acting as a scribe, and she only brought one cross with her."

"That's bad?"

"Yes. When she started out so blunt, I was figuring she'd ask her hard questions first, and then swing the tone of the meeting to a more positive nature. Surprise, surprise, surprise; she acted as if the longer that meeting could go, the meaner she could get."

"That is what is called, 'beat them down while they are down." They taught that to all of Hitler's officers, I read somewhere." (Laughing softly)

"Since I knew what the subject of the meeting was about, I knew the questions were not going to be easy. What I didn't expect was that I was going to be the victim of a public flogging."

"Now you got my curiosity what are doing in a meeting with Emily that she is attacking you? Even though she is the department head of Human Resources, she normally handles the cost unit stuff and let her individual team leaders handle the actual relationship matters. So for her to be involved, what did you do? Curse out a vice-president in the middle of a meeting?"

"No, I didn't curse out a VP. It was about a termination."

"So what did this terminated employee do? Call Serif and gave him your name?"

"Close. He emailed damn near everybody in the company except him."

"So, who is this person that has that type of balls to do that?"

Since it had been four months since he left the company, and Paul hadn't mentioned him, she thought it had to be someone that he had fired lately. She was very shocked when he answered her.

"Joshua Harrington."

"I thought that was over?"

"So did I, but Emily informed me that EEOC had sent a questionnaire and TEC is still investing his case as well."

"So he is filing an EEOC suit?"

"I didn't say that, because the reasons behind his firing are solid. But she feels that he may try to file some other type of suit. Her main concern is answering the questions of why some of the big boys were copied on Josh's email."

"Oh, I thought by the way you were talking, she is scared that he could win?"

"No, there is no way that bastard can win."

"Let's change the subject. How about me putting on some steaks and you going up and drawing me a bubble bath."

"I can't stay. Allison has a ball game at eight. Her little league team is in first place, and her daddy, the third base coach has to be there."

When she heard that, reality set in again with her. She was only his Saturday morning wife. She had to choose where this relationship was going and from where she was sitting, that was nowhere.

"I understand. Oh, by the way, this weekend I won't be in town."

She didn't say anything about leaving town last Saturday. "Oh…. so when will you be back?"

"I will be gone the entire weekend; I going home to see my folks."

17

After leaving the EEOC that afternoon, Josh scheduled a meeting with his attorney for the next morning. That night when he talked to Ronnie on the phone, he never mentioned the reason for his being fired to her. She was out of town at another office working. She normally would work fourteen-hours a day, so he just briefly had the chance to say, "Hi" and that he missed her. Since she had only been gone a couple of days, her reply was she hadn't been gone long enough to be missed.

The next morning, he met with Nicole Singleton, his attorney.

"Nicole, I need you to refer me to a good law firm that could handle a defamation of character suit for me."

"Joshua, and why would I refer my client to another firm, may I ask? Who are you suing for defamation of character: your company or someone else?"

"My former company."

"I didn't know that you had changed jobs. When did all this take place?" She asked.

"I haven't changed companies. I walked in one morning and they told me that they were terminating me without a reason."

"What do you mean without a reason? You mean you were caught in a downsizing?"

"No, they are growing. I mean no reason. Then when I file with TEC, they call telling me it was because of performance. It doesn't stop there; next thing I get from TEC states that it is for professional misconduct. Wait. It's about to get even better. So then I get mad and I go to EEOC, right?"

"So far I am following you; so EEOC does an investigation, and they are suggesting that you file a defamation of character suit?" Nicole asked

"Not exactly. Actually EEOC tells me that they improperly handled my termination, but they should have fired me," Josh answered her.

"What, EEOC tells you that the firing was improper, but they are saying that your former employer should have fired you? That doesn't make sense. If they found that the firing was improperly handled, then they should have filed a case against them."

"Well, as Ms. Taplin told me, I should be thankful that they only fired me."

"What?"

"See the reason she is saying that is because in their investigation, EEOC states that my old company says that I misappropriated company assets, which is a new way of saying that I stole something," Josh explained.

"So, your old company is saying that you were stealing but you don't know what you stole?"

"Right, Nicole, but that isn't true. This lady, Ms. Taplin, at EEOC says that they don't even have to show me their so-called documentation, unless it is evidence in court."

"Well technically she is correct. Do you have any idea what they are saying that you stole? Did Ms. Taplin say, EEOC saw documentation to support the charges?"

"Yeah, somebody saw something, but what they saw—that I don't know. That is why I am asking you to refer me to someone who could handle this. And I figured with your caseload that you may not be able to do this for me and this is probably going to take more than one attorney?" He replied.

"Oh, so you are more than a client now? You know my caseload? I am too small for you, since I am a one-person firm?"

"Nicole, do not go there with me. What I was trying to say is this case is going to be tough and, knowing my company, it is also going to be lengthy in time too?"

"Oh, I am your easy case lawyer?"

"No, but this may take a while to settle, and it will require a lot of hours."

"Josh, all joking aside, I appreciate your concerns that my office is not staffed or that I appear not to have the resources to fight this type of case. However, Josh, you also have to remember, that those large offices started just as I did. Then one day their Josh Harrington walked in and the rest is history. Just maybe you are my blessing that I have been promised."

"I hope that was true, since we have this great relationship and all, but my future is at stake here. Do you know the amount of time this would require, and you know they have deep pockets so they will try to drag this out to whenever?"

"Josh, you haven't given me all of the facts, and I don't want any client's business if they are not comfortable with my abilities. I am a damn good lawyer and if the evidence is there, then any lawyer worth their salt can win a case."

"Nicole, there is something else that I forgot to mention."

"What is that? That my fee would have to be based on my winning the case? I knew that from the start. Look, man, the truth of the matter is this: too often we think that because we are small, that we lack something in ability. That is not the case. What we are trying to do is provide service to the average guy so the system can work."

"But, Nicole, what about investigators, computer experts and the rest of those types of people that I may need?"

"That's my problem to figure out. But I'm not going to try to convince you to use me. I know of several firms that handle what you want. Do you have access to a fax?"

"Yeah, but I will be on this side of town for most of today, so can I pick up that list around 3:00 P.M.?"

"Sure. Taquitha should have it for you then."

"Thanks, Nicole, for understanding."

"I did not say I understood. You are not the blessing that He had intended for me. I just got to wait a little while longer."

After leaving Nicole's office, he did some running around town, picked up a couple of books on civil law and got Nicole's list. Returning home, he made a couple of calls trying to schedule some appointments. The first available openings on the calendars of the first few attorneys that he called were ninety days out. He was successful in scheduling two appointments for the following week.

The weekend for him was uneventful: church, golf with his buddies.... But Josh was starting to feel the pressures of being fired. The spark of being excited on what he would do was leaving him. Actually except for those appointments he made on Friday this was the first time he had opened his planner in over a month. He was finding it harder and harder to find something to pass his time. Too, add to his state of mind, there were no inquiries of his availability to be interviewed from the hundred or so resumes that he had sent out. No prospect of returning to the workforce— he couldn't think of anything that he might want to try as a business venture and he felt that he was beginning to accept his role as a victim.

Depression was getting to be a reality, but then he thought to himself, *"This is only a brief rest stop for him."* Since he was eleven years old, Josh had had some type of job— newspaper boy, janitor, grocery store clerk and countless others. Not having a job or interacting with people on a daily basis was really out of his comfort zone. So he decided until the right opportunity came along, he would read. He bought books on several subjects, but the one that got his attention the most was his Bible.

He thought he knew his relationship with God because he had been in church all of his life. This was the first time that he began to question what his purpose in life was. Where God was in his circumstances and when would God show up? He came to understand that there wasn't a separation between his professional life and his spiritual life, and to his surprise, God controlled them both. See, he was like so many, thinking the accomplishments that he saw or the things that he had were the tolls of his labor. To him at that moment in his life, Josh came to the conclusion that God provided the abilities for him to have, but it didn't belong to Josh. It was God's. So he pondered, *"what had he done or had not done that God was taking everything back from him."* Then his mind would change directions altogether and he would think that God was just preparing him for his next level in his life. This was just his *'Job experience.'*

At a baccalaureate service for his niece, Josh heard the speaker tell a story about an airline flight that he had been on, that story inspired him.

"He had been traveling in South America and on his return flight from there the ride became very rough. Since the speaker normally did not like to wear a seat belt, going through whatever the plane was going through, the ride was very uncomfortable. After experiencing what seemed like several minutes of being tossed to and fro, the pilot of the plane finally came over the intercom system:.

"Ladies and Gentlemen, this is the captain. We are experiencing some unexpected turbulence at the moment, but we should be clear of that in a few minutes. Please be advised, that you should remain seated; all overhead compartments should remain closed, and your tray tables should be in their upright position. Again, sorry for the uncomfortable ride, but in a moment we should be clear and hopefully resume to a smoother journey."

After that, the bumps and the shaking of the plane continued and to the speaker those few minutes seemed a lot longer than he had wished to experience. Shortly after that, the ride became peaceful again and, except for that brief moment of discomfort, the trip was uneventful.

Well, he forgot to mention when the captain informed them that we should have our seat belts on, he was already ahead of the game. He was wearing not only his, but he was trying to use the one next to him as well. But after the plane landed, he looked up the meaning of *turbulent* in the dictionary and discovered the most amazing piece of information. The word implies that hot and cold winds are interacting with each other. Because of their differences, this causes an unnatural wind shift in the atmosphere.

He also learned that when pilots fly into those types of conditions, to get out of them, they have to change altitude. The amazing part about that was planes can't go lower, because the unexpected drop in pressure could do serious harm to the it. When a pilot hits turbulent conditions is faced with only two choices—first, to continue flying through the turbulence and be bounced left, right, up and down; or secondly, to change the plane's altitude. Since he cannot fly lower than where they are at that moment, then it to means to change altitude, the pilot has to climb up. Thus when the plane is above the turbulence, the ride becomes smoother.

What Josh took from the story that the speaker was saying was: 'If you feel that your life is in some type of turbulence, God is just changing the altitude of your existence. Further, when He gets you to the altitude that He wishes for you to be, then this plane ride that we call life will become smoother.'"

Josh then thought how life was just a collection of experiences, and those mishaps that everyone goes through mean that God was only raising the individual to a new altitude. He reminded himself that even when he reaches his new altitude this time, again somewhere along the way he might encounter more turbulence. When He does that, HE will be just taking him even higher.

That speech inspired him and he had a new focus to regain both his life and dignity. So since he was changing altitude with God's intervention; his only choice was to buckle up.

18

Gayle and her audit team arrived at the building bright and early that Monday morning. After having a brief tour of the facilities, the team was taken to the Security Department for pictures and badges. Leaving Security, they were taken to their temporary home of cubicles on the fourth floor directly across from the Finance department.

After they got settled in, Gayle met with her team in a conference room and laid out the objectives and the proposed deliverables to the team. This was going to be a four-month engagement for Chapman & Chapman and the critical areas in this audit were accounts payable, payroll, the general ledger system and cash. If the time allowed, the team would then audit account receivables, but that should not be considered in the assignment of anyone unless all of the other areas were completed.

Corporate Deceit

She reinforced the need of teamwork and the potential impact of future business. This was their chance to take Chapman & Chapman to another level in its growth. After her introductory speech, she handed out the first set of assignments to her team. When she asked if there were any questions, one hand rose from the back of the room.

"Yes, Angelica, what is your question?"

"Gayle, I just want to make sure this is a true audit and management understands that we will identify everything in errors, questionable and does not comply with GAAP."

"Of course they do."

"What I really mean, Gayle, is just because we are a minority owned firm, do they understand that we follow the rules?"

"Oh. Let me see if I can answer this once and for all. People, we are a certified accounting firm, not a bookkeeping service, but the new breed of the old Big Eight. And yes, treat this engagement just like we have done all others. If you find any irregularities, document them and the corrections to those issues. Your corrections will follow the guidelines of GAAP without exception. Angelica, does that answer your question?"

"Gayle, it does and the reason I asked is because I have a friend in Oklahoma working for a firm like ours and they had an opportunity similar to ours. My friend told me that during the audit they found some issues. That company wanted them to over look those problems and tried to intimidate them."

"Angelica, I know of the situation that you are referring to. I had a conversation with one of the senior partners of that firm and I gave them my personal opinion on the matter. We, each of us in this room, when we took the state exam to become certified public accountants, we swore that we would uphold those rules and those of the Security and Exchange Commission to the fullest. If anyone in this company or any company where we are engaged tries to intimidate anyone of you, it is your responsibility to inform me or your team leader of that immediately."

When she finished her last statement, her entire team stood and gave her a round of applause for not only stating her beliefs, but also for the passion that she showed in giving her convictions to them. With that they left the room knowing that they had the full support of Gayle and Veronica. With a sense of pride, each member went off to begin his or her assignment, and to introduce themselves to those individuals that they would be interacting with while they were there.

The first order of business for Angelica was to schedule a meeting with Debra Kelly, the department head of Accounts Payable. Debra was a University of Texas graduate and has been with the organization for ten years. She had already obtained a Master in Finance from the University of Dallas. Sharp, articulate and an able manager, Debra exhibited the qualities that Gayle wanted in every member of her team. Debra with her degrees and understanding of both accounting and finance was over qualified in the position that she was currently holding, but her personal inner fears of failing had blocked her ambition and drive to rise in the company. Actually on raw talent along, she was an untapped jewel waiting to be discovered.

Her counterpart Angelica Giddings was totally the opposite from that of Debra. Where academics were easy for Debra, Angelica had to study night and day to pass the simplest of classes while she was attending North Carolina A&T University. Her drive to prove the system wrong was the driving force for her quest to success. The fourth of six children of a single mom, she was never encouraged that she could ever achieve any portion of the so-called American dream. Even while receiving her secondary education, she was told that she should be a beautician or go to some other type of trade school because she just wasn't college material. Too often she wanted to slap those who instead of encouraging her to reach for the brass ring of life, tried harder to make her accept the plight of her upbringing as her destiny.

Using all of the available financial aid sources known, not only did she go to college, but also with the victory of surviving her first semester, she used that as the catalyst to finish her degree plan in record time. After graduating in the top ten percent of her class, she took the next natural progression and obtained an MBA from one of the top business schools in the nation. Her goals did not end with her obtaining academic success, but her goal was to prove those who discouraged her early on, it is the individual responsibility for his or her destiny, not the conditions in which they were raised. Angelica had a dream and no one was going to stop her from achieving it.

Debra and Angelica had an instant bond even though their personalities were different— how each reached this stage of their respected careers— and even their political affiliations were as opposite as night and day. Both women sensed the integrity of the other and the positions that each held. Debra in the beginning would watch from a distance as Angelica went about her duties for this audit. Debra admired how Angelica could ask some of the hardest questions to a member of Debra's staff, but the way she would pose the question to the person, the individual did not feel any hostility or judgment. She observed the attention to detail that Angelica placed in preparing her working papers and how nothing got started until everything was organized in its proper stack.

Often the two of them would eat lunch with each other. Both saw qualities that the other had, so those informal gatherings gave each of them the chance to pick the other one's brain and to expand her knowledge base. At a typical luncheon the subject matter would range from the outfit either was wearing to why was a policy such as "X" ever instituted.

"Debra, and please hear me out first. When I was working with Steven and Renee today…. why are you having your two people check every expense report submitted? With the number of those things that you must receive daily that is a lot of duplicate effort. Beside your online system from a functionality standpoint it seems great."

"The reason being Angelica, around the first of the year, I had to fire a person."

"OK. So you fired a person, so you are punishing your staff because of that? That sounds kind of sick to me," (smiling).

"No, I am not punishing them, but you won't believe the trouble I got in over it."

"For firing someone! Hell, you are the department head, right? So, if someone isn't pulling their weight, *see you*!"

"No, it wasn't for firing them, but not being aware that they were stealing from the company and I did not have procedures in place to prevent it."

"Oh, so someone was submitting requests, this person was validating them and they were splitting the money, *got you*!"

"You are so smart. I would still be asking how they did it."

"So, how much did they make off with before you caught them?"

"About a quarter of a million."

"Damn! Instead of being put on the carpet, they should have given your team and you a medal for catching them."

"My team did not catch them."

"Well, who did? I know that they weren't stupid enough to pull up here making $30K a year, in a S500 Mercedes fully loaded? Actually, another client of ours in Florida had two accounting clerks do just that, except they were E320."

"No, they didn't. Actually, the guy's manager discovered it."

"How?"

"When he was reconciling his financial."

"Well, a quarter of a million would kind of stand out in his financial?"

"Yes it would, but it wasn't like that. See, it was after several months that he started to inquire and that was odd to me."

"Because those charges impacted his margins; this company is driven by margins."

"Name me a company in this country that isn't and I will show you one that is no longer in business." (Laughing)

"No, what I mean is those dollars would have impacted his margin sharply, and when that happens you have go to the WCFM meeting and that is not good."

"The WCFM meeting?"

"Who Can't Forecast Meeting."

"Since I have to attend those and they are ugly, I still can't remember that manager ever being in one. Anyway enough work stuff; where in the world did you find that suit? I just love the color of it."

The Monday that Chapman and Chapman started its audit, Josh Harrington had a meeting with the first law firms to talk about hiring them for his potential lawsuit. Dressed for success, it was the first time in a while that he had put on a shirt and tie on a weekday morning. As he was getting dressed, he remembered how he used to take the time in picking out his attire for the day for the right impact that he wanted to present. In his his dark navy blue doubled-breast suit with the right matching accessories. He had a flair in his dress and he always believed that in that particular suit, with a light green tie, he was untouchable. Of course, in the heavily starched white shirt with his Monte Blanc pen, you automatically assumed that he was the CEO of some organization.

Even though he was impeccable in his dress and articulate in describing his need for an attorney, he found in his first meeting and those that would follow that the lawyers would be foaming at the mouth to ratify this injustice. Then when they learned the name of his former employer their interest in the case would vanish. Until he got to that point of naming the company, everyone was reassuring him that they were the champion that he was looking for.

It really had nothing to do with him and the conditions, but if they could prove the charges that he laid out, the damages could range on the low side in their minds at a minimum of $10 million or more. Furthermore, if they received the industry standard of thirty percent, this one case was $3 Million, plus expenses. But to go against that company was political suicide in their mind. The name recognition of that company alone scared every attorney that Josh talked to.

After he found this was the reception that he was getting firm after firm in the city, he even went to Houston, Austin, and even made a trip to Oklahoma City where he found a firm there that specialized in this type of case but still no takers.

Dejected, he called his friend Keith one more time explaining that he had a cloud of bad luck above his head and he was at the end of road.

"Keith, it is totally useless. Those bastards have ruined my life and there isn't a damn thing I can do. Man, I say the name and the fear just shows up in their eyes. I don't believe these people."

"OK. Let's go to Plan B," Keith suggested.

"Plan B! Hell, I didn't know I had a plan-B?"

"There is always a Plan-B."

"So Plan B is what?"

"Plan-B is finding someone who is not afraid."

"Have you been listening to me? Everyone I have talked to is afraid."

"I mean there has got to be someone who is not."

"The only person who might not be afraid is someone who just finished law school, barely passed the bar, can't get hired anywhere, and driving up and down the freeway looking for a wreck, so they can pass out their business cards."

"No, I mean someone who is good and is not worrying about their political future."

"So, do I put an ad on the NET, Wanted: Lawyer with Balls? If this is you, call me at 1-800-HIRED."

"Cute, but there is someone like that. I just know it!" Keith replied.

"Well, since you know them, please have them call me."

"Josh, just listen to me before you say I am crazy, promise?"

"From where I am at the moment, what else can I do?"

"Maybe we have been approaching this thing the wrong? Look, all of the big firms are white and this is the South, so a white firm might not be your savior. So, we need to find a minority firm that will take this case."

"Keith, do you understand the access to resources a minority firm would have to have. I am not just talking people, but also money to fund it. And then there are no guarantees that we will win."

"OK. Is that your problem or theirs? What you are doing is what everyone does: you are assuming that a minority firm doesn't have or can't get what it needs. You have bought into the system, that we can play but we can only play so far."

When he heard his friend, he thought back to the conversation with Nicole. She too told him not to worry about how she did it; just step out on faith that she could do it. But this was his future. Was he really willing to trust his future to a minority firm and limited resources?

"You sound like my attorney." Josh interjected.

"You already have an attorney?"

"Well, she has done some work for me in the past. Remember when my Dad died? She did the probate thing for me and a couple of other small things that I needed legal assistance on."

"Is she sharp?"

"In those matters, she was on top of her game. Remember, my dad had some property, and Shirley, his, girlfriend was trying to claim to be his common law spouse. She beat that woman, her children and their lawyer down." (Laughing)

"Why don't you give her a chance?"

"Man, do you know what you are saying? This is a woman with an office the size of your guest bathroom, with an assistant/receptionist name Taquitha. Now, can she fight the kind of battle that I need her to? I don't think so!"

"So, you are basing you judgment on the size of her office and her assistant's name? The real question is where did she go to law school? What was her ranking in her class? Did it take her six tries to get her license and does she want your case?"

"Oh, she wanted the case, but I passed."

"Well, my boy, are you hungry; because I see some humble pie being prepared for you. Call this lady back and then call me."

"Keith, I don't know about that. Do you understand the gamble of trying to use her for this?" Josh was having serious concerns about Keith's suggestion.

"Then what are your other options? If she's qualified and after she hears the details, she might pass on it too. But is it really that or the thought of your using someone other than some big name firm? Man, get real; are you trying to win or just show up and make a statement?"

"Look, if what that woman at EEOC is telling me is in my personnel file, yeah I want to win and clear my name. Does it matter who fights the battle for me? To be honest—yes. See, Keith, you don't understand the real world at all it is all about name recognition."

"That is where you are wrong, because those so call big names that you're referring to were little names once. *Think* ,Josh! The Hell with name recognition; get somebody who will have the passion to fight this for you." Keith could not understand his friend's logic.

"I still haven't bought into the idea that a small fish can swallow a whale yet."

"You might need to read about a little boy that killed a giant with a slingshot."

"I know where you are going, but how many years ago was that? B.C.?"

19

How does one prepare humble pie…. because after his conversation with Keith, that is what he was about to do? Looking in the back of his planner to find her number in his address book, he called Nicole. Taquitha put him right through. He was wishing that she would have to call back so he could have time to formulate his words and not sound like she was his last hope.

"Josh, how are you and why am I being honored with your call this afternoon?"

Josh could tell in her tone what she was thinking: so you got to call me anyway. He thought for a moment to say he was on some committee and wanted her buy a table or something. But she knew, so why prolong the suspense of seeing if she would just look into his case.

"Nicole, the reason why I am calling is………."

"Is what?"

"You know this is very hard for me, so help me out." He was trying to interject some humor so the taste would not be that bad.

"Josh, lets get real for a moment. You have been across this city, talking to several firms and there aren't any takers, correct? So, now you want me to look into this for you, right? But what I am sensing is this: you don't think a one-woman firm can fight the type of battle that you need?"

"On point! Except the last one you are correct. The issue, and it doesn't have a thing to do with your ability, is I am afraid that you can't support the expense of taking on my case without some type of guarantees, I think."

"Oh, the money that you think it will take to fight a major corporation is substantial. No, I don't have a couple of millions lying around in my checking account collecting dust. But I tried to explain this to you— that is my problem to deal with, not yours."

"But to win this, I am thinking we will need some experts, an accounting firm, a whole team just to write and answer briefs alone."

"Mr. Harrington, when did you go to law school? I know there are a number of TV shows on, and the average person buys into that drama. Of course there was the O.J. case, so they got a dollar figure in their minds from there as well."

"No, mine is closer to home than that. See, about five years ago, I sat on a jury in a civil case and the trial alone was five months."

"Really! So you are thinking your case will take five months in court?"

"No, but I do know there will be a ton of briefs to get information out of them, to prove my case including briefs for particular records and such."

"Josh, here it is plain and simple. Do you want or need a lawyer to fight this for you?"

"Nicole, to be truthful, no I don't want an attorney; all I really want is my life back."

"I understand what you are saying, but to get your life back you need a lawyer. Look, after I really understand your case, I might not want it either, and I might not be the best attorney for you. What I do know is that you won't find a sharper legal team that has more passion than mine."

"Legal team, I thought you were a one-woman office?"

"True, I am normally, but from the bits and pieces that I already know about your situation, you need my team."

"Where have you been hiding this team of yours?"

"All over the state for the most part, and there are several members of my team in other states."

"So, you got multiple offices; I didn't know that."

"I didn't say that either. What we need to do is get you in here, get all the facts that you have in your head, emails and papers documents—the works—and plan the strategy around your case. When can you come see me so we can get started?"

"I am available whenever you are?"

"How about my office—around five? What we will do is have a conference call with some of the other members of the team. That way they will have first-hand knowledge of what we will be facing, if we decide to take your case."

"Can I get some resumes of the other members of your team?"

"When you were talking to the other firms, I bet you didn't ask for resumes, but I understand your concerns, so it shouldn't be a problem. The real question that you must ask yourself is if you can trust us. Then can you do what we tell you to do, and never second guess us because we are the experts."

"Why would I second guess you or your team?"

"Because you have so many built in doubts coming into this. Its normal, but we are awesome when we go after people."

"How many cases has your team been involved in, and what is your record for winning those cases?

"In the last five years we have had— I think this number is correct— forty-three cases. We won them all but two. Actually, we won them all. The two we lost were when the cases went to appeals."

"So, you can win hands down in open court, but lose in appeals."

"All of them were appealed because of the amount awarded; the two we lost were lost because the client themselves lied."

"I will see you at five."

Corporate Deceit

Five o'clock Josh is sitting in Nicole's office. The phone rang promptly at 5:15 and the operator informed Nicole, that her conference call was ready to be started. Twelve attorneys joined in that initial call from across the state.

What Josh learned that afternoon was each member ran their own practice, but they had formed this team about seven years ago while at a conference. What they knew that collectively they had the experience, the knowledge base and access to numerous resources to take on a wide variety of cases. Even though they were highly qualified to represent both large and small clients, they didn't have the corporate client base to form a firm.

But ever so often, a case would come their way that required a joint effort from the team. A little known fact outside of the legal community is that this group had successfully negotiated the union contract for the AFL-CIO against the trucking industry. They had won the largest civil award in the state of Louisiana in the death of a worker killed at an oil refinery accident, and successfully won several civil rights violation cases. Their cases varied just as much as the members of the team.

At first glance, a client would assume that most of the team had attended a historical black college or a state university. This was not the case at all. Some had received undergraduate degrees from colleges and universities that were known as some of the top schools in the land. Even where they had received their law degrees varied just as much. Southern Methodist, Harvard, Stanford, Texas Southern, Boston College, Georgia, LSU and Georgetown are examples where they had attended. And the point that impressed Josh the most was each member was in the top half of his/her class and most were recruited heavily to join some of the top firms in this nation. Three members had clerked at the Supreme Court of the United States after receiving their law degree.

This was not a collection of low achievers, but a group of individuals who not only wanted to practice law, but also wanted to make an impact. They also did not want to be part of the establishment in a large firm. They wanted to be recognized for their talents not because of their ethnic background, but because they were excellent at what they did.

Surprising to Josh, the conference call lasted some five hours, because after hearing his side of the story, there were inquiries of what his expectations were, and questions from the group regarding who knew him and who hated him this much. Several members tried to estimate how many individuals could be part in this and all assumed someone high up the food chain was involved. One member, who he thought was named April, said their first steps after filing the lawsuit would be to file a motion for depositions from all of the senior managers. Her logic was this would scare the hell out of them because that action alone would hit all of the major business news services. Under no circumstance does a corporation want negative media attention, especially with the way the market was. That tactic alone would force them to the conference table for a sit down almost immediately.

Josh's mouth was agape as he heard this array of talent strategize the way they were going to attack them. He never would have thought that Nicole had access nor was she a member of such a team. As he asked questions, he was ensured that when they gained access into their computer system that the truth would be found. They also told him that they first were going after the corporation, and then after the individuals separately. Someone remarked, depending on the number people involved, that Josh could own a bunch of property in that city when this is over. They all laughed.

It took several days reviewing and modifying the initial draft before the team agreed that they were ready to file suit. Someone in Alabama was selected to prepare the final document to submit to the 256th Federal Court on behalf of Josh. The initial brief would be ready in about three weeks and a committee was formed to review it prior to filing it with the court. Nicole would be listed as attorney of record and all correspondence from that point forward would be sent to Howard & Howard Attorneys at Law, San Antonio, Texas. Josh was asked to be available to sign all documents and he would contact Nicole directly with any concerns.

Josh was also instructed from that point forward that all matters between his former employer and him should be conducted and handled by Nicole. That included the EEOC, Texas Employment Commission and, of course, anyone who contacted him on behalf of the company. If he received any electronic mail from the corporation, all correspondence should be immediately forwarded to Nicole. He was also advised not to contact anyone including personal friends for the time being at the company, and not to discuss the status of his case with anyone except his legal representatives.

If someone called, he was advised to tell them to contact Nicole or the Law offices of Howard and Howard. After he had given that information he should end the conversation politely as possible. By no means should he answer or give statements to anyone without a representative from the team. If the person insisted on requesting information or tried to extend the conversation, he should hang up the phone. If they ask for phone numbers, email addresses, fax numbers, etc, repeat the instructions that he gave them initially and hang up.

Nicole warned Josh that when he saw the initial brief that they were submitting to the court, first he couldn't faint; and secondly not to think they had lost their minds. She explained that the amount was not for shock purposes, because the team had reviewed the financial of the company and the company had the ability to pay what they were seeking and more. Based upon the information that he had given, the suit amount fell in line with the act and they felt comfortable that they would win his case.

Josh did almost faint when he saw what the team felt was proper, but he didn't. It took about half an hour for him to sign all of the documents both for submitting his suit and those retaining the team as his attorney. After he laid down his pen, Nicole offered him a glass of wine, but she said the real celebration would be after the settlement.

On July 1st, the clerk in the 256th Federal Court in Dallas, Texas, logged the brief in the case of Joshua Alexander Harrington vs. Cavanaugh Inc., the parent company of Cavanaugh's Consulting Inc.

20

Because of the July 4th holiday, Josh's suit was not delivered to Cavanaugh's Industries until the morning of July 6th. It was not unusual for someone from the Dallas County Sheriff's office to be at the building serving a brief of a pending lawsuit against the company. Since a suit had to be signed for, those who regularly visited the company normally—at least once a week—were on a first name basis with the receptionist in the legal department.

"Good morning, Officer Edmond. What exciting documents do you have for me today?"

"Just the usual, Rebecca, with the exception of one being a Federal case."

"Really! We haven't had a Federal suit in a while. Well, whoever thinks that filing in Federal court will scare us is in for a big surprise."

When the receptionist was handed the petition, the document was fifty-two pages, and it listed sixteen attorneys representing the plaintiff of this action. Thinking it was a client of Cavanaugh, she was somewhat taken when she opened the brief:

IN THE UNITED STATES 256th DISTRICT COURT
FOR THE STATE of TEXAS

)
Joshua Alexander Harrington,)
6713 Clarington Drive,)
Frisco, Texas, 75652))
Plaintiff,))
v.)
2
)
Cavanaugh Inc,)
999 E Street, N.W.,)
Garland, Texas 77029;))
Cavanaugh Consulting Inc,)
2100 W Street, N.E.,)
Garland, Texas 77029;))
Defendants.)
)

FIRST AMENDED COMPLAINT
FOR DECLARATORY AND INJUNCTIVE RELIEF

Plaintiff bring this action for declaratory and injunctive relief, alleging as follows:

Richard Carter

INTRODUCTION

1. This is an action challenging the wrongful termination and the defamation of character of Joshua Alexander Harrington who was an employee of the Cavanaugh Consulting Inc., which is a subsidiary of Cavanaugh's Industries a publicly traded corporation that was incorporated in Delaware. Cavanaugh Consulting Inc. actions and those actions are in violation of numerous provisions of the First Amendment rights of the petitioner who is before this court. In accordance Cavanaugh Consulting and its parent Cavanaugh Industries willfully and knowingly violated the petitioner rights that are protected by the Reform Act of 1973 (Cavanaugh Consulting) as violating the United States Constitution. The limits and criminalized speech and related activities were done knowing of the potential impact and harm to the petitioner. In doing such actions it dramatically caused the petitioner in this action refutable harm and impeded the petitioner the ability to obtain employment and defamed the character of the petitioner both in seeking employment and his standing within the community. The defendants exceeded the scope of the Federal Fair Disclosure Information Act of 1971 (FFDI).

PRAYER FOR RELIEF
Wherefore, plaintiffs pray for the following relief:
1. an order and judgment declaring the aforementioned provisions of the actions of Cavanaugh Consulting and its parent Cavanaugh's Industries actions as unconstitutional;
2. an order and judgment enjoining defendants from enforcing the aforementioned provision of Cavanaugh Consulting and its parent Cavanaugh's Industries;
3. costs and attorneys' fees pursuant to any applicable statute or authority;
4. any other relief as this Court in its discretion deems just and appropriate;
5. The petitioner is seeking damages in the amount of $15,000,000 plus punitive damages because of both the physical and mental effects of the actions of the defendants who are before this court.
Respectfully submitted,

COUNSEL FOR PLAINTIFFS

Elizabeth Nicole Singleton (Bar No. 2743145)
Dallas, TX 75123-9281

Kathleen A. Sullivan (Bar No. 879177)
Houston, TX 77305 1776

James Baker, Jr. (Bar No 7621989)
Baker, COLESON & BOSTROM
Austin, TX 78807

David Coleson (Bar No 78922121992)
Baker, COLESON & BOSTROM
Austin, TX 78807

Samuel Bostrom (Bar No 4587768591989)
Baker, COLESON & BOSTROM
Austin, TX 78807

Nicholas Cunningham (Bar No 87543691995)
Cunningham and Associates LLP
Dallas, TX 75276-09209

Robert Howard, Sr. (Bar No 756000621989)
Howard & Howard
Austin, TX 78807

Brandie Howard, Sr. (Bar No 7565785219947)
Howard & Howard
7800 Lovers
Austin, TX 78807

After she read who the plaintiff was, she walked into the office of the lead counsel for the corporation, Timothy J. Hardy. Hardy, as he was known throughout the company, briefly looked at the documents and then asked her to log it in just as she would any other suit that had been filed against the corporation.

Hardy understood that any suit that was not properly prepared for the corporation could be found liable, so every matter that crossed his desk was taken seriously. He added a note to his Outlook calendar to schedule a meeting with his legal assistant to discuss the matter. He returned to what he was doing, which was reviewing the annual 10-K document for the SEC.

After the receptionist logged the brief, she placed a call to Pauline Calhoun.

"Pauline, have you had your morning break yet?"

"No, actually I was just thinking, I do need a muffin or something. Were you thinking about going down, Rebecca?"

"How about I meet you at the little store in about 10 minutes?"

"Make it fifteen; I need to schedule a meeting or two before I leave. What is going on here? Finding a conference room has been almost impossible lately."

"I really feel thankful that Legal has its own. OK. I will see you then."

Fifteen minutes later she met Pauline.

"Don't you look cute this morning?" Rebecca said.

"Thank you; I went shopping this weekend and bought a couple of new pieces," was Pauline's reply.

They purchased gourmet coffee and muffins and found a table away from everyone and began to talk. Hardy's receptionist's name was Rebecca and after a couple of minutes of casual conversation, Pauline began inquiring the real reason for their taking a break together. Pauline knew when Rebecca called that something big had happened and legal was involved.

"Rebecca, since we are miles from everyone else, this really must be good?"

"Pauline, what on earth are you talking about? We just had lunch two weeks ago and it was just lunch. Right?"

"Yes, it was just lunch."

What Pauline forgot to mention, Rebecca said in just passing conversation that Hardy was concerned how some of the big whigs were exercising their options. Normally, that didn't bother him, but this quarter 10-K might give some future investors the opinion that some were cashing in thinking this may be the right time to do so.

"So, this is just a break, with no additional news or headlines?" Pauline asked.

"Well, we did get a new suit this morning."

"Don't we get suited everyday for something by somebody?"

"Not like this one. Josh Harrington's attorneys filed suit."

"Really? Well, protected class or not, that is still an uphill battle to prove," Pauline replied, but she really wasn't surprised.

"He didn't file on either race or age. His suit contends defamation of character and wrongful termination."

"Really. Defamation of character, huh?"

"And would you believe they filed the suit in Federal court."

"Federal or State, does it matter? I heard EEOC was out here about a month ago inquiring why he was terminated. So if they have been looking into it for him then a Federal court seems a likely place where it would be filed."

"Even when EEOC investigates a claim, the person could still file the matter at the state level. I think…. No, I know it is because of what he is asking for. That is why this is done in Federal Court if it gets to that point."

"So, there are limitations on what you can sue for at the state level? So, how much is his attorney asking for $100,000, or a million at the most? That would be the Josh Harrington that I know. The boy is sharp, and he always thinks big."

"Hardy *wishes* that was the amount. Josh Harrington's attorney is asking for $15,000,000 plus damages."

"Girl, you got to be kidding. I thought that since Congress passed some legal liability limits bill, people couldn't ask for that type of money any more?"

"In Federal court, if who you are suing has the ability to pay, you can ask for any amount of money you want."

"Girl, but defamation of character? I wonder how his attorney came up with that!"

"Attorneys!"

"So, he hired a law firm?"

"I don't know about that, but there are sixteen attorneys listed in his brief."

"Josh has a legal team? They really must think that he has a case. Are they from here? Normally, I would think no firm here would touch him even if he had a case they felt they could win hands down because of the Cavanaugh's name recognition."

"Maybe so, but apparently his attorneys are not from here or don't care."

"Look at the time; I got to run. Call me later this week and we will do lunch."

"I will, and I better get back too."

Walking back to her office, she was thinking, $15 million, a team of attorneys, and they are not afraid of the Cavanaugh's name. Either they got an airtight case, or they think that they can build one. Either way, what will Alex and Paul Copeland think when legal begins to ask questions? Why was Josh fired? There were plenty of theories of why, but to the best of her knowledge no one involved in it had been quoted, as this is the reason why. Not even off the record.

She stopped by Alex Mann's office, but as usual she found his computer on and no sign of him. She placed a post-it-note on his computer screen that simply read:

Josh is suing the company.

Call me,
Pauline

When Alex returned to his office, he noticed the note. Checking his watch, he note it was a little past six, so naturally Pauline was already gone. He dialed Paul Copeland's cell.

"Paul, Pauline left me a note in my office that says Josh is suing the company."

"Well, I expected that would happen. He probably found some lawyer who won't have a chance with Hardy and his team."

"I wonder what he is stating in the suit."

"Knowing him, it will be either racial or age discrimination. But as soon as Hardy gives his two-bit lawyer the cause…. case closed!"

"Well, whatever the reason he is trying to do it; don't be surprised if legal calls you, since he reported to you."

"Thanks, Boss. Only thing I have to do is send them a copy of my report and the recommendation from HR. Then, they will call his lawyer and that will be that."

"You are breaking up on me; I only heard bits and pieces of what you just said."

"Alex, Alex, can you hear me?"

Alex hung his phone up, because he could not hear him. Well, either he would call him back on a land line later, or they would talk first thing tomorrow. So he packed up his briefcase and left his office.

As Alex was walking to his SUV, he was surprised that Josh would think he could sue? He was fired because he was billing his clients for work that he never performed. Boy, the nerve of some people!

21

As soon as Nicole was notified that the initial brief had been served, it seemed that her team went into overdrive. For the next five days, Cavanaugh's Industries were served with ten additional briefs, injunction orders, and motions.

Those briefs ranged in request from depositions of the Board of Directors, the Senior Officers, and executives of the corporation, motions to gain access to the corporation's computer system, telephone voice message logs, emails, and access to all correspondence in regards to Joshua Alexander Harrington. There was even in those few days an appeal to the 256th Court for a restraining order asking the court that everyone on the deposition list not be allowed leave the country. The rash of documents was overwhelming to Timothy Hardy and he tried unsuccessfully to arrange a meeting between himself and Nicole.

While Nicole and several members of the team were filing briefs and appeals in Federal Court, other members were working behind the scene, arranging a war room in the offices of Howard & Howard and getting the team's Internet site and chat rooms ready. Because each member in most cases owned or worked for different firms, they did not have access or the means to create their own personal Intranet. But to ensure the security of their website, you either had to be pretty darn lucky or a privileged member to know where to find their site.

So with all of the wheels in motion, it was time for the first meeting with Cavanaugh's Industries. Arriving at the Cavanaugh's building they were met by Tim's legal assistant and they were escorted to a conference room. Just as in the TV shows, each legal team sat on one side or the other. Pleasantries, introductions—and for a moment it seemed like a happy hour mixer—as business cards exchanged hands. Timothy Hardy opened the meeting, thanking Nicole and her team of five for taking time from their busy schedule to meet.

"Ms. Singleton, we have reviewed all of your briefs and motions and we are unsure why your group feels there is any validity or merit in these actions," was Hardy's opening statement to the group.

"For starters, Mr. Hardy, after our interview with our client, it appears that his First Amendment Rights were grossly violated, and someone should be held accountable for this miscarriage of justice," Nicole fires back.

"First let me assure you the Board of Directors, the Executive Staff, Directors and Managers within this organization would never impede the rights of any individual of this organization. Secondly, the corporation has a very strict code of ethical standards that every employee must review each year and sign. Those guidelines are followed and practiced by everyone here at Cavanaugh."

"No disrespect, Mr. Hardy, but someone this corporation does not practice those policies, and because of his or their actions our client's rights were infringed and irrefutable harm to him has been done."

"Ms. Singleton, it is our intent to investigate fully the allegations brought by you and if what is being stated in your briefs is found to be true, then all responsible parties will be punished appropriately."

"Mr. Hardy, I commend your staff and you on conducting an internal investigation, but those actions will not satisfy my client, since it has taken six months for those actions to commence."

"Ms. Singleton, until you filed the original brief the officers and the executives of this organization assured me that there have not been any irregularities in the dismissal of any employee in this company."

"Mr. Hardy, as I stated earlier, we applaud your efforts of conducting an internal investigation. I am not trying to offend you or any other member of your company; however, senior executives within Cavanaugh should have noticed the red flag as early as April of this year. An internal investigation should have been done then, when members of your organization denied my client's rights of retrieving his personal property. Would you care to have the list of those individuals?"

When, Nicole asked Hardy if he wanted the names of the senior executives that Josh included in his email, Cedric Green a member of her team, looked in his briefcase to retrieve those documents.

"Ms. Singleton, that won't be necessary at this time. What I am looking for is a fair and equitable closure to this matter."

"Write a check or give us drafting instructions for $15 Million dollars, and we will consider this matter closed. Actually, we have the necessary documents prepared and a non-disclosure agreement with us today, if by chance you or an authorized officer of this company wishes to end this matter now."

"Ms. Singleton, I would like to end this incident as quickly as possible, but I am not prepared to approve your proposal or submit that recommendation to my superiors at this time."

"Well, I guess the next step then is the negotiation of access to your facilities both here and at any satellite offices deemed necessary for our experts and the submission of the deposition list for scheduling."

"My assistant, Matthew Killabrew, will be contacting your office before the close of business Wednesday with all of our Security forms for access. As for the scheduling depositions, my office has submitted a motion to the Court for relief and that hearing is pending. Until the Court offers its stance and the validity of your motions, the scheduling for depositions we cannot support or comply with that request."

While Timothy Hardy and the senior legal team were meeting with Nicole Singleton and those with her, Matthew Killabrew, Hardy's legal assistant was meeting with Security chief Tim Eldridge.

"Tim, Hardy wants to know everything you have on Josh Harrington. I also need your investigator to do background checks on sixteen lawyers and their associates."

"Are you requiring them to have drug test as well?"

"No."

"What kind of turn-a-round do you need?"

"For access, twenty-four to forty-eight hours, if possible. I don't want to give the impression that we are deliberately dragging out feet giving them access; but I don't want instant access either."

"Understood."

"About this Josh Harrington investigation— what do want from that?"

Tim already had done one, so to get the updates he felt should not be a problem. He also knew he shouldn't tell Killabrew that he had done one for Russell Smiley a couple of months ago. Let them find out for themselves; and it also kept him and his team from being in the middle of whatever was going on.

"I need the works. Add the works to one or two of those lawyers as well. I know one name for sure, but I better check with Hardy later on this morning or this afternoon to see who else he wants."

"Okay. Anything else?"

"That's a good start for now. As I said, I will drop you an email later today about the lawyers."

"Question? You said sixteen lawyers *plus*; Harrington has a full legal team on his side?"

"Yeah, and what I have seen so far from the five or six of them this morning, they are far from being your average attorneys.

22

He had signed all of the documents that afternoon in Nicole's office and it was now his attorneys who went to work fighting this battle for him. So he was still as lost as he was before, but he knew that this to was a long shot. He was still asking himself what would he do and would his life ever go back to something like it had been? He tried desperately to stay positive, but that was hard when his life was nowhere close to what it had been, and it didn't seem to be heading in that direction either.

To add to this state of mind, his relationship with Ronnie had not been on the best terms the last several weeks. She was trying to be supportive but his mood swings were beginning to affect their relationship as well. Since it was appearing that his life was a downward spiral, she was going the other way. Chapman & Chapman was growing. At dinner one night she told him that Gayle had landed a huge audit job with a major corporation in the city. Since Dallas was the Southern version of New York, in Josh's mind, a major corporation could be one of so many, so Cavanaugh Industries did not cross his mind.

After the close of the last quarter both sisters made some major salary adjustments to their personal salary along with some key individuals within the company. With this new influx of cash, both bought new luxury cars and of course, they were loaded. Gayle hired an interior decorator, per Ronnie she was contributing the max into her 401K. Then there was him—filing every other week for unemployment. *Why?* was the question he kept in his mind and the constant theme of his prayers? He had been embarrassed the last couple of times when Ronnie and he had gone to dinner. When the check came, she would go into her wallet and offer to go Dutch, and his male ego was crushed.

Beginning the second month in this new chapter of his life, he began to notice that Ronnie was finding more and more things that she needed to attend to and she would get back to him later. Where before all of this began they were, in his mind, a couple, but now instead of picking her up for dinner, she would suggest that she would meet him here and there. Finally, he had to ask the hard questions and her answers, carefully chosen, did not give him the warm feeling that they were on solid ground.

"Ronnie, are we okay?"

"Of course we are okay, Josh. Why would ask such a silly question?"

"Well, I've been noticing that, well over the last several weeks, it hasn't appeared we are as close as we have been."

"Well, the last couple of weeks I have had one of those weeks which I hadn't had for a while. Since Gayle started that new audit and she isn't in the office as much, everyone is coming to me. I can't get to the things on my desk because I am spending the majority of my day answering questions or dealing with other people's issues. I even told one guy that is what we pay him for— handle it."

"I understand your workload, but I was talking about us."

"Well, at the moment, I can only focus on one thing at a time and I know you need my support and you have that. But my primary thoughts have to be on Chapman."

"Sorry, I brought it up. I guess I was making my story up in my head?"

"I've told you before about those stories." Laughing.

"I still don't understand; it is always stories in *my* head, but in *your* they are reflections?"

"That is what makes us different. I have reflections; you have stories."

After arriving home from their dinner, Ronnie sat quietly in her den and wondered why she couldn't tell him what was really on her mind? Early on she felt she had finally found what she only had dreamed of before in Joshua Harrington. For so long as she could remember she wanted this type of relationship. She had seen it in other couples and she envied the women who were showered with both love and affection from their spouse or lover. She wanted to experience those feelings from someone who really cared for her.

But life, in her mind, had not dealt her that hand, so when Josh came into her life, after many years of searching for it, she thought she had finally found it. He gave her what she had always wanted but in the back of her mind she questioned something. Was this real or was she only making it the way she wanted it to be. When she found that he had some faults and he wasn't perfect, she began to create her own story. What she did not know was the dream she wanted was before her, but the fear of being hurt scared her so much that she had to protect herself.

Actually, she was more afraid than she would admit to herself. So, she placed this shield up just in case. This included Josh too, and when his life changed it validated the story in her mind that she wasn't supposed to be happy. No matter how much she loved him, she had to be a realist and understand this man might never be able to afford the lifestyle that she wanted.

Just as Veronica was having second thoughts and evaluating their relationship, so was he. Here he was before her believing that he had some control over his destiny and in a matter of months he didn't. Yes, he had relationships in his past, and yes he had used the "L" word, but until her those other relationships— no matter how special—they were just passing episodes in his mind. Until he met her, he thought he knew what he wanted, but his prayer to God was to make him the man that she wanted. Even those who were close to him saw that this relationship was nowhere close to those others, and he, Josh Harrington, was truly in love. Not just in love, but blindly in love to the point that he would do almost anything for her.

That's not saying that it is bad to love, but Josh, to his friends, was losing his own personal identity for Veronica. He began slowly to change and alter his activities to accommodate her. He gave up on doing those things that defined him as a person, but to him, he was showing to her, to the world, and to God how important she was to him. But what he failed to understand was the man that she loved was leaving and what she was seeing was another person taking his place.

Who he was becoming was not the self-assured individual, but a man who was reacting out of fear of losing what he wanted. Josh had to understand, if it were meant to be, as he had often quoted to others, it would be. What he didn't understand was it is the faith of a man that makes things happen, not fear. Fear is the by-product of not thinking one is worthy to have what has been given to him. So, if this relationship was causing him fear, it would not last, and then he must not be worthy to have her because he might not be good enough. When those thoughts first crossed his mind, he wasn't aware, however, that that was the day trouble began in the relationship.

But he was beginning to take a new stance that what is meant to be will be. His prayer included a passage from the Bible, beginning with Psalm 37:4

> Delight yourself in the Lord
> And He will give you the desires of you heart.
>
> Commit your way to the Lord
> Trust in Him and He will do this
>
> He will make the righteousness
> Shine like the dawn;
> The justice of your cause like the
> Noonday's sun
>
> Be still before the Lord and wait
> Patiently for Him
> Do not fret when men succeed in their ways
> When they carry out their wicked schemes.

For once in his life, Josh began to know that no matter which road he was traveling at that moment, just as he had heard before, his God was preparing him for a higher plane that even he could not ever dream of.

23

When Paul Copeland learned that Josh was suing the company, he tried to figure out what was the basis of the suit. Learning that Josh was suing, alleging that his termination was not justified, Paul wanted to make sure that their scheme was foolproof. He wasn't alone in being concerned because the rumors surrounding the suit were traveling faster than a brush fire on a hot still day. Russell and he had met to discuss the matter, and Paul ensured him that everything was fine. Russell wanted to know how many individuals were involved because depending on that number the chances of someone becoming unglued and revealing what they had done could become public knowledge. Also, if this was ever exposed, not only would they lose their jobs, but also they could face both civil and criminal charges.

Paul assured Russell there was only one other individual involved and he could be trusted. There was not a trail of their activity because of the way they had done it. And the company prided itself on their own internal security safeguards. One of the major assets that the company sales team pointed out to prospective clients was that the Cavanaugh's data security was above industry standards. Consequently, other companies were trying to duplicate Cavanaugh but at this point no one had not been successful in doing so.

After a meeting to reassure Russell that everything was in control, Paul had touched bases with Monty Cooper to assure himself that what he had told Russell was correct.

For several weeks right after he had a meeting with Emily Simmons he tried to reach Monty and had been unsuccessful. Then he decided not to follow-up because he remembered that she was not a technical person and the thought that she would go through all this trouble would not be on her radar screen. Her fishing expedition was policy and procedures, which he admitted to himself, he had blown. She had given some feedback that he needed, some additional training in policy and procedures. Emily advised that he should enroll in the next available class on employee situations. But after his meeting with Russell, he knew that he'd better check with Monty.

He met late one afternoon with Monty at a bar near the office, over a beer. Why not kill two birds at one time?

"Monty, have you heard Harrington is suing the company?"

"Paul, you know that I am too far down the food chain to hear about what you big boys do. So, is he suing on the basis of race or age?"

"Neither. His suit alleges that he was fired for something he did not do."

They both laugh.

"Well, according to my data, he is a guilty bastard."

"That is what I wanted to know. Does your data support that, and can anyone, even the sharpest people figure out that it is your data?" Paul asked.

"No way. To most people the stories of systems having backdoors are just rumors. To top that off, if the system is in production, then it is almost impossible to alter it."

"That's what I was thinking too. Since there isn't an audit path to follow, how could they trace it?"

"Especially since we caught it before the data was back-up. They would have to be very smart to figure it all out . Not only did I change the data on the files; I even changed the transactions that feed the AP system."

"The transactions file too?"

Corporate Deceit

Paul knew Monty was sharp, but to alter the transactions was brilliant. What he had done showed that the system had processed and paid Josh what they said he had taken.

"See, man, if an auditor ran reports and didn't have the supporting transactions, all kinds of RED FLAGS would go off in his head. So it must be true—case closed."

"Like I told you at the beginning, the man wants to be sure we haven't left any loose ends."

Paul had never told Monty who the big shot was that wanted Josh gone, and Monty really didn't want to know. After Monty had explained to Paul what he had done, their conversation turned to sports and women. After another couple of beers, they said their goodnights and ended their boy's night out on the town.

Before going home, Paul called Lori and asked her could she get away the next afternoon. Since that afternoon that he had gone by her place after his Emily Simmons' meeting, Lori had not been the same. But she was the best second wife a man could have and he wasn't ready to divorce her right now. Normally, she never demanded his time and she always understood when his schedule did not permit them time together, so she was ideal. Now she was always having something else to do, so maybe she was seeing someone else besides him. Now that did not settle right with him because if that was true, what would he do between 7 and 11 every Saturday morning— go to gym? He didn't think so.

When Lori talked to Paul she really wanted to know the details of his meeting that day. He had never told her who he had gotten to set-up Josh, and since she didn't know that many technical people she would have been clueless. But, what if Paul's scheme became known? Paul was clever, but to save his neck, then he might tell how he got involved and that would lead back to her. To make matters worse, she was tired of their relationship—if you call what they shared a relationship. Over the last several weeks it wasn't even that because she now wanted more than what he was providing, but until this Harrington matter was put to bed once and for all, she knew she had to continue. The last thing she wanted was a scorned lover exposing the details on how he became involved in this whole mess. So for at least at the moment, she needed to get her head right, keep everything as it was and then end this relationship and move on with her life.

24

The audit team from Chapman and Chapman was getting close to ending their engagement at Cavanaugh's Industries and, except for a few minor issues, everything was above reproach. The things that they had found were the normal things expected in a corporation the size of Cavanaugh and the number of people inputting data into their financial system. Most of what they were finding was that most managers had little or no knowledge of accounting. The only requirement that most colleges and universities have is that all graduates take one accounting course. Most did not know or had never heard of GAAP.

In one of the weekly meetings when the team brought issues and concerns to the group it was just the usual: have you seen this or that and nothing to stop hearts or raise the eyebrows of anyone. So, Gayle would ask each week if there was any thing that she needed to know prior to meeting with the senior executives and as usual there was no response. After she asked that question, then the procedure was to go around the table and have each member give his or her status report and the expected completion date for an assignment. All things were normal until they got to account payables and Angelica gave her status.

"Gayle, well AP is almost through…. just as soon as I get my hand on one issue."

"Do you need some help, because Garry is about finished over in accounts receivables, right, Garry?"

"Gayle, I should be out of there by mid-afternoon tomorrow at the latest," Garry interjected

"So, Angelica, do we need to schedule Garry to help you beginning Thursday?"

"Gayle, it's not people; it just one thing that is looking weird and everything supports it, but it doesn't make sense."

"You are totally losing me. Either the documentation supports or shows there is a problem. Simple Accounting 101! So what is it?"

"That is just what I said, but this one doesn't. Documentation supports the books in AP and AR to the letter, but cash doesn't balance."

"OK. Are we over, or short on cash?"

"Short! And the number isn't just five grand or so either"

"How much is cash short?"

"About twelve million, give or take ten grand or so."

Those who were bored and wanted to get back to their own assignments all looked up with amazement at the conversation that was taking place. Even the summer interns looked up in shock that a CPA couldn't figure out her error. Because it had to be an error, somebody in this company would know that they were missing or had twelve million too much. Regardless the size of the company, $12,000,000 was not petty cash.

"Angelica is there something wrong with your calculator, computer, hard drive, mother board, memory or something… because how in the world could you be off twelve million dollars? Did you fat finger an account? There has to be a logical answer to this."

"Gayle, everyone on my team has looked at my results. Joyce and Ross made copies of my documents and worked on them all last weekend. Then this morning they are telling me that they can't explain what we are seeing. We are twelve million dollars out!"

"Are you sure that you have the latest data and reports from cash?"

"Yes, and you can send whomever over there and let them start from the beginning, but I am telling you: at the end they are going to out that amount."

Everyone in the room just a sat there and tried to think how or what could cause that type of condition. Since Garry prided himself on being the best problem solver on the team, he was the first to step up to the plate.

"Gayle, I have a suggestion. Let Toby finish the loose ends that I have left, and let me help Angelica out.".

Angelica knew how Garry was, so she challenged him.

"Garry, you think it's something we have done wrong, *right?*"

"Come on, Angelica, we are a team, so I am only being a team player. But there has to be a logical answer to your problem."

"Okay. Bet you dinner at the Mansion; no limit for you and five guests."

Since the average meal for a couple was $300-$350, Gayle knew that placing a bet of dinner for six was a huge bet because she knew their salaries. She and everyone else knew that Angelica was wagering a $1800 bet on the table. Everyone in the room was thinking Garry would not take that bet. After thinking for a moment, Garry's reply was that she was on. The team burst into loud laughter and even a couple of the guys on the team started to make side bets. Everybody asked to be included on the winner's guest list.

"Guys, quiet down before we are put out of here before when finish," Gayle said as she was trying to get control of her meeting.

"OK, you two; and as your boss I cannot support your little wager, but one of you is going to have a long two weeks between checks. Seriously, Garry, thanks for stepping up and being willing to help out. To both of you, I know that I am one of the guests. Maybe I should encourage this kind of competition more often; I could eat at some of the finest places in the city on y'all's money," Gayle said.

They all got one more laugh together and the meeting ended.

Gary stopped Toby and they scheduled a working lunch so Garry could get her up-to-date on where he was. Garry also asked Maria to send him the latest cash reports and he told Angelica he would see her at 1:00; and he also wanted to know if their bet included transportation. Her reply was to make it heavy or light as his AE card could handle.

His reply to her was, "If you think you can afford it, the card could hold it." They both laughed and were looking forward to meeting at 1:00 in one of the conference rooms near Angelica's cubical.

25

After his meeting with Josh Harrington's lawyers, Timothy Hardy scheduled a meeting with Emily Simmons. In his meeting request, he asked her to bring all personnel-related information concerning Joshua Harrington. He knew that he had heard the name but he couldn't put a face with it. Then his legal assistant described Josh to him and immediately he had a face to place with the name. That image made him think: now I know who my enemy is, so I will now know how to attack his weakness.

When he met with Emily, she explained that the actual termination did not follow policy or procedures. So Hardy questioned the basis of this suit, how did his manager screw up in firing him, that is now worth $15 million dollars. Emily explained she personally had reviewed the documentation. In her opinion, Josh Harrington should be glad that he was only fired and not prosecuted by Cavanaugh for his actions. When she said prosecuted, Hardy looked directly into Emily eyes and asked: "Prosecuted, for what?"

"Theft"

"What in the hell did this guy do steal a laptop or something?"

"No, he was stealing using the AP system."

"So he said he was staying at the Hilton but actually he was staying at what the Days Inn?"

"Bigger than that, over the course of several months, he stole about a quarter of a million dollars."

"What! How does a person steal a quarter of a million from us?"

"Falsifying expense reports is how. At first we were under the impression that he was only cooking the books, so his margins looked acceptable. HR normally just recommend, that we take the person out of a financial manager's role, reimburse the client, and place a written notice in the person's personnel file. And that is what his leadership brought us to investigate. We discovered that not only was he over-billing, but that money was going into his pockets. His scheme wasn't about improving his margins, he was robbing our clients using our billing system."

Hardy became very angry because if what he was hearing was true, then instead of meeting with her, he should have been meeting with the DA. "You have documentation that shows what he stole?"

Emily hands the documented proof to Hardy. Handing it to him, she wonders why no one had informed the head of legal the charges against Harrington. Then the question popped into her head, *"Does anyone in legal know about this?"*

Seeing that this was the first time that he had any knowledge of this, she became very concerned. She had just assumed that Paul Copeland and his management had discussed the entire matter with legal before they came to Human Resources. She also had assumed since this happened just as the quarter was ending, legal or someone did not want any bad press when the company's numbers were not the best. The worst thing from a stock market point of view would be bad quarterly earnings and a scandal.

"Emily, leave me this with me and do me one more favor. I want a meeting within the hour with this guy's manager and his manager, you and the HR rep that handled this in my conference room. I want to know why this guy isn't in jail."

After he made his request, the meeting was over. Emily called Helen and asked for Paul Copeland's manager's name and told her to schedule the meeting and who to invite and for her to join them as well. At that moment, her stomach became a giant knot and she asked one of the ladies in legal where the closest ladies room was.

From the time that Emily left his office, Hardy looked over the documentation. He sent out a memo requesting an immediate response to all of the lawyers on staff, if anyone had been contacted about an employee named Josh Harrington and he wanted answers within an hour.

Pauline called Rebecca to tell her that Alex would not be able to attend because he had a meeting off-site. Rebecca politely asked her to hold, and transferred the call to Hardy.

"Timothy Hardy, may I help you?"

"Mr. Hardy, this is Pauline, Alex Mann's admin, Alex is out of the building the remainder of the day. So he is not available for your meeting, could he reschedule the meeting with you? I can check his calendar for available times, if you wish?" Pauline asked.

"Has he been in this meeting all day?" Hardy asked.

"Actually, the meeting starts in about thirty minutes. Alex just left the building about five minutes ago," she replied.

"Good, I will try to reach him on his cell. Could I have his cell number, please?" Hardy asked.

Pauline gave him Alex's cell number, which he quickly dialed. Calling Alex's cell, he answered on the second ring.

"This is Alex Mann."

"Alex, Tim Hardy here. Alex it appears that we have a serious problem here and I need you in a meeting in the legal conference room in about thirty minutes," Hardy responded.

"Tim, there is no way that I can do that. I am on way to a client meeting and this meeting is very important. Can you check with my admin, Pauline Calhoun, and see if she can rearrange my calendar, so that I will be available first thing tomorrow?" Alex asked.

"Tomorrow is not an option for me, so I must insist that we meet this afternoon. I am sorry and I know I am asking a lot, but this is a major issue. I need some answers and some clarity about a termination that your organization did. So do whatever you need to do, but I need you in this meeting," With that Hardy ended the conversation without giving Alex a chance to reply.

When Hardy hung up, Alex quickly called Pauline, and asked her to open the meeting request for whatever meeting Tim Hardy was insisting him to be in. He also asked her who all of the attendees were. Pauline provided him the information, telling him the subject line was titled 'Termination' and that he and Paul were required attendees. She also told him that Emily Simmons would be attending. He asked her to call his client and cancel his meeting and reschedule. Quickly, he knew that this meeting was about Josh, so he thanked her and dialed Paul. "Paul where are you?"

"I just got on the toll. Did you want to ride with me?"

"Get back to office; we have a meeting in legal in about thirty minutes."

"In Legal? What about our meeting with Cedar and didn't you explain to whoever is calling this meeting that we are on our way to client meeting?" Paul asked.

"I had Pauline cancel and reschedule for later this week. From the attendee list that she read to me, I am assuming this meeting is about Josh. So turn around and I will see you in legal."

"The client comes first, so we should reschedule this meeting with legal."

"Those were my wishes, but Timothy Hardy made it very clear that this is where we will be this afternoon. By the way, bring all of the documents and emails concerning Josh with you to this meeting. That way we should have all of the supporting documentation to answer whatever questions that Hardy has," Alex responded.

"Ok, I will stop by my office first and meet you where?" Paul asked.

"We are meeting in legal's conference room."

When the meeting started, Timothy Hardy was not polite and very blunt with his first question concerning Josh Harrington.

"I am not going to thank you for attending, but I will say someone better have an explanation of what happened and why wasn't Legal involved in this matter?"

Emily was the first to answer, "It was the understanding of my department that this had been approved by legal first. I was a little taken by surprise that no one on your staff had informed you."

"Well, I have sent an email to every lawyer in this company and no one can recall being contacted about this matter. So, if anyone has a contact name, may I have it now?"

Alex was sure that Paul would interject his comments, defuse this situation and give Hardy the lawyer's name that he had spoken to. Paul was the next person to speak, but Alex wanted to choke the breath out of him when he heard his response.

"Mr. Hardy, I just assumed that Human Resources had a standard practice to touch base with legal before they recommended termination. So when I sent all of the documentation to them, I was very confident that legal was in the loop."

If Alex was thinking about choking Paul, he would have to first get pass Emily Simmons, because if looks could kill, Paul Copeland just died.

"Paul, how on earth could you assume such a thing? It was Helen's impression that you had been to legal," Emily Simmons shot back to Paul's statement.

Helen Sparks picked up right behind Emily "Paul, you know that I didn't document our conversation, but you gave me the impression that you had been to legal. Actually, I believe I asked you, what was their stance on how we should proceed with this matter," Helen, who was normally soft spoken, wasn't ready to take the blame for not involving legal.

Paul saw that this was getting ugly and he had better think fast. He was jammed in a corner with no way out. What on the earth could he do? His only choice was to continue to lie.

"First, that was six months ago, I am very sure that I spoke to someone in legal on the evidence of him inflating his finances, the action of what should be done, I left that in HR's court."

"You mean you spoke to someone in my office about a person stealing a quarter of a million dollars and you cannot remember who that person was?"

"What quarter of a million dollars are you talking about?" Alex asked.

"The quarter of a million that this Josh Harrington stole from this company," Hardy shouts back

"There has to be some type of mistake here. The action that we took to HR about Josh Harrington was evidence that he was cooking his financial and over charging his client. How did he steal a quarter of million dollars?" Alex asked.

"I am not aware of any money being taken. I only saw where he was over billing his clients," Paul stated.

"The matter that we took to HR was that one of our managers was over charging his client. Since, I know of three other occurrences of this being done in the past, I was somewhat taken when HR recommendation was termination." Alex points out.

Paul asked the next question. "How did Josh steal that type of money and can we prove he was stealing?"

"He was using the expense reporting system to steal. Overstating his revenue was the means he used to hide the inflated expense numbers for his department. And, Paul, why are you looking so surprised; I know when I discovered what he was really doing. I know we had a conversation around this," Helen says. Actually, she is mad at herself, since this was a verbal conversation with Paul, and she doesn't have any supporting emails to prove that he knew.

"Everyone, if I had been aware that Josh had done that, I would have been the first person calling the police to have him arrested. The question should not be who dropped the ball on this, but what can we do now since we know." Paul retorts back.

"That's fine, but I am still not sure how two departments knew that this type of behavior was going on and no one had the common sense to walk up here and find a lawyer. Does Finance know that we may be a quarter of million dollars short in our bank account?" Hardy is probing for the truth.

"Since it was so obvious to me when I inserted the actual revenue, I assumed his managers had done the same thing? I was also assuming that we did not want him arrested at the building, so we first would fire him, and have him picked up at his home." Helen is now being like Paul Copeland— trying to think quickly on her feet— so she won't be named in the next termination letter that is written.

"Well, I guess that since, legal had no knowledge, then his arrest is not forthcoming is it? Alex, how did this get by you since he should have impacted your organization's financial?" Hardy pointed out.

Alex is lost for words and can't find the right response to Hardy's question. Since Paul has been doing his monthly reporting— and based on his projections from his managers prior to close his organization was never more than two points off of their organizational goals.

"I just don't see how he could beat our accounts payable system. Actually, even when I took the impact of reimbursing his client, my margins were still in line with my projections. So, if what Emily is saying is true, then Josh must have had another way of expensing those claims and not through the normal channels?" Alex fires back to the group.

"Then which is correct? Did the guy walk out of here with a quarter of a million or not? Who is that lady in accounts payable?

"Deborah Kelly?"

"Yes, did Deborah have her department pull the expense reports in question, and was Harrington's signature on them? Did we pull whatever bank files showing direct deposits, or checks being written to Harrington, and do they add up to that amount?" Hardy wanted hard proof.

"Tim, AP pulled all of that information for us and that validated our claim that he was stealing. Actually, HR contacted his bank and asked was there any way that we could reverse those transactions." Emily was trying to show Hardy that HR had done everything.

"Don't tell me, when you called, Harrington's accounts did not have the type of balances to support that he had that type of money sitting in his accounts? If I was him, then I would have moved that money within minutes of it showing up in my account."

"Emily, when you saw that Josh was stealing, why didn't you come to me or go to legal with your concerns?" Paul asked.

"It doesn't matter who came to legal with this, HR: your team Alex…. Hell, AP could have brought it up here. The matter is no one in legal knew that this person walked out of here some way, somehow, with a lot of money. Should he be in jail for this? Of course! But is he? No! That is what is really bothering me.

This guy is walking free and has the nerve to ask for more." Hardy's blood pressure is at a boiling point.

"Can't we have him arrested now? Then we could start investigating what he did with the money?" Paul asked.

"Hardy, I trust Paul and if he says that he had a conversation with someone on your staff he did. Therefore, when he came to legal the only issue that he had was that it did appear that Josh was inflating his financial. Now, I am not trying to place blame, and we all want the truth to be known, but we can't turn back the clock. The issue before us now is how we proceed," Alex responded.

"I have ten briefs or more in my office from the attorneys for this guy, ranging from asking for depositions from senior managers, motions for injunctions to stop or impede the daily operation of this company, and one even asking for Sr. Managers to surrender their passports, so no one can leave the jurisdiction of United States. However, now I find that I am tying up resources, court appearances, preparing answers for lawyers who are representing a person who stole. That is insane."

"If we have proof that he was stealing, can't we take that documentation to the judge?" Paul asked.

"That is my point! His suit is that he was wrongfully terminated; in other words, he is saying that he didn't do anything to be fired. Since, he hasn't been charged with any crime, it is up to the company to prove that he was stealing and him being fired was correct."

"The documentation that Ms. Simmons says she has proves that he was stealing," Paul interjected.

"No, it doesn't. It says someone was stealing and used his name. Until he is either convicted or he confesses that he stole he is innocent. Now what I have been doing for the last hour is looking at documents from HR, and it does appear that he did. The question for all of you is who said just fire him? If you felt that you didn't have the authority to call the police, then you should have escalated to whatever level that was needed. If your manager didn't want to take the responsibility then that is what legal is here for. I want each of you to go through email, notes in planners, whatever and look for someone's name that you may have talked to in legal. I also need to know who approved the payment of unemployment," Hardy was becoming angrier because this should never have taken place in his mind.

Paul spoke up, "Well, sir, I did; and HR was aware that we were."

"I thought when TEC called about the reason, and you sent that documentation, the matter would have gone to their appeal process," Helen remembers Paul requesting documentation for TEC.

"You sent TEC documentation that he was stealing, and they still approved him for benefits?" Hardy asked.

"I didn't go through the whole file because I thought I knew the reason for his termination; so I found the form that said for professional misconduct and sent that," Paul tries to explain.

"Well, correct me if I am wrong, but professional misconduct disqualifies a person from receiving benefits in this state. If you sent that form then he shouldn't be receiving unemployment from us?" Hardy responds.

"When I sent that form to TEC the lady explained that this would automatically go to appeal. An appeal date was set, but on the day we had production problems which I was involved in, and the hearing skipped my mind," Paul says.

"So, we appealed the ruling, but we didn't show up for the hearing, is that what I am hearing?" Hardy asked, directing his eyes on Paul.

"Why are we paying unemployment to someone who we say allegedly stole a quarter of a million dollars? Is he cash poor or what?" Hardy's anger was showing both in his choice of words and in his body language.

"Well, Alex and I weren't aware that he actually stole money. We also didn't want to impact him financially while he was seeking other employment," Paul stated.

Everyone in the room looked at each other when Paul finished his explanation of why the company was paying someone unemployment who may have stolen money. Alex was so embarrassed by Paul's comment that his head dropped for a second. Emily was thinking that her feelings about Paul Copeland were right on target.

"Let me get this straight. He stole from us and we want to ensure that he can eat, pay his utility bills, car payment or whatever. Additionally, to top that off we also want to help him while he is looking for another job. I personally don't care if he ever eats again and that should have been your mindset. Either case, if he was over billing his clients or stealing from us, he was stealing. I am telling you, the decisions around this have got to be the worst anyone holding the title of manager could have ever made. Consequently, I am making it a point to talk to your individual senior leaders about this. They need to know what type of people they have empowered to make decisions for this company."

Hardy was thinking, this guy Copeland could be lying and hadn't talked to anyone in legal, but then someone on his staff could be lying too. But could he really find the truth? Maybe not. What if Copeland is telling the truth and since there were three attorneys that had left the company since the first of year, it could have been one of them. Damn, in one way his gut feeling was this guy is lying through his teeth, but then there is this doubt of maybe not. But he had to do something because he had a $15 million dollar lawsuit on his desk. He had better talk to Serif and get his opinion on this.

As they all left the conference, they were all puzzled and wondered if their careers with Cavanaugh were in trouble. Outside in the hallway, there were two side-bar conversations between Alex and Paul, and Emily and Helen. If you had passed them it would have looked like boxers waiting for the next round.

"Paul, go through your notes and see if you scribbled this lawyer's name down anywhere. Think. Did you come up here, or did you call someone? If we provide Hardy with a name, it will validate his team screwed up and not us," Alex requested of Paul.

On the other wall, Emily was asking Helen to do the same exact thing and see if she had anything.

Luckily Serif was in town and was available to see Hardy almost immediately. You could always tell when Hardy was going to the CEO of the company. The first thing that he would do is put on the jacket to his suit. He did this out of respect. Serif seldom wore a complete suit unless it was a Board of Directors meeting.

"Good afternoon, sir. I have a couple of issues that I need some input on," Hardy said as he sat at the conference table in the CEO's office.

Serif Wali was American born, received his MBA at Harvard Business School,

Corporate Deceit

and in most people's eyes in the industry, he was a highly effective CEO.

"Hardy, what are these issues that are concerning you so much that you need my assistance?"

"First, sir, we are being sued for $15 Million by a former employee."

"$15 Million?. We must not be a very nice company to work for?" asks Serif.

"Well, from the amount, I guess you are correct. But it has been brought to my attention that the person who is suing us may have stolen from us while employed."

"Interesting? He stole and we fired him; now he is suing us? So did he feel taking company assets were within his rights?"

"Don't know the answer to that one."

"So what was he caught stealing?"

"Money-using the expense reporting system."

"What are we talking? A few hundred dollars? A thousand dollars? How much?"

"Quarter of a million."

"I beg your pardon! A quarter of a million? So, he found a lawyer after he got out of jail that would sue us?"

"We never pressed charges."

Serif, who was always in control, looked at Hardy in disbelief, as he told him no charges had been filed.

"Someone stole that sum of money and we didn't do anything?"

"Sir, I just had a meeting with all of the parties involved, and I have contacted my staff and no one is saying they had no knowledge of this."

"Legal has not been in on the loop at all and the reason being is what?"

"No, sir. One person says that he did speak to someone, but he could not remember who it was. However, when he came to legal, the matter of this guy stealing was not known. He was overstating his financial, so his manager only wanted to know their options."

"Hardy, can we still have this person arrested and charged? Moreover, can we prove in court that he was stealing?"

"From the documentation that I have seen the guy is guilty; so, yes, we have the rights to press charges."

"So, call the authorities."

After that meeting, Timothy Hardy placed a call to the Collin County District Attorney's Office and scheduled a meeting for the next morning. Following that meeting, the Assistant D.A. Julia Morales, issued a warrant for Joshua Alexander Harrington for a first-degree felony theft.

26

Today was the first day in the 256th Federal court to hear the arguments of the motion to grant the petitioner's request to obtain depositions from the Board of Directors, the Senior Management of Cavanaugh Industries, and it's subsidiary Cavanaugh Consulting, Inc. Nicole Singleton and seven of her team were outside of the judge's chambers and were met by Timothy Hardy and his assistant. The presiding judge was the Honorable Allison D. Hathcock, who had been appointed to the court in 1997.

Judge Hathcock, who received her law degree from Stanford, served in private practice for ten years, specializing in immigration law and was nominated to the Federal bench by former President Bill Clinton. Her nomination to the

Federal Bench had been strongly challenged by the conservative wing of both the House and the Senate for her perceived liberal views. She had several written opinions that were liberal in nature when she was State Supreme Judge for the State of New York.

Timothy Hardy had spoken to several other attorneys who had appeared before Judge Hathcock and was told she was very sharp and articulate, but most of all she was fair. She did try to remove her own personal opinions that were before her, but she did follow the intent of law to the fullest. Believed to be ultra-liberal, Judge Hathcock was respected by all who had appeared before her.

Nicole Singleton also was familiar with the Judge's reputation, and that is why the suit was filed in her court. While she served on the bench in New York, she had offered two opinions of affirmation concerning the rights of employees against corporations. Both were appealed and one was appealed and heard by the U.S. Supreme Court, where the high court rendered an opinion that supported the verdict of the lower court.

In her private chambers, attorneys for both sides presented their arguments of why this and subsequent motions before the court were either necessary or frivolous in an attempt to disrupt the activities of the defendants.

"Your Honor, the motion before this court to obtain depositions from parties who had no knowledge of the events in said matter and to ask for a restraining order to keep those individuals within the states until that time is undue hardship. Furthermore, your Honor, this impedes the operation of the corporation and the officers in fulfilling their obligations to the shareholders of said corporation," so elegantly spoken by Timothy Hardy.

"If it pleases the court, the intent of this motion is for the discovery of the truth concerning this matter. It is the contention of the petitioner that Sr. Executives and or Board members constituted this fraud and injustice against the petitioner willingly and with malice," Nicole Singleton responded.

"Your Honor, the allegations proposed by my worthy colleague are ludicrous, to say the least, and the foundations for those allegations do not pass the acid test for validity." Hardy quickly responded.

"However, the rights of the accused to seek from all parties who may have been involved testimony to that cause is a right protected under the First

Amendment." Nicole answered.

"Granted, but to subject undue hardship was not the intentions of our Founding Fathers, nor the implied right to use retaliated methods of his own to hinder the operation or injury is iniquitous," Hardy pleaded.

Judge Hathcock had read both briefs and she was granting this hearing to see if either side had additional arguments prior to her ruling on the matter.

Judge Hathcock spoke: "Counselors, each of you has made elegant statements for your respective clients; however, the law is very clear on the rights of the petitioner and those of the defendants. Under the rules of discovery, all parties who may have knowledge of any matter before the court are subject to give testimony in such actions. Just as those are rights for the claimant, the claimant cannot with malice for the purpose of harm, cause undue hardship on the respondents in said action.

It is my opinion the motion to receive testimony from the Senior Executives of Cavanaugh Industries and all subsidiaries of the corporation is dutifully within the rights of the petitioner in this matter. So I am signing the motion for depositions to be given by the Senior Executives. I am also reminding the attorneys that those individuals should be given notice that failure to render testimony will be seen by the court as act of contempt. The motion for the Board of Directors is not being granted, because justification was not proven sufficiently in either written or oral arguments to warrant their involvement in this matter. Are there any other matters that you wish to discuss before the court this morning?" Judge Hancock asked.

Both sides agreed that there were no issues at that time. Judge Hathcock adjourned the session, and thanked them for their briefness in their arguments. As the attorneys were exiting the judge's chamber, Judge Hathcock had one last word.

"Ms. Singleton, from this point forward, do not try to influence this court by bringing so many attorneys into my chamber's. Further notice is also given that this matter will not be a circus, so the number of attorneys for both sides that will be seated at one time will be no more than three. Is that understood?"

So round one had been a draw, since both sides had accomplished something Nicole from the outset had no intentions of taking depositions from the

Board of Directors, but the threat of it would cause Hardy to scramble. Now the Sr. Executives were another matter because her team knew that someone had to authorize this or had knowledge of its doing.

While Nicole was in chambers, the Collin County Sheriff officers were in route to the residence of Josh Harrington with a warrant for his immediate arrest. When they arrived at his home, Josh was in his office updating his resume and talking to Marilyn. His attorneys requested him to cease all communications with employees for the time being, but this was Marilyn, his dearest friend while he was employed. Actually, Josh had shared with her the details of what Nicole and the rest of team planned to do. They had had a great lunch one day, visualizing the reaction of the management team and legal when the mountain of briefs started to arrive at corporate.

"Marilyn, this is driving me crazy; everybody has something to do except me. The ironic part is their actions will influence my life forever and I am not a part of it."

"Josh, so that is why we hire the best regardless what it is for."

"Yeah, I know that, but there should be something that I am supposed to be doing too?"

"Just do what you have been telling me that you do—keep reading in the Bible, wait and be still!"

Just at that moment, the doorbell rings.

"Who in the world....? Hold on, Marilyn; someone is at the door."

"Can't you walk and talk at the same time? Isn't your phone cordless, dummy?"

"Habit, and *yes*, I think I still have those skills? Now, there are some others because I haven't used them in a while that are in question." (Laughing and walking toward the front of the house).

"That's too much information, Mr. Harrington."

"Marilyn, you got bail money for me?"

"And why would I need bail money for you?"

"It's the police at my door."

"So buy two tickets to whatever they are selling and they will be gone."

Opening the door, "May I help you?"

"Joshua Harrington?"

"Yes, I am Josh Harrington, and how may I help you?"

"Mr. Harrington, we have a warrant for your arrest, sir."

"I beg your pardon! You must have made a mistake?"

"Sir, the warrant was signed by Judge Cole, who is the judge for the 75th Criminal Court of Collin County."

"What are charges?"

"First-degree theft."

"What!!!!"

"Mr. Harrington, please comes with us. If this is some mistake, it is up to the court to sort it out."

"My I call my attorney?"

"You will be given that opportunity to do so at the station."

Marilyn, who has been hearing the whole conversation, is holding her breath and cannot believe what is happening.

"Josh, Josh! Calm down and ask them where they are taking you?"

"Sir, where are we going? Will I be allowed to lock my house?"

"Yes, we will make sure the premises are secure. Sir, we are going to escort you to the Lew Stewart Justice Center."

"Marilyn, they are going to take me Lew Stewart."

The officer read Josh his rights and took him to jail. For the next seventeen hours Josh sat in a six-foot by six-foot cell on the tenth floor of the Lew Stewart Justice Center until Nicole bailed him out.

27

The next morning Nicole phoned Timothy Hardy, but he wasn't available to receive her call. She asked the receptionist to have Mr. Hardy to phone her at any one of the three numbers that she left. Her next call was to Thomas Lackey, a member of her team that specialized in criminal law. After a brief conversation with Tom Lackey, she phoned Daniel Hampton who prepared the original brief for this case.

"Dan, do you have a second; it is important?" Nicole asked.

"Sure Nicky, what is the problem?"

"I want to amend our suit to Cavanaugh."

From her tone, Tom knew something must have happened, and it was not good. Nicole learned early in Law School, that if your adversary sensed that you were angry, the odds were they would beat you. As her instructor said, law is a game. The only difference is, it is played with people's lives, but it was still a game.

"What kind of amendment do you wish to add?"

"Malicious prosecution and I want a rider on that issue seeking an additional $5,000,000 with punitive damages."

"What did Cavanaugh do? I think already know; they arrested Josh for theft, right?" Daniel asked.

"Yeah, they picked the guy up at his home yesterday morning. I called Tom Lackey and he is going to handle the criminal case. What I think we need is to put on a full court press against them and get our ducks lined up in a row."

"Since you have the game plan, what are the next steps?"

"Can we get the computer and finance people in their office this week? I know I am working about two to three weeks ahead of our project plan, but if they want to play hardball they'd better know we invented the game."

"I can't promise the computer people, but the finance team is ready and waiting to go."

"If they are ready, drop them on their door steps as soon as they get into town."

"Nicole, I got to take this call. I will setup it up and confirm with you later today."

After being booked, finger printed, and photographed, he was being placed in a cell. No contact with anyone, no interviews, one phone call and that was the extent of it. He was just locked up. Up until that moment, he had *imagined* what he thought going to jail might have been like. While in college he had bailed out a couple of friends, but his imagination fell way short of the actual experience. The sound of the cell door closing, he felt as lonely as any human could. The freedom that he had taken for granted had now been taken from him.

Arriving home, he sat for a moment because his faith in both God and man was gone. What had he done in this life that he was paying the penalties for? Why should he be exposed to this? At this moment in time when he needed a support system the most, there seemed not to be one for him that he could rely on.

As he sat, he asked for understanding, mercy because he was at his lowest. Sitting there he didn't realize that he was crying and praying for heavenly intervention for his plight. As he prayed, he experienced a knowing that he wasn't alone, but God was just getting him ready. If this was making him ready, his mind could not comprehend what the next level would be like. He did know one thing; he was too afraid to ask what would happen next.

Later that afternoon, Timothy Hardy returned Nicole Singleton's call.

"Ms. Singleton, you called?"

"Mr. Hardy, I was under the impression that we could handle this matter in a civil manner, but I see I was mistaken?"

"Ms. Singleton, I am not following you. Is there something in particular that you are referring too?"

"You filed criminal charges against my client?"

"Ms. Singleton, Cavanaugh Industries does have an obligation to the stockholders to protect their investment. Since the evidence supports the charges, the corporation had no choice other than to turn that information over to the proper authorities."

"Well, Mr. Hardy, I would not normally tell opposing counsel our next move, but in this case I am making an exception. Our intention is to amend the brief that is before the court to include a claim for malicious prosecution."

"That action is within your right, but I must warn you: you have to prove intention to harm."

"That I will do. And please make all of the necessary arrangements for our finance experts. They will be at your office tomorrow morning promptly at 8:00. Have a good day."

Tim Hardy sat back and thought this may be easier than what he first anticipated. The first time the fire was turned up just a bit she cracked and became angry, and I thought she was sharper than that. I wonder how she and her team will respond when the stew really begins to boil.

He left the office that afternoon thinking he did accomplish something and that was a good feeling. He learned that Elizabeth Nicole Singleton did not like playing hardball.

The strange part that Tim Hardy didn't know was that hardball was her best game.

28

In their next staff meeting, Gayle Chapman asked when she was going to get her dinner invitation. She was told the results were in and that she should ask Garry since he was handling the reservation. Learning that Garry had lost took Gayle totally by surprise, and she wanted the details.

"Well, Gayle, there is a problem here. Their books are showing about twelve million higher than cash. About seven of us have searched for voided transactions, typos, the entire works. There isn't any supporting documentation to explain this."

"It has to be fraud or theft?" interjected Angelica.

"Well, what are the people in finance saying?" asked Gayle.

"Robin in finance— you know the one that looks like she's from West Texas and rides a motorcycle—is saying we must be mistaken, and she's taking this very personally." Garry answered.

"Has anyone done full bank reconciliation?"

"Yes, and those accounts balance to the penny except the months in question," Angelica answered.

"You know, Gayle, there was a conversation that I had one day at lunch that didn't mean much then, but now it might have some merit," Angelica posed to the group.

"And what piece of information do you think is important now?" Garry asked.

"Well, one cost center had some huge expenses that should have caused the margins to just look ugly. But the lady I was having lunch with had to attend this meeting, and she couldn't remember the manager to be in those meetings when his margins were rock bottom," Angelica recalled.

"So, this manager didn't attend a meeting; so what's the big deal? Managers miss meetings all of the time," Gayle said.

"It is what folks around here refer to as WCFM: Who Can't Forecast Meeting. It is a mandatory meeting if your monthly margins are off, and I mean *off*, not just one or two points," Angelica replied.

"So, this manager who was your lunch companion—can't remember if he ever attended— how far off were his margins and money?" Garry asked.

"How about this, his should have been something like a negative sixty-nine percent and around a quarter of a million," Angelica replies to Garry's question.

"Negative what? Well, I bet we can't talk to that person; they're probably no longer with the company, if those were his group's contributions to the company," Gayle replied. Everyone in the room broke out with laughter.

"Yes, sir," Paul answered his phone.

"Paul, are you available to meet in my office in about twenty minutes?" Russell asked.

"Yes, sir, I can be there."

Alex's phone was ringing about the same time that Paul was accepting his call from Russell.

"Alex, I need to talk through this whole Josh Harrington thing, from the top. Do you have a few minutes? Hardy asked.

"I have a moment." Alex replied.

"OK, I guess the first order of business is do you trust Paul Copeland?" Hardy asked, and he was always blunt.

"Paul is one of my senior managers; so, yes, I trust him. And why are you posing that type of question?"

"I just didn't get a warm and fuzzy feeling from him. I just don't believe that he spoke to someone in legal."

"What I am hearing is you think that Paul lied to everyone in that room."

"Alex, think about it. If you had an issue this important, I am assuming, not only would you talk to someone in legal, but also keep dates and times of those conversations. I am also assuming there would be some type of written communications copying several others including Human Resources as well?"

Hardy's points were not only valid in Alex's mind, but were the same thoughts he had, *"Why would you not go to legal and explain the circumstances around the matter?"*

"Your points are valid but maybe at the time of the conversations with legal, Paul may not have been aware of the magnitude?"

"No way, because he had the full story and the documentation to support the charges; then if he disagreed with the original recommendation, then he would have supporting evidence to challenge the decision. This would have been a no-brainer for someone to make the right call."

"So are you suggesting that the documentation was not presented to legal?"

"Right!"

"So either Paul came to legal without the full story and this person based his decision on partial information, or Paul never came to legal at all."

"He might have gone to legal, but the documentation that HR has was never seen by anyone in legal until I saw it. I would bet my life on that."

"So let us assume Paul came to legal first. Then when he had the full scope of what had been done, why didn't he come back to you guys and tell you that this is bigger than what he had first assumed. Or, since he had been to legal and started thinking that HR would automatically get legal involved and there was no need for him to come back again?" Alex stated.

"Why legal wasn't involved is only part of this. If they had been involved, when the whole story was known, they would have done the proper thing. But if legal was only involved when he was believed to be changing his billing, then why didn't either HR or Copeland come to legal then if they had proof of theft? That is an internal issue that we will address at a later date. My main focus right now is how did someone do this and our systems did not detect that it was happening. I need to understand not what was done, but how. We need to know how he got the system to accept those payments without being discovered," Hardy stated.

"To figure how it was done…. I think I know who could solve that for us." Alex replied.

"Alex, this conversation for the time being needs to be held in the strictest of confidence, for several reasons. First, because Harrington's lawyers will be here beginning tomorrow and they have an injunction to have access to a lot of information. I don't want them to paint a picture that there was a type of system error and their client didn't know that it was taking place. Moreover, if he did this, I need concrete evidence of how he did it for both the civil and criminal trials."

That same afternoon Paul Copeland was meeting, to his surprise, with Russell Smiley and Mike Jefferson, Russell's boss. The door was quickly closed as Paul entered. Mike was the first to speak and he was not a happy camper, neither in his tone nor in his body language.

"People, we have a serious issue on our hands and I need to understand the impact of the events of today to us."

Since Paul wasn't sure what Mike was referring to, a very perplexed look came on his face, so Russell brought him up to speed with one sentence.

"Josh Harrington was arrested today at his home for first-degree theft."

The room became unbearably quiet and it took several seconds for Paul to grasp the statement that Russell had just made.

"Who filed charges and what was presented to the police to arrest him?" Paul asked.

"The district attorney's office of Collin County was given photostat copies of the documents in his personnel file. I hear that Hardy took them over there himself. After that meeting between Hardy and the DA's office, an arrest warrant was executed," Mike answered.

"So, Harrington, instead of suing us, is now in jail on theft charges," Paul said.

"Jail, or by now he may be out on bail, but that is not the issue." Mike replied.

"The issue is can the DA or anyone else determine that the documents are fake? Also, can those documents be traced back to your guy?" Russell asked.

Paul was flushed because he wasn't that affected by firing Josh, using compiled documentation that painted the picture that he wanted it to. This wasn't the first time he or any other manager had done the same thing. When you want to get rid of an employee, the manager can create his or her story showing that the employee's performance is no longer with the acceptable range. So the person gets fired. They cry for a moment, go online, find a position with another company and life goes on. But getting the authorities involved includes other factors that all of them must consider. At that moment, Paul felt that he made a pact with the Devil because this was way too far out of his comfort zone.

"I don't think anyone could prove that the documents and the files were altered," Paul replied.

"We need a better answer than I think; we have to be sure," Russell spoke up.

"What I mean—the backdoor to the AP system is there—so maybe a programmer, thinking there has to be a way in could find it. I got Harrington out of the company like you wanted. You wanted proof so he could be fired and I did that," Paul said.

"Paul, it was us who wanted him out of the company including you," Michael was becoming angry by what Paul implied.

"Okay, I stated it wrong; we wanted him out of here," Paul said.

"People, why are we thinking the worst? This could be the answer to all of our problems. First, Harrington is gone. Second, knowing this company, its philosophy is one hand washes the other. By that it means what if someone offers Harrington to drop the lawsuits and we drop our criminal case? Now Harrington is no fool so to get his life back he will make a deal.," Mike injected that theory.

"But instead of giving in, what if he decides to fight?" Paul asked.

"The evidence proves his guilt; he loses," Russell answered.

Paul was taken by the attitude that Russell took. So he goes to jail! Big deal! In Russell's mind it was better for Josh Harrington to go to jail than them.

"But what would happen if he can prove that the evidence is false?" Paul wanted to know.

"We all will be unemployed, possibly facing criminal charges and never work in this industry ever again in our lifetime," Mike answered.

"So now it is a question of us standing together and having a chance of staying employed, not going to jail, and having our lives return to normal in a couple of months. Or, our next option is go to the authorities confess what we have done, be unemployed and in jail within an hour of that conversation," Russell said.

"I won't let everything that I have worked so hard for go down the drain over one person. No damn way! The way it is right now, nobody knows what we are doing or have done. The only guilty person known by anyone is Josh Harrington. So, if they think that he is guilty, let them think that. They will focus their attention on that and leave everything else as it is," Mike was red and angry.

29

Nicole Singleton and the accounting experts the team contracted arrived at the Cavanaugh's building promptly at 8:00 am. The accounting firm was based in Port Arthur, Texas, and the president, Kay Boutte, was a sorority sister of Nicole's from college; so their relationship extended beyond the basic business boundaries. Nicole had explained that what the legal team needed most was evidence that either the documents were falsified or proof beyond a doubt that her client had been lying to her.

Kay's practice extended beyond the city limits of Port Arthur, and by all accounts, the legal address should have been 6721 West 610 Loop, Houston Texas. Ninety-five percent of the firm's clients were based in the greater Houston area. However, because Kay had young twin boys, she preferred that the family live away from the city and the boys would have a better opportunity to experience a childhood similar to one that most kids in the fifties enjoyed—Mom home, home-cooked meals, little league baseball, and boy scouts. To her surprise, during the introductory meeting, she learned that the Chapman's firm was conducting the annual audit for the corporation.

Corporate Deceit

Kay had met both Veronica and Gayle Chapman several years back at the National Black Certified Accountants Conference in Atlantic City. When a chapter was started in Texas, both Gayle and Kay served on the Board of Directors for several years. They weren't the closest friends, but because of their duties in the organization they had a warm and friendly relationship.

After the meeting, Gayle and Kay first got caught up on social events and then the two went to the business issues at hand.

"Kay, what is happening here that Cavanaugh is hiring you to come in and they already have us? Are they displeased with the way the audit is going and want to replace my company?" Gayle was a little nervous that another private accounting firm was on site.

"Cavanaugh Industries didn't hire us and if your guys are the same audit team that did Chevron's audit two years ago, then they are in the best hands that money can buy. Actually my team and I are here because of a pending lawsuit against the company," she explained to Gayle.

"Oh, so you are looking at their books because of a lawsuit? Well, Kay, I hope you have an idea of exactly what you are looking for because from what we have found, their people know GAAP better than most accounting firms. I mean, except for the normal mistakes, their books are immaculate; I mean no major errors including their 10-k reports are prefect."

"Really, I mean with the size of this company and I am hearing from his attorney that there are fourteen accounting teams supporting different divisions. They must have great communications between groups," Kay responded.

"I don't know how they are doing it, but they are top-shelf all of the way. I mean the only thing that has kept us here for the entire length of the audit was the size of the corporation," Gayle explained.

"Huh, that means that my job is really cut out for me because from your feedback they've got their ducks lined up in a row and in order."

"That's right; actually we should be out of here by the end of week; as soon as we resolve a few minor issues and one of the strangest things we can't put our hands around."

"That's good; only a few minor issues and you are finished," Kay was glad the audit had gone so well.

"The minor ones are standard, you know—, better procedures in payroll or getting their sale teams to document expenses better. Nothing that would stop the show or any major problems that will cause them heart burn with the SEC or the IRS. Then as soon as my team refocuses on that other issue and gives me an explanation, we can prepare the final reports and we are out of here."

"What kind of issue are you focusing on that is holding you up?" Kay asked.

"Well, it has to be a logical answer, and I keep telling them don't let me come and figure it out for them. That can't get cash to balance," Gayle explained.

"That's a normal in almost every company. When have you ever found that cash and expenses balance to the penny? You always have to do some type of prior period adjustment to reconcile the differences. Some transactions got deleted in error so why is that so hard for them to figure out?" Kay asked.

"Well, let me restructure that statement. They have less cash than expenses; that is being shown."

"Are you saying AP balances are lower than cash?" Kay inquired.

"No, that is not exactly what I am saying. Don't look too strange at me when I explain this. The expenses are higher than cash, but cash is lower than receivables," Gayle gave Kay a very brief explanation of the problem.

"How big are the differences?"

"That is what is so weird about this whole thing. AP is showing about $250,000 out but cash is twelve million short."

"Question: Why are you so interested in my problem?"

"Part of your problem may be what I am looking for."

"How?"

"We are looking to see if Nicole's client actually stole some money. Furthermore, the claim is he used their expense reporting system to steal it."

"Really?"

"Well, I am not real sure off the top of my head, but I would like copies of all of your working papers and documents."

"That shouldn't be a problem, but I need a copy of the court order stating that you can have them."

"I will call Nicole and get the paperwork to you. Actually, I will have her send it by a courier to your office?"

"The last thing I need is Cavanaugh to know that I was helping someone in suing them. Actually, the information shouldn't be brought to this building."

"Oh, I am going to play the game to the max. We will still make them go through all of the hoops in providing us all the information in the court order. Oh, before I use your documents, I will make sure that what you are giving us is protected under the order from the court."

After Gayle and Kay's conversation, Kay called Nicole to deliver to Chapman & Chapman a copy of the order from the court. Gayle in turn instructed Angelica to make copies of all documents surrounding the AP and cash issues and have them delivered by a courier to her office at Chapman & Chapman.

As Nicole was getting the finance team settled in, Kathleen Sullivan was about to conduct the first deposition for the case with Michael Jefferson, Sr. Vice President of Human Resources. Kathleen had flown in from Houston to do the depositions for the team. She normally wasn't chosen because she was so charming, but because of her ability to formulate the right questions they felt it would be beneficial this time.

Kathleen dressed in a tailored navy suit, high cotton starched blouse with her hair pulled back, and she had an elegance that everyone saw. As she entered the conference room, her radiant smile eased the tension that was heavy within the room. Kathleen thanked everyone for being prompt and explained the reasons for their being there.

Accompanying Michael was Timothy Hardy, the vice-president of legal, and two members of his staff. Hardy's role was to insure that Michael understood his rights and those of the corporation's in presenting testimony during these proceedings.

Kathleen started the deposition, just as she had countless other times, by asking the witness if he needed anything before they got started, and that he understood his rights that were protected under the First Amendment of the Constitution. Michael acknowledged that he did and with that Kathleen began with her first question.

"Mr. Jefferson, would you prefer that I address you as 'Mr. Jefferson' or may I be allowed to use 'Michael' or 'Mike'?"

"Ms. Sullivan, since this a formal deposition, 'Michael' will be fine."

"Very well. Then, could you briefly explain what departments of Cavanaugh Industries report directly to you?"

"I am the Senior Vice President of Human Resources and Associate Relations. My responsibility includes the implementation of policies, practices, and benefits for the corporation."

"So with the responsibility of policy and procedures, those include the employment and the termination of all employees?"

"Yes, that is correct."

"So are the policies concerning employment documented?"

"Yes."

"In that same regard, are the policies concerning termination?"

"Of course."

"So those in either Human Resources or Employee Relations are required to understand and administer the policies and procedures for both employing and terminating an individual within the corporation?"

"Correct."

"So could you please explain the policy surrounding employment?"

"First Ms. Sullivan, since I don't have the entire process memorized, I can only give a general overview of the steps that my area follows."

"That is fine; what I want is a general understanding of the procedure," Kathleen responded.

"Okay. An applicant must submit a formal application and a release that allows the corporation to conduct both a credit and background check. In addition, there is a release authorizing the corporation to give the potential candidate a drug test."

"Are there minimum and maximum levels of acceptance? Also, if the candidate passes those requirements, is he or she eligible for employment?"

"Well, I guess there is some latitude given concerning credit scoring; we don't want dead beats" (He tries to inject some humor in his response only to get a pleasant smile acknowledgment from Kathleen). As for the background and drug testing—those areas have very precise requirements. "

"In what regards?"

"Well, the potential candidate cannot have been convicted of a state or Federal felony. And at Cavanaugh we have a very strict no tolerance policy concerning drugs."

"Your company should be commended concerning your no tolerance policy concerning substance abuse. So, to the best of your knowledge everyone within your organization has successfully passed those requirements for employment?"

"Ms. Sullivan, we also know that even with the best policies and procedures in place, that occasionally someone we hire beats our best efforts."

"You are right, Michael, so the only thing you can do is try to enforce those policies. Now did my client Joshua Harrington qualify for employment under the guidelines that you described to us a moment ago?"

"To the best of my knowledge, yes, Joshua Harrington satisfied all of those requirements."

"When a person is terminated are there any specific procedures required by your department concerning policies and procedures that must be followed?"

"Yes, but those do vary depending on the reason the person is being terminated and the past performance of the individual."

"I understand there may be differences, but is there anything that is standard for every termination, regardless of the reason the person is being terminated?"

"Of course, there are because there are Federal regulations requiring the company to provide certain information to each person," Michael answered.

"Could you give an example of those?"

"Ok, let's see, COBRA, the right to submit an application for unemployment, if it applies 401k information. (Michael thinks for a moment, trying to make sure that he had not forgotten anything) Also, information on how to contact Employee Relations, Payroll and our severance agreement policy, if one is given."

"Is the person who is being terminated given the reason why he or she is being terminated?"

"Of course, the person is entitled to understand why he or she is no longer being employed."

"Is that a state or Federal requirement?" (Kathleen already knew the answer, but she was setting her foundation for the next series of questions.)

"Both."

"So if an employee who is being terminated is not given a reason, then both state and Federal statues have been broken."

Before Michael Jefferson could answer Kathleen's last question, Timothy Hardy stopped him and whispered into his ear. Michael, nodded he understood Hardy's advice.

"A reason for the action of terminating is explained to every individual unless the employee terminates the exit interview."

"Are there any guidelines concerning having a member from Human Resources or Employee Relations present in an exit interview?"

"Yes, again this is because of Federal statues, if the person is past the age of forty or considered a member of a protected class—yes, a member of my staff is required."

"Can you then explain then when Joshua Harrington was being told that his employment with Cavanaugh's Consulting was being terminated, why was not a member from either Human Resources or Employee Relations present?"

"I don't have knowledge to substantiate that a member for either HR or Employee Relations was or was not present at that meeting."

"In the termination meeting, are there are any required forms stating who was in attendance at that meeting?"

"Yes, there is a form that is placed in the employee's personnel file."

"So have you reviewed the termination file for Joshua Harrington?"

"Yes, I briefly reviewed his personnel file so I understood the reasons why I was chosen to give a deposition in this matter."

"In your review of his personnel file, do you recall seeing that form stating who was in attendance in Mr. Harrington's exit interview?

"I don't recall reading that particular form in detail."

"So you do recall seeing the form?"

"I can't absolutely say that I either saw or did not see that document, Ms. Sullivan. I can say that form is a requirement of the corporation."

"Let's change topics for the moment. Do you have any personal knowledge why Mr. Harrington's employment with this company, was terminated?"

That question concerned Michael Jefferson because if he was subpoenaed to testify in court his answer here could be introduced into evidence. But, he also knew that his involvement in this was too deep to have a certain outburst of conscience.

"The facts that I reviewed warranted the termination of Joshua Harrington."

"The question, Mr. Jefferson, was do you have personal knowledge of why Joshua Harrington was terminated from Cavanaugh's Consulting?"

"No!" Michael Jefferson emphatically answered Kathleen Sullivan's question.

The deposition continued for another half hour where general questions about responsibilities, positions and titles were asked.

Following the deposition of Jefferson, several other Senior Executives had their turn and most were unaware of why they were being asked to give testimony in this matter. Only a few knew Josh, so this exercise of getting depositions from the Senior Executives only accomplished the initial intent to cause some uneasiness within the corporation.

30

When Gayle went into the offices of Chapman and Chapman she found lying on her desk the courier's package from Howard & Howard Attorneys At Law. Opening it she found the motion of discovery issued by the 256th Federal Court. Quickly, she dialed Veronica's extension.

"This is Veronica."

"Girl, I am glad you are in the office; I will be right over."

Veronica hung up the phone and wondered what on earth had Gayle so excited? Maybe she has landed another big contract or her oldest child had received a full scholarship to Saint John's that her niece wanted so badly. Whatever it is, it is big, because….. And before she could finish her last thought, Gayle walked in, closing the door behind her.

"Ronnie, why haven't you told me that Josh was suing Cavanaugh's?"

"Suing them? Josh hasn't mentioned that to me. And if he is suing them, how in the world did you find out?"

"Because I ran into Kay Boutte today at Cavanaugh's."

"What were you doing at Cavanaugh?" Ronnie asked.

"Duh, that is the big audit job that my team has been doing for the last four months. Anyway, you need to pay more attention to what I tell you. But anyway, her company has been hired by some law firm, Howard & Howard, to go through Cavanaugh's books for this lawsuit."

"OK, so what does that have to do with Josh?"

"Josh is their client"

"So, Kay told you that Howard & Howard is representing Josh and they are looking for evidence?" Ronnie asked.

"No, I was telling her about my team's audit and something weird that we can't explain in Accounts Payable and she wants all of our documents and working papers. So, I told her I could only give her copies if that was within the scope of her client's motion for discovery."

"OK, so how did Josh's name come up?" Ronnie was thinking it has always taken Gayle so long to get the point.

"So, she (Kay) said that she would get the law firm to send the motion over from the court to me by a courier , and they did. Look!"

IN THE UNITED STATES 256th DISTRICT COURT
FOR THE STATE of TEXAS

)
Joshua Alexander Harrington,)
Plaintiff,))
v.)
2
)
Cavanaugh Inc, Cavanaugh Consulting Inc,)
Defendants.)

Motion of Discovery:

The plaintiff in this action asks the court to order this request to review, document, and copy all records of the defendants that support or prove that the defendant willfully and with malice with the intent to harm the plaintiff. This motion should include the review of financial, personnel, and department records of the defendant.

Respectfully submitted,

_____   _____

    After quickly reading the motion of discovery, Ronnie began thinking why Josh hadn't mentioned to her that he was suing his former employer.

"Gayle, why is Kay interested in their Accounts Payable issues? Josh wasn't in accounting so what does that have to do with his suit?"

"That, girl I don't know. What I am going to do is have dinner with Kay as soon as possible and find out why that made her ears stand up."

"So, what is the problem in AP?"

"Ronnie, my best people including Garry have been trying to understand that one. Their AP books and cash don't agree, and the strange part is that there is more cash than payables, but overall cash is short."

"So, how out of balance are they?" Ronnie asked.

"By twelve million dollars," Gayle responded.

This made Ronnie think harder than ever: "*What does twelve million dollars have to do with Josh? From the way he has been the last couple of months with his moods, he isn't a man with $2,000."*

"By the way, I knew Josh was let go from his old company, but I didn't know it was Cavanaugh Industries," Gayle expressed.

"Well, he worked at the subsidiary that is listed here: Cavanaugh's Consulting."

"So, exactly what did he do?"

"Some type of manager of some technical team, I think? But this thing about AP and Kay is the question of the hour. I know I would have remembered that he was fired for theft."

"I would have, so what reason did he tell you?" Gayle asked.

"He has never changed his story. He says that they did not give him a reason. His exact words were that based on an investigation by HR, they were firing him. From day one I have told him, that didn't sound right." Ronnie replied.

"Boy! This is something. Look at this list of attorneys! What is it? Ten or twelve lawyers representing him? They must think he has a case."

Ronnie quickly counted the attorneys listed in the document as being the attorney for the plaintiff. "Sixteen to be exact."

"Did you notice what he is seeking?" Gayle asked. After she saw who was suing, she wanted to know why.

"That is a number. But there is no way any company is going to pay that type of money to an individual; then after the team of lawyers get their share, it is my best guess that he may get a couple hundred grand at the maximum," Ronnie figured.

Josh still needed more than $200,000 for his financial future, but it was a step in the right direction. Of course, she wanted to think bigger, but she always followed a saying of her father: *"It is better to be surprised than disappointed."*

"Well, that is a shocker, but that is enough about Josh for now. You and I could speculate the rest of the morning what could or could not happen. So until we really understand what is going on, then I suggest we go back to doing Chapman & Chapman work." Ronnie said feeling they were only making stories up in their minds anyway.

"Yeah, I guess you are right, but boy this really is something. I guess the only thing we can do is pray for him and hope he is right," Gayle said.

Leaving her sister's office, she called Kay Boutte and made dinner plans with her for the next night. She told her that she had received the motion and she would have those items sent by a courier to her hotel later that day.

Michael Jefferson, after the deposition, called Russell Smiley and gave him a heads up on what to expect when he is called to give a deposition. After that call, he placed several calls with different head hunters that had called him recently to inquire if they were serious about his changing positions. His thoughts were if he left the company and relocated would his testimony be that important to either side's case for him to testify.

Alex Mann was entering his 10:00 meeting with his old friend, Sawyer Kelly, who owned a small consulting company in Kansas City. The purpose of the meeting was to go over the details of what Alex needed from Sawyer and to keep his engagement at Cavanaugh between the two of them for a while.

"Sawyer, I am so glad that you could fly in on short notice for me. How was the flight and, of course, how are Chris and the kids?" Alex was glad that his friend was willing to help him.

"Flight was fine; the kids are growing, and Chris? Alex, I am so lucky to have her in my life and she is more beautiful with each day," Sawyer had married one of the most beautiful co-eds at Texas Tech and they were the prefect couple in Alex's mind.

"Great and most of all, how is business?"

"Business is business. Some months we have more than we can meet; then as quickly as that happens it may dry up for a month or two. Overall, I would not trade the experience for anything. Now, what does Cavanaugh's Consulting need from a company a tenth in size?"

"Cavanaugh doesn't need you; I do," Alex quickly responded.

"Ok, what do you need my company for? Unless you guys have had a change in direction, you hire the cream of the crop out of school, so everyone else, including me, is like picking from the bottom of the barrel." Laughing as he asked Alex.

"Well, true; we do pride ourselves on recruiting the best talent available. And I guess I also need to rephrase that last statement, Cavanaugh and I need you."

"Okay, what for?"

"I need to know if someone tampered with one of our systems; how it could happen without being detected."

"That is not that difficult to find out. So why are you going to the outside to determine if that happened? I know that with as many sharp people that you have here, somebody could get that information for you."

"That is where it gets sticky; I need to know it can be done, but I don't know who I can trust."

"Really? This must be very important and have a strong impact."

"See, Sawyer, I don't know that if what I am suspecting really did happen. But if it did, then I need to know how they beat our security and most of all who did it?"

"So what is the impact if they did?"

"They stole a quarter of a million," Alex stated.

"So what system do you want to look at, and can you get us access?"

"Now, I may not be able to get you access because you are an outside vendor, but you can use my credential if need be. The system is our Accounts Payable, and the area that your guys need to concentrate on is the expense reporting sub-system."

"So, when do you need to start and can I charge you my premium rate?"

"Invoice what you feel is fair, and you started when you got on that plane to come here." After that Alex explained in detail what he needed from him and the timetable that he was on.

The next night Gayle met Kay for dinner at Mia's, a small Mexican restaurant that everyone in Dallas loves. Over dinner it was strictly girl talk about kids, school and of course, those men who were in or out of their lives at the time. After dinner they walked the strip mall that was close by and continued their general conversation from dinner. Gayle was the first to bring up business and she wanted all of the details of the lawsuit.

"So in this lawsuit, what is this guy saying?" Gayle asked.

"Now, I only know what I have been told, but this guy, Harrington, is claiming that he was fired improperly."

"Okay, so being fired wrong is worth $15,000,000?"

"If it was, I would have been fired from two or three places by now."

"So, his lawyers really think his case is worth that?" Gayle asked.

"The firing maybe a hundred grand or so, but if we prove what they think we can, $15,000,000 would be starters," Kay explained the logic for being there.

"What on God's green earth could a company have done to him to be worth that type of money?"

"Accuse that you stole money and falsify documents to say you did it."

"So, when I said I thought payable and cash were out of balance, that's why your eyes got big?"

"Well sort of, but when you said cash was short then I began to wonder. If you really didn't steal it, or even the people who set you up didn't steal anything, then the money would be there. So it kind of makes you believe this guy may be telling the truth. But when you then said that cash was short, maybe he did steal it. Now the question is this. 'Did he steal a quarter of a million, or twelve million?' Then if he didn't steal anything, somebody wants the world to think that he did."

"Wow, who did he piss off, that they had to go after him like that?"

"That, girl, is the million dollar question. So this guy gets fired right; then as soon as he files his lawsuit, they have him arrested."

Arrested; when was Josh arrested? Why didn't Veronica say anything about that? Then she remembered that Ronnie didn't even know about the lawsuit; so if Josh went to jail, she probably didn't know about either.

"So, I guess his lawyer and him are really mad as hell?" Gayle asked.

"*Mad* isn't the word to use. Nicole really went after Cavanaugh then. She amended the suit adding another $5 million for malicious prosecution," .

"You are joking?"

"Nope, so this brother is going after $20,000,000 *plus* if the jury awards damages too."

"Huh, this is very interesting. Boy, I would never have guessed that a corporation would go through that much trouble to fire someone. Think about it—the possibility of falsifying documents and everything."

"Yeah that is true, but if he wins, that will be a storm that was well worth the bumps. I wonder if the brother is married? If he isn't then he won't have a real big problem finding him a wife after this. Actually, if he *does* win, the boys and I are looking for a new daddy." They both laughed and after some more small talk they ended their evening.

31

Kathleen Sullivan's depositions of the senior executives continued for more than a month because of scheduling, and finally she was about to take the depositions of Alex Mann and Paul Copeland. Her deposition of Russell Smiley was very similar to that of Michael Jefferson, the Vice President of Human Resources and Employee Relations. The only thing that she noticed was Russell was quite uncomfortable when asked about his involvement in the termination of Josh Harrington. What caught her and everyone in the room that day was that all of the blood left his hands and it took him an extremely extended period of time to answer her. True, that is not something that you could offer as evidence, but it was something that she needed to remember when they draft the witness list.

Russell, even as a child, was told that one of his character faults—if you could classify it as a fault—was his inability to lie. He always used that as the reason that he had never considered to cheat on his wife, beside the fact that he was deeply in love with her. Kathleen asked him the question if he had knowledge of the reason Joshua Harrington was fired. At that very moment he needed air.

He felt a shortness of breath and he thought the left side of his body was becoming numb as if he was experiencing a heart attack. Just as Michael Jefferson had done, he lied that he didn't, but to the observers in the conference room, the majority of those individuals would place money that he was lying to her. Now, it was time for the key individuals in this case to give their account about the events leading up to and the firing of Josh. The first to give testimony was Alex Mann.

Kathleen started the exact same way as she had done with everyone else, but she wanted to explore the evidence that points to Josh's being guilty of fraud.

Kathleen asked, "Mr. Mann, who brought to your attention that Josh Harrington was stealing from the company?"

"Paul Copeland," Alex answered.

"So, did Mr. Copeland send you an email, call you on the phone, schedule a meeting to meet with you, or did he just walk into your office and say, 'look what I found'."

"I believe it was one of the topics on a list of issues that he and I were discussing that day."

"So was it first, last, or somewhere in the middle?"

"I don't remember exactly when in that meeting it was discussed."

"So in your initial conversation was the extent of the alleged fraud by Mr. Harrington known?"

"No, what I recall is Paul thought there may be an issue with some expense reports that Josh had submitted and he was looking into the matter and he just wanted me to be aware of his investigation. Which is…….."

Kathleen cut him off and asked him to only answer what was asked and if she wanted any additional clarification, she would structure other questions. She asked if he understood, which he acknowledged that he did, so they continued.

"So, did Mr. Copeland follow this up with any type of written communication?"

"Well, when his investigation was completed he did supply me and Human Resources a spreadsheet with expense numbers, dates, and amounts of the invoices."

"Did he provide photo-stat copies of the actual documents for your review?"

Corporate Deceit

"No, and the reason.............."

Again, Kathleen interrupted him, reminded him how he should answer, but Alex fought her because there was explanation that she needed to be aware of. She allowed Alex to answer the last question with his explanation.

"No, Paul didn't provide me photo-stats of the fraudulent expense reports, because our system allows me to look at those documents online."

"So, you reviewed the expense reports in question online on your personal computer, correct?"

"Yes"

"Now, does that system that you referred to show you images of the document or just raw data?"

"It shows an image that has been scanned into the system," Alex wanted to explain how the system worked and the security measures to ensure that all data within the system was accurate.

"So, you see an image including the signature of the person submitting it?"

"Yes."

"If I presented signatures on three sheets of paper that all bear the name of Joshua Harrington, could you identify Mr. Harrington's signature?"

"I believe I would be able to identify Josh's signature."

"Good! Mr. Mann, I am handing you three documents all bearing the signature of Joshua Harrington. Please tell me—and you are not being timed— but in your judgment, which of these three documents was signed by Mr. Harrington?"

Alex took all three documents and quickly eliminated one and closely looked at the other two. In what took less than ten seconds, he said he was ready to answer. "Ms. Sullivan, the document that is labeled Exhibit 1012A is the one that I believe was signed by Josh."

"Please enter into the record that Mr. Alex Mann identified Exhibit 1012A as the one signed by Mr. Harrington."

"Was I correct?" Alex asked.

"Mr. Mann, this was not a test and I am sorry but I am not at liberty to answer that question." Kathleen smiled, and from her expression Alex knew that he had chosen the correct document.

had chosen the correct document.

"Mr. Mann, to your knowledge, was Mr. Harrington in his exit interview given a reason why he was being terminated?"

Timothy Hardy stopped Alex before he answered that question, and whispered into his ear. Actually, Hardy was reminding Alex of the politically correct answer that they had rehearsed several times over the last few days in Hardy's office.

"Ms. Sullivan, as I recall, Josh became upset, learning that he was being terminated. Consequently, on several occasions during that meeting, both Paul and I tried to get him calm so he could understand the reason behind that decision."

"So, at no time was a reason was given?"

"As I stated, Paul was laying the ground work on how the decision was derived, but Josh continued to interrupt so Paul never had the opportunity to go into details."

"Ground work—is that like the story behind the action being taken?" Kathleen was seeing that this guy had been coached and she was angry. In her mind this should be treated in the same manner as a person giving testimony in court.

"By groundwork I mean that firing anyone, and especially an employee with his tenure, you try to be as humane as you can be. So, the ground work is the facts that drove the decision—nothing else."

"So, you told Mr. Harrington that you had evidence that he had submitted false expense reports?"

"No, as I said before, each time that Paul tried to explain what was going on, Josh would stop him, either saying it was a lie or something."

"So to the best of your knowledge, until Mr. Harrington was arrested, he had no clue why he was fired?"

"Since he submitted the false expense reports, he should have known if he were caught that he would be fired and arrested."

"That is not the question that I asked, and every person in this country is innocent until proven guilty. The question was, 'Did anyone employed at Cavanaugh's Consulting inform Mr. Harrington that he was being terminated for the alleged charges of submitting and receiving money, under false pretenses, by submitting false expense reports'?"

"To my knowledge, no." When Alex gave that answer, Hardy was upset, not because Alex answered the question truthfully, but his answer could harm the negotiations with Harrington's attorneys.

Kathleen continued, "Mr. Mann, do you recall at anytime Mr. Harrington asking for a representative from Human Resource?"

"No," was Alex's response.

"Let me rephrase it. Did either you or Mr. Copeland tell my client that based on an investigation by HR or Employee Relations that he was being fired on what they had concluded as being true?"

"Again because of time, I believe Paul or I tried to lay the foundation of the action and may have stated this was being done based on HR findings, but Josh interrupted us before that groundwork could be laid."

"So, did Mr. Harrington inquire as to why he was being investigated?"

"Yes, he asked what the investigation was about," Alex explained.

"So at any time was my client told what the charges were?" Kathleen was now applying pressure to Alex Mann, and Hardy was aware of what she was doing.

So, to stop some of the bleeding, Hardy interjected. "Ms. Sullivan, it has been established time and time again that before your client could be given a reason, he became upset so the exit interview was on a downhill spiral."

"Point noted, Mr. Hardy; however, Mr. Hardy, the question that is on the table at this moment is. Did my client ask Mr. Mann and Mr. Copeland to get those who made this decision in that meeting?"

Hardy didn't want this to get ugly, so he responded to her: "Ms. Sullivan, because firing anyone is not only hard and difficult, Mr. Mann in his judgment felt the situation was at that point uncontrollable, so he made the best decision at that moment in time; the least number of people was the safest."

Kathleen quickly responded, "Mr. Hardy, I wasn't aware that you were present in that meeting? So I am assuming that your last comment was truly speculation without any supporting documentation or accounts to substantiate your views?"

When she said that, Hardy's face became flushed. Here was an attorney, who probably wasn't as old as he had been practicing law, upstaging and challenging his views. He made a mental note to go over Alex's deposition prior to trial because in court some of his answers could really hurt their case.

Kathleen picked up just where she left off without skipping a beat. "Mr. Mann, did Mr. Harrington ask for the person or persons who conducted this investigation to be included in this meeting?"

"Yes, but because the way Josh was at that moment, we felt that was not a good idea."

"OK, next subject. In Mr. Harrington's severance package from this company does any document state the reason for his termination?"

"No." When Alex gave that answer, he was flushed too because he felt this was not going good.

"Is there an explanation that a member of your organization can give for the severance package not including a reason for termination?"

"I believe it was an oversight by HR."

"Or so that your company could say today it is performance, tomorrow theft, and next week professional-misconduct?"

Hardy was fighting mad. "I resent that last question, statement or whatever you intended it to be!" He stated angrily.

"My apologies; however, Mr. Mann can you explain why you or a member of your organization reported to the Texas Employment Commission several different reasons why Mr. Harrington is no longer an employee of this company?"

"Well, at first we wanted to do the right thing and not deprive Josh of any benefits."

"Your former employee is accused of stealing a quarter of a million dollars from your company and you want to make sure that he can get unemployment? So, what is the magic number that a person has to steal that you would fight his unemployment?"

"The unemployment was based on his length of service with the company."

"So if you become vested and then decide to steal a million dollars or so, you can still draw your unemployment from this company. Is that what I am hearing?"

Hardy and Alex both knew that Alex's last answer did not make sense, and she was not giving them any room to back track his answer.

"No, I was not saying that at all. I made the decision that I could take the expense of his drawing unemployment if he needed it." As soon as the words came out of his mouth he heard an inner voice shouts, "*Fool*."

"Is that decision rewarding an employee who stole from the company; does that make you a good manager, Mr. Mann?"

"Ms. Sullivan, I have always taken care of those who report to me. Yes, I am a good manager and if you must know, I considered Josh Harrington more than an employee, but also a friend."

"That's good, but then when TEC asked about the performance statement that someone originally submitted, your "taking care of my employees" attitude changed."

"Since, Josh wanted to fight and not move on, so if he wanted potential employers to know the truth, then he got what he wanted," Alex lost his temper with that last statement, and that was something that he never wanted. Not just here, but anywhere.

Kathleen had gotten the gist of what she wanted from him, so for the next hour she asked general questions about his management style, Josh's performance and several other topics that would never be used in court. When she had finished, she thanked him for taking the time to do the deposition and wished him a remaining good day.

32

Kay Boutte and her team used the living room in her hotel suite as their conference room away from Cavanaugh. Spread out across the table were the documents that Gayle Chapman had sent from the audit by her team. Just as Gayle had said—in their original conversation—the Accounts Payable documents and cash reporting were showing a difference of about a quarter of a million dollars. The strange part was even when Kay had the computer experts check the log files for the Accounts Payable system they too did not find anything out of sequence or anything pointing this treasure hunt to a different path.

On the third evening after they got back to the hotel, had dinner and were reviewing the accomplishment for that day, a teammate of Kay's asked the strangest question. "Kay, what could you do to a document without changing the numbers that would cause this error?"

"Mindy, I thought you had tea with your dinner? I didn't know it was Long Island tea." Kay replied.

The room burst into laughter. "No, seriously, maybe whoever did this to this guy knew accountants would be looking at numbers and not at what they actually changed. Look at what we have. The expense reports balance to the penny, and so do the bank transfer records. From just looking at those, this guy is guilty as sin, so why are we here? Problem is when we got the motion from the judge to get the bank files—no deposits? So how do you do that? You steal it, but don't take it; where did the money go?"

"That is what is so puzzling about this, on this end the guy is caught hands down, but somewhere between one system running and the bank, the money vanishes. Why would anyone go through that much trouble to break into a system undetected and not take the money? So, the logical conclusion is that he never did steal it," responded Page, another member of team.

"No, what I am saying is there has to be something that makes the numbers look right, but the accounting is all wrong."

About that time Justin entered the conversation: "Hold it, guys! Mindy could be on to something; let's step out of our boxes for a moment. Think about it; the signature belongs to this guy, all the information identifying him is his and there aren't any missing documents, so if what he is saying is true, then what did they change?"

"Well, first of all, *how* did they change it?" Page asked.

"That isn't the issue. First we prove that they changed it, then we figure out *how* they did it," Kay said.

"Could it be currency?" Mindy asked.

"Is anybody logged on to the Net?" Kay asked.

"I am," Page responded.

"Go and find me some exchange rate tables," Kay asked.

Going into the Internet, using one of the search engines, Page responded that the result from her search was 792 possible rate tables to choose from.

"OK, find one that I can use in any country I wish," Justin said.

"OK, got it, what are we doing?" Page wanted to know.

"Well, since we don't know what "X" was, this may take some time," Justin spoke out.

"Use the Euro dollars and tell me what the conversion rate is to US dollars."

Converting a quarter of million in Euro dollars gave the conversion to US dollars showed an amount of $305,901.44.

"Well that theory is shot in the foot," Page said.

"Not really, we only tried one. There has to be one that will give us the results that we are looking for?" someone else said

"Then again, who ever did this may have just pulled a number out of the air, so this theory may not be worth the time to investigate. So since we don't have any proof or logic to say we are on the right track with this theory, then why have all of us sitting here doing this?" What are your thoughts about this? Should we have someone continue to convert to different currencies and we really don't know what number we are looking for?" questioned Kay.

Everyone in the room looked at each other trying to see who would speak up first, but there was no one jumping in to answer Kay. After thinking about it for the moment, Justin saw no one else was voicing an opinion, so he voiced his.

"Kay, while it seems no one else is talking, since I brought this up, it was just a wild guess. I was just thinking what else could we look for? I was just taking a stab at something,"

"Well, since it's just a hunch, let's go back to what we know that will work, that is true research the old fashion way then," Kay replied.

That same night, Josh and Veronica were having dinner at Josh's. Since, for the last couple of weeks, making time for each other seemed to never work out. Veronica was just ending the second quarter of the year, so she and her staff were working at a minimum twelve hours a day preparing quarterly returns and preparing financial for their clients. Besides spending a night in jail, Josh was too busy meeting with Nicole, and being briefed by his legal team on how the depositions had been tied up. Finally, this was a night that they could enjoy each other's company without the problems of life that were surrounding them both.

The doorbell rang promptly at 7:00 as she had promised and she had spent a little extra effort in selecting her attire for the evening.

Opening the door, Josh smiled and his eyes took in a moment seeing the woman he loved standing there using the beauty of the evening sky as her stage. "Hi and may I have your name young lady?"

"My name is Veronica K. Chapman of the Mississippi Chapmans, sir." Trying to use a southern bell tone to her voice

"Well Miss Veronica K. Chapman, welcome to my home."

"Thank you sir."

As she came in, she kissed his cheek. Josh was thinking, well it has been two weeks or so since she saw me last and all I get is a kiss on the cheek. Oh well, that is Ronnie.

"What are you cooking? It smells just heavenly."

"The dish is called oven shrimp. Now, would you care for a glass of wine while we wait?"

"That's fine. Now, Mr. Harrington, I understand what I have been doing the last couple of weeks, but you, I've barely heard from you. Now, I told you up front, don't start anything that you are not willing to keep up. So, why haven't I received a quick hello from you?"

"Ronnie, have you missed me?"

"No, but I have gotten used to hearing your voice at least a couple of times during the week."

"I think I have spoiled you. Well the short of the story is I have been in meetings it seems daily with some folks, and their energy level makes ours appear that we have none."

"Oh, so what are you and your people talking about that is keeping me from receiving my daily call?"

"Just stuff at the moment that is more speculations, than reality."

"Business venture?"

"Kind of, but anyway until something breaks, it is pure speculations, but promising. Now what about yourself?"

Veronica thinking, "*It had something to do with his lawsuit, so that is why he is being mysterious.*" Since he didn't know that she knew that he was suing Cavanaugh, then he would talk in general without any concrete statements of what he had been doing.

"*Well he has his own reasons for not telling me, I'll leave it alone for the moment.*" She was thinking.

The timer goes off in the kitchen, so he goes and finishes preparing their dinner. While he was placing salad into bowls, the general conversation then and throughout dinner was centered on her quarter-end workload. After dinner, sitting in the den while a jazz radio station played in the background, the conversation turned back to what he was doing, and at that moment Josh wasn't sure if he was ready to answer Veronica.

"Ok, so when I got here tonight, you said you have been meeting with some people, right? So are you entering into some business proposal with these folks, or is this a real job that y'all are kicking around?"

"Well, it's sort of like a business deal, but it isn't. The people that I have been meeting with are very bright and their ideas sometimes just blow my socks off. To put it another way, for the moment, I have a Limited Partnership Agreement with these folk."

"LLPA, sounds interesting, to say the least."

"Yes, but is not your standard everyday partnership. Everyone is not equal, but everyone understands his or her role within the organization."

"Oh, is your group more like venture capitalists?"

"No, you got to trust me, if this works out to plan, well lets say what were ashes in my mind are no longer ashes. How does it go, what was meant to harm you, God will turn into a blessing for you."

"Well, since you aren't really saying what you are doing, I can only pray that you're right."

"Ronnie, I have been going through a lot and so I have this mindset that He is only preparing me for something bigger than I could ever dream of myself."

"Now I am being selfish with this statement, but whatever it is, will I benefit from it?" she asked.

"You know for a long time, now how do I say this? This will work, I think? You know for a long time, even some of my desires at Cavanaugh were driven by what I thought you wanted from a man. For the first time, this isn't about you, friends, or family, this time it is all about me. Therefore, for once in my life, I like being Joshua Harrington."

"That's what I have always wanted for you. See Josh, I see a man who could be whatever he wishes to be just as soon as he started to believe in himself and not what others tried to define him as." Veronica stood up, walked over to where he was standing and kissed him. She saw the potential, but she also saw that he was trying to be what he believed she wanted him to be. Strange part, the man that she fell in love with wasn't the man he was trying to be. It was with the man inside.

33

Paul Copeland was scheduled to give his deposition that afternoon. Sitting in his office he wondered how much reality was in those television dramas that he watched nightly on one of the cable stations. Could he invoke the Fifth Amendment if Josh's attorney asked him a question that he couldn't answer without exposing his involvement in this? Then if he did that, what can of worms would he have opened here in the company? Could some law enforcement agency prosecute him? Maybe he should reschedule the damn thing, hire himself an attorney, and then give his deposition.

Thinking that his options were slim to none, his phone rang. Looking to see who was calling he was surprised when he noticed the name Monty Cooper. Why is he calling? He had never done this before; it was always him contacting Cooper. Instead of speculating why, he picked up the phone.

"Copeland."

"Paul, this is Monty. What time today can you leave the campus for about an hour?"

"Well, I know this afternoon I am in a meeting for the rest of day. Then, before that I have another meeting that is slotted for an hour, then I……………"

"Sounds like if it is today that I needed to see you that just isn't going to happen?"

"Well, if you can cut it back to thirty minutes instead of an hour, then right now may work," Paul suggested.

"I take what I can get. How about meeting me in the mall by the skating rink in about fifteen minutes?" Monty asked.

"See you there."

Monty rushed to the copier room, copied about four sheets of a report he had ran that morning. From the copier room, he went down a back hallway because he didn't want to be spotted leaving the building. Walking to his car, Monty was thinking, *"As long as this guy has been in management, I'm surprised that he still kept his technical skills this sharp."*

Paul picked up his keys and casually walked out of the building as if he was on his way to a meeting at a client site.

Driving to the mall, he thought: *what has happened that Monty wants to talk about?* The first question he had been asked—to give a deposition—really scared him. Not saying he felt that Monty would expose the entire plot on the first question asked of him, but Monty was a follower, not a leader by any means. Arriving at the mall he found himself a parking spot and was standing by the rail when Monty got there.

"OK, Mr. Cooper, what is so important that we needed to meet here like we are two spies?"

"Well, I think someone is trying to figure out what we have been doing. Also, they may have found our backdoor into the Accounts Payable system?"

"Found the backdoor? You told me that the person who may have a chance of finding that entry point would have to be really good and have an idea of what he was looking for?" questioned Paul somewhat angrily.

"Well, this guy is getting too close. I am almost sure he has found the backdoor, but from what I am seeing he isn't anywhere close to the files that we modified?"

"Someone has found the back entry point to the system? How did that happen?"

"Like I told you, if you have an idea that it may be there, you could find it.

There's just no way you could conceal it completely unless you got rid of it entirely. Finding the entry point did not alarm me; it was who was doing it."

"So, who is this geek that discovered our own little private entry point? Some hot shot employee from MIT or Duke?"

"Oh, you were like me thinking the person would have to be one super stud to find it. That's what I was thinking until I found his credentials."

"OK, who was it?"

"Alex is the one who found the entry point."

"Alex who?"

Paul knew that somewhere in the organization there had to be another Alex besides Mann that Monty was talking about. Sure in their manager's meetings occasionally Alex would mention or ask if they had read this book or that book; so he read a lot— big deal. But Alex had been in management for the last six or seven years and with those positions he didn't have the time to keep his coding skills up-to-date. So whoever this Alex was he needed to find out some kind of way why he was looking for a backdoor into the Accounts Payable System.

"Alex Mann that is who. Here, (handing him a copy of the log files that he printed that morning) see for yourself. Alex had been in the system several times each day for the last week or so. I mean he has been into Source Safe to retrieve the actual code, so he knew what he was looking for."

"If he has been doing this for a couple of weeks and hasn't found your trail, then that means he will never find it. So let him look."

"I think he is still searching."

"OK, so he is still searching; if there isn't a trail for him to follow what can he find?"

"There are always some footprints, even when you try to erase them all."

"But you said that you got rid of all evidence that you had been there. You even said you had modified the back-ups too. So he finds out there is a back door. That can be explained, but modifying the system—that may take some work. Look, how often are these reports running? If you aren't running them daily, start and make that a priority to do so. Then if you think that he or whoever is getting too close, call me."

"Man, if he finds out what we have done, they will fire us on the spot."

Since Cooper was just a hired hand, he didn't know that what they had done had gone beyond being fired. If what he saw every night on TV was close to reality, then Cooper may be asking the court system for mercy before sentencing. Actually, since he only knew the one side, the DA would give him a deal; but for his part, that would be a totally different story altogether.

34

Sawyer Kelly was good at what he did as a security consultant. He was contracted by both large and small firms to evaluate the quality of those companies' software security systems. When the Internet became a major player, data became more priceless than gold. If someone could gain access into a corporation's data center, then those individuals could steal anything from client lists, trade secrets, patents, and even money.

That is why Sawyer recognized when the personal computer was first introduced to the corporate world, there was a need for another type of computer expert and he thought he knew what was needed. He went back to college and obtained a degree in accounting and he also sat for the CPA examination. See—using his computer skills and now his new degree in accounting, he became a computer auditor. His understanding of systems, multiple computer languages and the rules of GAAP, made him an invaluable asset to his company.

When he and another auditor were talking one day over lunch, they realized that the services that they were performing for their current company could be marketable, so after some research Sawyer and the other auditor formed System Security Technologies in St. Louis, MO. Initially, the business did not fare as hoped, but an incident in New York at Chase when someone hacked into their system and transferred $500 million, gave them the break they needed. That amount of money stolen without a person physically walking in and pointing a gun to someone's head was unbelievable. After that incident SST was being recruited from both those in the financial world and other industries.

Using Alex's credentials to gain access, it took him and two of his employees to discover the back door into the Accounts Payable system at Cavanaugh. So, they had found an entry point, but Alex had not told him what to look for if it was found.

"This is Alex Mann, may I help you?"

"Alex, this is Sawyer, how is it going this morning, buddy?"

"Sawyer everything is fine; what about on your end?"

"Great! I have some good news for you, I think? Well. it might *not* be because of what I have found?"

Marty English, one of Alex's direct reports was sitting there in Alex's office hoping he didn't have to sit there through an extended conversation with Alex and somebody else. Alex—remembering that he did have someone in his office—asked Sawyer to hold on for a moment. Alex then apologized to Marty, asking him to reschedule their meeting and to shut his door on his way out.

"Sawyer, sorry about that, but I had someone in my office. OK, give me the good or bad news that you have for me."

"There is a backdoor into that system that you wanted us to look at. So your hunch was correct, but trying to figure out who has access to that and the last time they were there may take a little longer."

"Sawyer, are you telling me, even with us backing up data, restoring files, and such that you can still go back in time?"

"Not bragging, but yes we can. See, your application people have always thought that if I restored it to some state that it would be a new beginning. But the truth is unless you bring in all new disk packs or such, that old data is still out there somewhere."

"But can you find out *who* and *what* about the data?"

"Oh, ye of little faith. Let me explain this once and for all to you. The original data may still be there, the updated data has the pointers so you can access it, but the original data may still be available. The question is this: I need to know the time span that we are working with and exactly what I am looking for?"

"Give me a couple of days to get that information to you. Until then, go get in someone else's pockets until I get back to you," Alex told Sawyer.

"Will do. Do you have a clue what you are looking for?"

"That's the hard part; I was hoping there wasn't a backdoor then I wouldn't have to deal with any more issues, but since it is, oh well. Now I got to hope that my worst thoughts are not true."

"Sounds as if this is really tearing you up, Alex? I have known you for years and normally you take the approach that it is just a part of business."

"That's the way it should be, but this time it does seem that someone is trying to create his version of truth and that is not settling with me. The hard fact is that more of what I am thinking is this may affect a lot of people and cost this company a large sum of money."

"Details—I don't need to know, but if you are really looking for something that is on that system, then there is a good chance we can find it."

"That is why I called, because if it could be proven either way, your company has the best track record in the industry of doing just that. Look, I will be talking to you in a few days with that information, but I got to run," Alex says.

"Bye, Alex."

There is a backdoor into the system, then who has been accessing it? Could someone who really wanted Josh out of the company do this? But why? Would Sawyer really discover who had gone into the system and what they had done? So if this really did happen, am I really helping the company or exposing it if the truth comes out?

Finishing his conversation, he called, Timothy Hardy but to no avail. Because Josh's attorneys were still doing depositions, Hardy probably was where he had been for the last month: locked in a conference room as Kathleen Sullivan tried her best to slice and dice the next witness on her deposition list.

Actually, Alex was right about Hardy and his focus. Hardy was in a conference room with Paul Copeland going over how he should answer Kathleen.

"Paul, the most important thing you can do this afternoon is to maintain your composure. Do not let this attorney rattle you. There isn't a time limit on how long it takes you to answer any question. Remember: if you don't understand the question, you are entitled to ask for clarity or for her to rephrase the question."

"Got it!"

Trying to reassure himself more than Hardy had tried, Paul's response was quick and to the point. He wanted to ask if he could have his own personal attorney present, but what he needed more than an attorney was a drink to calm his nerve.

Kathleen Sullivan was in Nicole's office meeting with Josh before she went to Cavanaugh to do the deposition with Paul Copeland. From the first interview when Josh told his version of that day, Kathleen felt Paul was a key piece of this puzzle but she did not know exactly where he fit in.

"Josh, this afternoon I will be taking the deposition of Paul Copeland. What I need is for you to tell me some things about this guy. What makes him tick?"

"Paul is a strange guy exactly. From a technical standpoint he is good, but his people skills are lacking. See, the best way I can describe him is he is a follower more than a leader. The guy probably hasn't made a decision in his life that wasn't the idea of someone else."

"So, if he is involved as much as I think, then he is following the orders of some one else? Is he loyal to his superiors or if he feels his neck on the block, would he sell them out?"

"Oh, in my opinion, he would jump ship quicker than a rat on a sinking boat. The guy wants to move ahead, but in his mind that can only happen if whoever he is following takes him with them."

"I know the type. Now during your exit interview, who was driving that meeting—Copeland or Alex Mann?"

"Oh, that day, Paul was the man. Now, when I started to ask tough questions, he *did* look to Alex to see how he should have responded, but overall it was Paul."

"In your opinion, was Alex really driving that meeting and Paul was just the puppet doing the talking?" Kathleen asked.

"That one I am not real sure about because when Paul told me that I was being terminated, my anger was directed to him. I wasn't really focused on Alex much."

"Do you know any reason why Paul Copeland wanted you out of the company? I mean does he feel that you made too much money? Your position? Anything?"

"I mean I reported to the guy, but I had very little interaction with him. I mean I reported to him, so my salary hit his financial, so from an expense side it could?"

"Answer this: who gets charged with your expenses?"

"Normally, it would be my home cost center, which in this case would have been Paul. Now suppose I was doing something for another group; then those charges would be routed to them."

"Is there any way that you know of, that an expense report could bypass the manager who had P&L responsibility?"

"If you mean, does the expense report show on the FOP? Of course it does and the entire supporting transaction file that supports it."

"FOP?"

"Financial Outlook Plan is the full description. Actually an FOP is nothing more than an accounting income statement, plain and simple. Financial managers are responsible for their department's financial health. Now usually, division managers set goals for every department's revenue, expense reduction, and margins before taxes."

"What happens when a manager fails in any of those areas?"

"That is not good. See, at the division level, well, what is the best way to give you the right picture? This should work. Remember Amway? Sorry, you are too young for that analogy. How about the new grass roots marketing thing—Legal something?"

"I think I know what you are talking about—Prepaid Legal. Is that the one where you see people with signs on their cars, talking about they can provide you a lawyer anywhere, anytime, or something?"

"Yeah that is the one. Well divisions within Cavanaugh work on the same principle as that does. Those income statements are rolled up to the division level, every department within a division. Now, that can be good or it could be bad depending on the departments that are in the division. Now, divisions have goals too and that is why you can't have some departments not pulling their weight."

"You still didn't finish answering my question. What happens to a manager who is failing to meet his goals?"

"Off to the WCFM. Before you ask what in the world WCFM is, it means who can't forecast meeting. It is held every month after closing and those meetings are ugly. Actually, every financial manager does everything in his power not to be included on that invitation list."

"Then for an example, if my expense exceeds my revenue, am I candidate for the WCMF?" Kathleen asked.

"That is WCFM bound and yes, you would have an invitation for sure."

"One more thing, to the best of your knowledge, is Paul Copeland a racist?"

"Let me put it this way: he drives a pickup that has a gun rack in the back window, chews tobacco, listens to country and grew up in West Texas. Now my grandmother always told me this. If it looks, walks and quacks like a duck, then in most cases it could really be a duck."

They both laughed. Kathleen, who was doodling while they were meeting, circled the center of the piece of paper that she had been writing on. In the center she had two words there; "**RED NECK**."

35

The bailiff for the 256th Federal Court announced the entrance of Judge Hathcock as she entered the courtroom. "All rise!" The judge was a petite woman standing barely five feet in height, but she had an elegance and grace that magnified her presence. All in the courtroom recognized not only the judge's authority, but also her statue defined by her presence and self-proclaimed inner power.

"You may be seated," she said from the bench after she rearranged the folders and papers that were before her.

"This is in the matter of case number 7820-781784-90782 docket number 1902-2005-1122 in the civil matter of one Joshua Alexander Harrington v. Cavanaugh Industries and its subsidiary Cavanaugh's Consulting Inc. for a motion to obtain a restraining order against Cavanaugh Industries to cease the malicious prosecution of the petitioner in this matter for the crime of first-degree theft and to obtain an order of injunction for the 75th Criminal Court of Collin County to halt all legal proceedings against the petitioner in the above fore mentioned actions.

Are the attorneys present and are you ready to state your bequests before this court?" Judge Hathcock asked.

"If it pleases the court, your Honor, I am Assistant District Attorney Erica Crenshaw of the Collin County District Attorney Office representing Collin County."

"So noted."

"If it pleases the court, your Honor, I am Kenneth E. Walton, representing Cavanaugh Industries today standing in for attorney Timothy Hardy. Mr. Hardy had an emergency matter of a personal nature, so he was unable to attend today's proceeding."

"So noted."

Nicole thinking to herself, *yes Hardy had a personal emergency I bet. I am willing to bet he is in the same conference room with Kathleen listening to Paul Copeland deposition.*

"Are the attorneys ready to proceed, and if so you can begin, Ms. Simmons," Judge Hathcock stated.

"Thank you, your Honor, and good afternoon. The defendants in this matter after being served by this court willfully had my client arrested for a crime, of which they are aware he did not commit. Your Honor, they knowingly and with forethought are trying to intimidate my client from seeking justice and restitution demonstrated by of their actions in the wrongful termination and the slander of his character.

The petitioner lies before this court today, asking the court to enter an injunction halting the criminal prosecution of my client. If those proceedings are not ceased, their actions will contaminate the jury pool, instill predetermined bias and do refutable harm to my client while he is seeking the truth in this matter. This is why my client Joshua Harrington begs for the court's intervention for both motions before the bench today," Nicole's opening statement to the court.

"Ms. Crenshaw."

"If it pleases the court? In the stated matter concerning Joshua Harrington, the Collin County District Attorney's office does not nor has ever had any affiliation with Cavanaugh's Industries or any of its subsidiaries in this or any other matter before this court. The Collin County District Attorney's Office, as the duly elected official of Collin County duties includes the enforcement of both state and local laws and statues of it citizens and prosecutes to the fullest extent of those laws those accused of committing a crime or crimes within its jurisdiction of Collin County." Erica Crenshaw replied.

"Your Honor, the petitioner is well aware of the duties of the Collin County DA's office, and supports their commitment to our judicial system; however, said matter was only presented to their office, post the petition and pending lawsuit before this court.

In Clingman v. Beaver, No. 04-37 (2003), CERTIORARI TO THE UNITED STATES COURT OF APPEALS FOR THE TENTH CIRCUIT, JUSTICE THOMAS delivered the opinion of the Court, and in his opinion states.

That the intention to defray from the court the rights of the petitioner or intimidate the stoppage of action by using the criminal justice system against said party is invalid. That all proceedings that will be before any court shall be heard in the order of filing and process in said order. Those subsequent cases either civil or criminal are to proceed after the conclusion of the first case and the order will continue in sequence of filing.

Kenneth Walton spoke: "If it pleases the court, Your Honor, Cavanaugh Industries is innocent of the allegations brought before this court on behalf of Mr. Harrington. Cavanaugh Industries has not used its standing within the community to apply pressure to the Collin County District Attorney's Office in their investigation and subsequent indictment, and arrest of Mr. Harrington. Cavanaugh Industries did turn over documents and supporting evidence of the possible crime by the petitioner, which are the rights of the citizens. After Cavanaugh turned those instruments over at that time Cavanaugh became a third party to any actions that the Collin County DA deemed appropriate at the conclusion of its own independent investigation," Kenneth Walton states.

"I find it very hard to believe that Cavanaugh just determined that the petitioner in this matter may have been a party in actions of a criminal nature. Furthermore, that that information became the knowledge of the corporation after this matter was submitted to my court does appear that the actions were postured to intimidate the petitioner," Judge Hathcock said.

"Your Honor, even though it does appear that a serious allegation should have been known prior to this matter, it was not discovered until these proceeding began. The defendant's plea before you today does not penalize Cavanaugh, because such actions of the petitioner were so devious that the discovery of those actions may have gone unnoticed if the petitioner himself had not stirred up this hornet's nest with his frivolous lawsuit," Attorney Walton replied.

"I will take into consideration that point, but to use your influence to get the DA's office to issue a warrant for Mr. Harrington with the sole intent to use as leverage will not be tolerated."

"Your Honor, I beg to differ that the actions of the DA's office was based on the evidence presented without any influence of Cavanaugh Industries" Ms. Crenshaw said.

"Ms. Crenshaw. Correct? Do you expect this court to believe that within an hour of receiving said evidence that the DA's office could review, come to a conclusion of a possible crime, and issue a warrant without any outside pressure? Please Ms. Crenshaw, think before you answer, because this court does not like or tolerate being lied to."

"Your Honor, since I was not present when the evidence was presented to my office, I am assuming that the procedures established by District Attorney Davis were followed to the letter," Erica was very careful in responding.

Feeling that Judge Hathcock was siding with her, Nicole spoke.

"If it pleases the court, Your Honor, it is the petitioner's wish to have his day in court surrounding those charges; however, the petitioner begs the court to sanction both Collin County and Cavanaugh from trying to leverage their independent power against one individual."

"So noted. I am taking this matter under advisement and will render my decision at 9:00 A.M. tomorrow. I am also scheduling that court appearance and trail date for this matter to begin on the 27th of August. Court is adjourned"

"All rise."

As Judge Hathcock exited the bench and the courtroom, the three attorneys huddled for a moment.

While Kenneth Walton was standing before Judge Hathcock, Timothy Hardy was sitting in on the deposition being given by Paul Copeland. Hardy had given Kenneth instructions to call him as soon as the hearing was over. Depending on that outcome he could formulate a way to end this and get on with his life. If Ms. Singleton hadn't done her homework and wasn't prepared, then he might for the first time in this case have the upper hand. Then again, if she did have her ducks in a row, he needed to see what his next strategy would be. The jury was still out with him on Paul Copeland. Copeland's story and his actions had left a number of doubts in Hardy's head, but he hadn't been able to put all of the pieces together.

The deposition had been going on for about thirty minutes with Kathleen Sullivan asking her usual opening questions. They were general in nature, so there was no way not even Paul Copeland should have any problems in answering. Then Kathleen turned her attention first to Paul's responsibilities as a department manager.

"Mr. Copeland, exactly how many departments or sub-departments report to you?"

"In my organization, there are five department managers that report to me directly, and I manage two departments personally."

"Are all of these departments, revenue-generating departments?"

"Yes. Sorry, all are revenue departments with the exception of one."

"So, your revenue departments—do they have revenue and profit margin goals?"

"Yes, they have margin and revenue goals. Just like every revenue-generating department in the company."

"Is your degree in accounting? You do have a degree? I am assuming that either you have a degree or that you may have a minor in accounting?"

Paul began to turn red with anger, but he was trying very hard not to become upset. *What right did she have to imply that he wasn't educated or didn't understand accounting.*

"Yes, Ms. Sullivan, I graduated from Texas Tech with a major in engineering and a minor in computer technology."

"So what is your knowledge of accounting and the principles of GAAP?"

"Our finance department trains all managers to work with our monthly accounting responsibilities, and each department has a financial coordinator who is degreed in accounting so all rules are followed, including GAAP."

"But who is responsible for the department financial, the department head or the coordinator?"

"The department head is the one who is ultimately responsible."

"Those that include expense vouchers?"

"Yes, unless it is a complete pass through to a customer, or the expense was incurred while performing the duties for another department."

"So you had to approve Mr. Harrington's expense reports?"

"No!"

His answer caught Kathleen by surprise. She was positively sure that she asked Josh did he report to Copeland and he said he did. *Has our client been lying to us?* she wondered.

"Who approved Mr. Harrington's expense reports then?"

"Josh was a level 7 manager, so he could submit his expense report without additional approval."

Josh had the authority to submit his own expense reports without anyone seeing or approving his request. What other details had our client forgotten to mention? Kathleen thought.

"So, Mr. Harrington also had financial responsibility?"

"Yes, Josh's team was in my organization so the financial responsibility fell under me."

"So his expenses hit your Profit and Loss statements, correct?"

"I suppose so, when he actually had expenses that were incurred doing work within my org."

"How many times have you been invited to WCFM, and I believe I have given the right acronym?"

"Once in three years."

"Once in three years! Congratulations! Do you remember that one time? Was it this year, last year or three years ago?"

"I think it was about two and half years ago. We had a project that went totally south and there was a ton of un-billable time. By that I had to pick-up the labor, overtime and benefits for about seven people. So, that's how I got to the WCFM."

"Then explain to me how Mr. Harrington could submit the types of reimbursements for fraudulent expenses and his expenses are in your financial, (1) how you could overlook those line items, (2) why those expenses did not affect either revenue or expenses, and (3) how your margins stayed within the goals and you didn't have to go to the WCFM meeting?"

Paul knew when she finished asking that question, that he had to be really careful in answering this. Actually, he gazed to his left and saw Hardy waiting for his response. *Boy, if they pull my financial right now for those periods and followed the trail upward, even Alex's numbers would go negative.*

"Ms. Sullivan, I can't explain it. Maybe your client had modified some system that allowed the payment of those expenses, but didn't create the proper accounting transaction updates to the general ledger. So, I never saw the effects of what he was doing in my financial. When I answered that last question, because my margins were as they had always been, I had no reason to be invited to that meeting."

"If your theory is right, that would explain why you weren't invited to those meetings. But then, since I am assuming that since others have given testimony, you are the one who brought the allegations against my client?"

"I did not bring any allegations against Josh or anyone else."

"Aren't you the person who first saw the possibility that there was something wrong in Mr. Harrington's expenses to Alex Mann?"

"Well, no. What I saw was that his client was being billed an excessive number of man-hours that I did not see supporting 'time entered'."

"Then please explain, since your financial did not reflect anything in error, how did you discover it?"

Thinking of an answer to her question. "Another individual brought it to my attention."

"Who was that?"

"A programmer on the Billing team, I think."

Corporate Deceit

"And his or her name?"

"I don't remember."

Hardy looked at Paul just as strangely as Kathleen had when he answered. Hardy thought *"How does a person forget something that important, especially if you start looking into it and it appears to be true?"*

"Mr. Copeland, do you expect us to believe you don't know the name of the individual who brought such damaging information to you?"

"Well, it has been over nine months since that report came to me. I don't remember if the person actually came to see me or just sent me an email with an attachment."

"Mr. Copeland and Mr. Hardy, could you gentlemen provide me a list of names of everyone who has worked on the billing system within the last year by COB today?"

"Ms. Sullivan, we will compile those names for you as quickly as possible," Tim Hardy said, before Paul shot himself in the foot.

"Let's change the subject for the moment, Mr. Copeland. When my client asked for a Human Resource representative, why wasn't his request acknowledged?" Kathleen asked and she saw him becoming flushed.

"I don't remember the reason, but I am assuming that at that moment Josh was not being rational."

"Mr. Copeland, when TEC asked for a reason for the termination of my client, you stated that it was performance issues, is that correct?"

"Alex wanted to make sure that even if Josh had lost his job being stupid, we wanted him to be eligible for his benefits for unemployment."

"You give Human Resources documentation that an employee has billed his client wrongly, which is actually stealing, and you want to make sure he gets his unemployment. Is that what you are saying?"

"Ms. Sullivan, my immediate manager, Alex Mann, wanted him to receive his unemployment, so I did what I was instructed to do."

"Then why did you later change that to professional misconduct?"

"Well, I guess TEC contacted Josh, and he fought the original reason. When they contacted us, we figured, 'oh well he doesn't want our help, so put down the real reason."

"Then why wasn't my client ever told why he was being terminated?"

"Your client became upset and stormed out before we could conclude the exit interview."

"Are you aware that on his final paperwork there is not a reason for his separation?"

"No, I wasn't aware of that fact."

"As his immediate manager, do you have copies of his final separation paper?"

"I suppose so, somewhere," Paul was becoming uneasy with this line of questions.

Kathleen continued with several general questions and ended the deposition. As Paul and Tim Hardy were leaving, she did remind them of the list of names that she was expecting.

36

One of Kay's team members, Justin kept trying to think outside of the box and he had explored several approaches of how accounts payable and cash were not in balance without any luck. Then a thought came to his mind, so he found Kay and told her there maybe another way to solve this puzzle.

"Kay, these are the facts that we know: Accounts Payable is reflecting more money than cash, right? And we know when this started and ended, right? We have only been looking at AP documents and the cash balancing reports so we haven't seen this error in accounting? I tell you why….. because these financial coordinators are not out of balance."

"Justin, where on earth did you go to lunch? Was your lunch totally liquid? How could AP and Cash not be out of balance and the coordinators don't know?" Kay asked.

"Because only the files in AP were altered. See, whoever did this only wanted the documentation to frame our client; they weren't really trying to steal any money. So what I am thinking is whoever did this only wanted him fired. Simple."

"So if we pulled other supporting reports that receive feeds from AP, and then recreate the activity, we should see a vast difference that was originally shown on our second run."

"Do we know that for sure?"

"No, this is just a theory, but I am betting that this will hold up."

"Where is Page?"

"She is sleeping in and won't be into the office till 10."

"Get someone to pull all of the AP data, and then create me a list of all departments. Next, pull everything with Josh Harrington's name on it. Then I want a spreadsheet with the following column headings: date, expense number, name, amount, and description. I also want sub-total breaks denoting when the months change. We need something else; we need all of the transactions for that same period. Then we can back into our missing X if there is one."

"I'm following you; if we validate the coordinator's figures, then we can tie something together. Kay, we need a beginning point," Justin said.

"We need someone with pull who can get the coordinators to do their part. They aren't about to do all this work for someone who is trying to sue their company. Can't go to Senior Management and ask them to put some pressure on the coordinators. Who has the power to help us?" Kay was trying to figure whose name or position to make the FC's (Financial Coordinator) jump through hoops for them, Kay pondered.

"How about your ex?" Justin asked jokingly.

"First, my ex-husband knows nothing about accounting. There has to be somebody?"

"What about your friend that we met when we first got here? Justin asked.

"Gayle doesn't have that type of power?"

"Why doesn't she? Her company was doing the audit for Cavanaugh. She also has to have buy-in from the top executives, so she does have the power. Call her and see if she will help," Justin told Kay.

Calling Chapman & Chapman she was told that Gayle was in a meeting and she left her number. Twenty minutes later Gayle returned her call.

"Kay, this is Gayle; how is it going?"

"Gayle, one of my guys is making us think outside of the box, and what he is putting on the table makes sense. We have one small problem and we can't pull this off without your help? Kay said.

"So how do I or Chapman & Chapman play in this theory?"

"Listen for a moment and I will explain."

Kay then explained that approaching the differences by only looking at the documents available, they would be able to see what the company was seeing with or without Josh's expense reports.

When Kay had finished her team's theory, Gayle responded. "Kay, I think you are on to something there. And to think about it, we should have done the same thing. I do know someone there who could get the coordinators to provide you the information that you need. Now, the question is how do I pose the request as if it is part of our audit versus your investigation?"

"Gayle, I wasn't sure if I called you that you would agree to help. I understand that I am asking a lot, since Cavanaugh is your client. But if this proves what we think it will, then this guy may be telling us the truth."

Gayle hadn't told Kay that she knew Josh. In Kay's mind her friend was stepping out on a limb to help her.

"Look, regardless of who it is, no one should be set up to lose everything based on a lie. Normally, the system only allows us to go so far; then this invisible ceiling appears. This time someone went too far and that isn't right."

After making sure of what Kay and her team wanted, Gayle placed a call to her contact at Cavanaugh. Gayle had given Kay the email and password that was given to one of the members of her team, and had the coordinators forwarding their information to that email address.

Within an hour of the email, several of the coordinators either had sent the desired documentation or a response stating when that information would be available. Justin and the remaining of Kay's team began assembling their information.

Working through the rest of the afternoon the first breakthrough came. Page was looking at income statements and noticed that Paul Copeland's margins had not deviated more than a half of a percent each month, which included those months that Josh was supposedly submitting false expense requests. Page found Kay and Justin in a team room going over the transaction files that the coordinators had supplied them.

"Justin, Kay, explain this, because I think this is just too weird. How can this one department's profit margin stay constant when those exorbitant expenses should have been hitting the bottom line and there wasn't a significant increase in revenue? Do you have the Accounts Payable transactions for the Enterprise Development Group?"

Shuffling through the mountain of spreadsheets that were spread across the conference table, Justin found the spreadsheet for that department. Looking at the report he saw Josh's name and running his hand across the page he found an amount of $562.11. Using the document number, he looked through the copies of expense reports on the floor looking for document #76827. After finding it his eyes quickly went to total reimbursement amount and saw $23,327.65 and his eyes lit up.

"What?" Kay asked seeing the expression on Justin's face.

"What if I told you two there is a $22,000 plus difference between what was reported and the expense report? He told them gleefully.

"Justin, your out of the box thinking is heaven sent. I just love you!" Kay said.

"Well most of the credit has to go to Page, because it was her idea first."

"I don't care whose idea it was, but it proves that one of these documents is false. Now let's see what the other months will tell us," Kay instructed them.

Sending out for pizza, the team worked the remainder of that night, but cold pizza and sodas were worth it. When they called it quits for the night the first part of the puzzle was solved. Beginning the previous August all of Josh's expense reports had been altered in the Accounts Payable system. When they finally reconciled the total amount matches the excess what was being shown in Cash Balance Report. The difference was $254,439.89.

Closing down for the night, they returned to the hotel and said they would get a fresh start in the morning, documenting what they had found. Kay told the team what a great job that they had done and she would call Nicole first thing in the morning with the news. Everyone was on a personal high because they had figured out what had been done, except Page.

Sitting in her hotel room, Page started her computer and studied the spreadsheet that she had put together before they had left Cavanaugh. She questioned: why *those* amounts? As she sat there she added columns to her spreadsheet and

Corporate Deceit

divided the number and saw there was a factor of 41.5 times what Josh had submitted. This was too bizarre; why that number? Using the first entry and entering the same calculation as she had done in the total column caused the same results. She repeated the process on every line and got the same results.

Page logged on to the Internet and searched again for currency conversion applications. After going into several sites, she found one that she could use. Testing her new theory she found a currency that for every US dollar converted, you would receive 41.5 times of that country's currency. She then went to the Cavanaugh's home page and read about the company. There she found another piece of the puzzle. Whoever did this used the conversion rate of the country that Cavanaugh also had offices in. Immediately, she called Justin's room excited.

"Justin, wake-up! I know the mindset of whoever changed those expense reports. The conversion factor is constant for every entry."

When Justin awakened, his head was still not clear, so it took him a moment to understand what Page was saying. "What are you saying Page?"

"Whoever did this used a rate that they were familiar with. They used the conversion rate of the same country that Cavanaugh has offices in."

"Yeah that's what they did. I bet you whoever did this either worked there or had to go there for some reason. Because the rate of difference is the same, they knew that would inflate his expense report to some big number."

"Okay, that makes sense, but we tried Euro dollars and that didn't work."

"But we never used Ringgits," Page told him.

"What is a Ringgit?"

"Malaysian's currency. See Cavanaugh has an off-shore operation there. So, that is the conversion factor."

"Okay, so we know the currency; that still doesn't tell who or why," Justin responded.

"Yes, it does; well maybe not who, but sure does tell us why. See, they didn't care what the final total was, but they knew the exchange factor was so great that it would really look as if this guy was cleaning up like a bandit. Somebody wrote a program looking for his name, multiplied each line item by the same factor, and overwrote the total column."

"Great theory, but how did they get into the system to do it?"

"Now, since I am not a programmer, somebody else would have to tell us that. What I do know is they changed his expense reports to show Malaysian dollars instead of our currency."

"Page, go to bed. I like your story, but it is 2:00 A.M. and I got to get some sleep."

"Justin, this is the fun part that alone should keep you running on pure energy. Boy, I am so hyped I'm going down to the pool and swim. Good night! I will see you guys in the morning."

With that she hung-up, changed and went to the pool to relax.

37

If they had been working together this puzzle would be almost complete, but each group had their own agenda with bits and pieces, so no one had the complete picture. Sawyer had received the information that he had asked for from Alex, so his treasure hunt had begun.

Robert and Joe, two of Sawyer's guys unknown to the Cavanaugh's Network Security team, had made a full copy of the Accounts Payable disks and downloaded that information onto their system in Kansas City. When Sawyer explained to Alex what they were about to do, Alex became very concerned and asked Sawyer was that necessary. Sawyer's explanation was with the data in KC, so they could do a lot more without being noticed.

Alex understood that they could copy the current information, which was a normal process, but could they really copy data that was supposed to be altered or erased? Sawyer ensured him that they had the technology to do just that and they would destroy the information just as soon as they were completed with it.

After they had downloaded the data, Sawyer's team ran a series of programs that they had created and within four hours they had found what they were looking for. They pulled the information and compiled a report that outlined the chain of what happened, but also who had done it. Calling Alex, Sawyer explained to him what they had discovered.

"Good morning Alex, I think we have something for you to work with? In fact, I know we have something for you to work with. We know who may have modified the data and when."

"Sawyer hold-on for a moment," Alex asked. Quickly, he closed his door.

"Ok Sawyer, who changed the data?"

"Well, we know ID of the person who changed the data. Now you will have to get your network security group to give you the actual name."

"What is the ID?"

"The id is CCIMDC. Whoever this is, what he or she did was run a program that changed the data on December 18th," Sawyer told Alex.

"That proves that somebody had actually done this to Josh, but why?" Alex said out loud forgetting that he had Sawyer on the phone.

"Yeah, that's right. The data was changed. But you also have another problem there too."

"What other problem do I have? Don't tell me there is another security issue with one of our systems?" Alex asked.

"Yeah, and this one is really a problem. You got someone robbing you guys blind and you don't even know it," Sawyer explained.

"What in the hell are you talking about? What do you mean? Are you telling me someone is actually stealing? So why hasn't AP found this person too?"

"Because the guy isn't using your AP system, they are stealing on the front end as money comes into the door, not the back where most would look for it to happen."

"On the front, but where?"

"How about your receivable system?"

"Sawyer you got to be wrong about that one, because that is a secured socket. Unless you have the password there is no way that anyone could steal from the receivable system."

"They could and they have because their program is just in front of the secured socket. Your clients are logging in, this program runs the transactions first, takes what it wants and then gives Cavanaugh the remainder. The client is unaware, the receivable system is unaware, and so they are making off with thousands like bandits."

Alex was flushed, *"what was happening to this company."* The one thing that continued to get deal after deal signed was the testimonies that your data was safe and secure was a lie. Could Sawyer be right about this? No way! Because some report from the billing system would reflect an out of balance condition.

"Sawyer, you got to be wrong about this? Let me explain why I am saying this. First, the billing system and the receivable system would be out of balance. Then the client would get a reminder from the billing system that there was an outstanding balance, then the client would send supporting documentation showing that they had paid the bill in total. So, if there was a program out there running and stealing money before it got here, then the audit trail would find it."

"Well my boy, your thief thinks the same way and he worked around his audit problem. What this person is doing is trapping the transactions on their way out and balancing everything on both ends. Your finance people are seeing what they expect, the client is paying what is actually owed and the thief is getting his. In his mind everybody is happy."

"Sawyer? Do you hear what you are saying? First, the transactions that I sent for you to verify as being true or false, you are telling me are false. Then since that is enough information to make me wonder about the entire day, then you tell me that we actually have someone else or the same person robbing us blind. Is there anything else you wish to share before I have heart failure?"

"Well, whoever is stealing is smart, but I know where the money is going."

"Great, so all our security people and the FBI has to do is find out whosename or names are on the bank account?"

"Now that may be a problem. See, and we haven't done it yet, but what we are thinking is that this may be a little harder trail to follow. We know this guy is smart, so logically then you assume that the money is going to bounce around before it lands where he wants it to."

"Can you and your guys follow that?"

"Yeah, we think we can."

"Do that and keep me posted."

"Will do. Sorry for bursting your bubble that you guys had your data locked down so no one could do this," Sawyer was really being sincere.

"Question, can you send me copies of what the data looked like before it was change?"

"Yeah we can do that, but its raw data, so you will have to write some type of quick and dirty program to make it look pretty."

"When can I expect it? I need this really quick because I got a trial starting in a week and I need to get with the company's attorney."

"Look, we can pull it in about a day, download it to a CD and overnight it to you. Best guess, you should have it in a couple of days."

"Thanks for being able to do this for me. Man, I guess when you first told me five years ago that this was a service that companies would one day need, I thought you had gone off the deep end."

"See, Alex when technology changed about ten years ago, companies opened themselves up for this type of fraud. I don't know the story around Cavanaugh, but this same person could have stolen millions and be out of the country before you found out how or how much."

"Man this is scary to think about. Actually, what you did scares me just as much. How did you pull data out of here without our Network people knowing?"

"Trade secret old buddy, but you saw it can be done. Furthermore, you don't have to be a rocket scientist to do it either," Sawyer said while laughing.

"Look, I have to inform a couple of people what you found out, so I have to go."

"Understandable, I will call you when I Fed-Ex you the package. Talk to you soon."

After he finished his conversation, his first call was to network security. He asked the person to send him the name of the person whose system id was CCIMDC and he needed that information as soon as he could have it. The person on the other end told him to hold on for a moment and he could look it up in a matter of seconds.

"The id CCIMDC belongs to Monty Cooper of the Enterprise Development Team."

"Thanks," Alex acknowledged.

Corporate Deceit

He logged on to the company's Intranet network, and he searched the organization chart for this person's name. Monty Cooper, who ever this person was, reported to Daniel Stevenson who reported to Paul Copeland. Did Daniel get this guy to do this, or did Paul? He knew one thing, he had to tell Hardy what Sawyer had discovered.

That same morning, Kay Boutte was trying to reach Nicole and tell her what her group had found the night before and what she had learned while eating breakfast with Justin and Page. Calling Nicole's office, Taquitha, her receptionist informed her that Nicole was in San Antonio and she could be reached on her cell phone.

"This is Nicole."

"Nicole, are you in a meeting?" Kay inquired when she answered.

"No, I am lost that is what I am. This will be my third trip around the Riverfront Hotel this morning. I am trying to get to Beacon St., but I don't see a street sign of that name anywhere," Nicole said, sounding somewhat frustrated.

"Nicole, if you are by the Riverfront Hotel look for Avenue K instead of Beacon. Avenue K and Beacon are the same street. They did everything by the River Walk to have letters, and then the street names start back a couple blocks up," Kay told her.

"How in the world would somebody know that if they didn't live here? That has to be the dumbest thing I have every heard of. Oh, I see Avenue K, now which way do I turn?" Talking out loud to herself.

"You can only go north from where you are. It is alright, you will be where you are going in a couple of minutes. See Beacon itself is only about six or seven blocks long, and then it changes to Grapevine."

"Glad you called, but since you didn't know that I was lost, what's the problem? Still no luck in finding evidence to clear my client?"

"Well, we do know what they did, but we are clueless on how they did it."

"What! You can prove that somebody changed the books?" she exclaimed.

"Yes, we have the documentation and everything. What somebody did was changed his expense reports into Malaysian currency."

"What? Malaysian! Why Malaysian?"

"Our theory is whoever did this knew that the exchange rate is like 42:1. So, we are guessing, they wrote a program, modified every line item on the real expense reports. When they did that instead of documents showing about six thousand of expenses over six months, you now have a little of a quarter of a million."

"Ok, that alone when I present it to their attorneys will get the ball rolling on a settlement. But the truth of the matter is I still need to know who did this. If we knew that, then no way could they say that they aren't liable. Now the real question and I don't know if we will ever find that is, why?"

"Can't answer that, but we do know how it was done. He will still get paid and his job back if he needs or rather wants to work after this."

"Courier your information over to my office, and I will look at it first thing in the morning when I get back."

"Ok, enjoy the city and I will come by tomorrow afternoon and explain what we have put together."

"How about 1:00 tomorrow?"

"That's fine, see you then."

Finally at her destination, Nicole regrouped and on her way in called Josh. "Josh, are you busy?"

"Am I busy? Let me think about that, no I am tired of looking at reruns of I Love Lucy," Josh said laughing.

"The accounting team feels that they know and can prove that your expense reports were changed by someone."

When he heard that he sat down and calmed himself before he asked. "So somebody changed my expense reports?"

"That's what Kay is telling me."

"So how did they do it?" This was a rhetorical question on his part. Josh had a better grip on how, but he couldn't understand why it was done.

"Don't know that yet. But this clears up some things, give us some bargaining power. To have an airtight case we still need know who and why. But this is major, believe me. We should be able to get the criminal charges dropped easy now. Now how much is this worth to Cavanaugh is still another matter," Nicole explained.

"Do you have their report yet? I can come by this afternoon. I want to see for myself what someone is trying to do to me."

"Josh, if I didn't tell you, I am not in town. I am in San Antonio and won't be back into my office until tomorrow."

"That's fine. I can be in your office first thing in the morning."

"Make it around one o'clock, that is when Kay Boutee will be there, so you can hear it first hand," Nicole told him.

"Ok, I will see you at one."

She walked into the conference room to settle another matter that she was handling; this $40,000 car accident was peanuts compared to the negotiations she would be in with Cavanaugh in a week or so, she hoped. Just think, whoever was behind this did not realize the liability that they had placed that company in.

Alex had not been able to reach Timothy Hardy that morning, because Hardy was off-site at a Senior Management Conference. When Hardy returned to his office late that afternoon, he found four messages on his desk that were all from Alex needing to talk to him. Thinking he must have some proof that Harrington was guilty, he quickly looked up Alex's cell number and dialed.

"Alex, Hardy here what is the news? Harrington did do this, so I can tell all of his lawyers, auditors, and whoever else here to get out?"

"Wish that was the news, but it isn't." Alex responded.

"What, did we set this guy up? Do you know what the impact of that would mean?" Hardy asked.

"That is only part of our problems. We have a bigger problem. Sawyer has found someone stealing from the company and we don't know yet for how long."

"What in the hell are you saying? Somebody is actually stealing using the AP system too?"

"No, whoever is doing this, is stealing from us on the front end and it appears that we aren't the wiser because everything balances."

"I am totally confused. What dollar figure are we looking at here?" Hardy needed that information for when he went back to Serif.

"That I don't know yet."

"Find that out as quickly as your guys can and call me day or night when you have that information. Send me an email explaining the full details of what you are telling me now."

"First, let me call Sawyer back and see if he can give me a rough number, then I will send you that email," Alex says.

"How did they make it look as if Harrington was guilty?" Hardy asked.

"Well, somebody changed the data in the Accounts Payable system to make it look like Josh stole the money. I know who did it, but this guy is just a programmer, in fact he works for me in my organization, but I don't have a clue who he is."

"So, he did the work, but we don't know for who, right?" Hardy asked.

"Right, he works for a manager that reports to Paul, so it could have been his manager, or Paul or both. I don't know which one."

"That is a problem. Can you prove this guy did this?"

"Yeah, the outside firm that I contracted is sending me the evidence in a day or two on a CD. I just got to figure out why this was done."

"No, that is not your problem to figure out. Your problem is to figure out how this doesn't become public knowledge."

"What are you saying?"

"We are international, and we are on the New York Stock Exchange, but we are small and up to our eyes in debt. See, we have leverage almost everything to compete against the Big Boys, the company is stable, but it doesn't have the means to lose twenty million of it in a lawsuit. Tell me what you know right now," Hardy asked.

"What I am saying is, we got to stop this bleeding and I don't care at the moment how that happens," Hardy's voice became very loud and he was very angry.

"You want to cover this up?"

"No, I want everyone fired, blackballed in the industry and prosecuted if I had my way, but I also got to protect other people too. It is either one person

Harrington, who is hurt behind this or 2400 other people losing their jobs because of this. You do the math and tell me what you come up with."

"We are going to try to cover up the cover up."

"I didn't say that, I said we got to figure out a way to save the company. I am the corporation's senior counsel, but I am also an officer of the court, so I can't condone anything illegal."

"No, you might not be able to condone it, but you sure in hell can imply that it happens," Alex was angry now.

"No, I am asking you to help me uncover the truth and at the same time figure out how to save the company too." Hardy told Alex.

"How do I do that without breaking the law?" Alex asked.

"Alex, you are a very smart man, a senior leader who makes tough decisions just treat this as another item on your plate. I want you to also get all of the information from that person who changed the data and keep me in the loop. Wait a minute, better yet, find this guy first thing in the morning, I mean go to his office, then tell him come with you. Bring him straight to my office and we will talk to him. That way he won't have time to call and get their stories lined up."

"Ok, then we should know who is behind it, but as you said, that's only part one."

"Right, then we may know how we can handle part two. I don't know about you, but how long can you look for a job in this market without feeling some pain?"

Alex understood what was at stake, but could he really do what Hardy was suggesting? Calling Sawyer back, Alex needed to know one answer from him in a hurry. "Sawyer, that ID that you gave me, is this guy also involved in the Account Receivable theft?"

"From all of the data that we have found so far, no this guy is clueless about that."

"Thanks, I needed to know that," Alex said and ended his conversation.

38

The next morning Alex stopped by one of his managers Daniel Stevenson's office, spoke briefly about his kids, work and such and then he asked to be shown where Monty Cooper's office was. Dan of course asked him why, and Alex gave him the song and dance that he needed to get out more and meet those who indirectly reported to him. When they got to Monty's office, Alex introduced himself, excused Dan and sat for a moment and talked with Monty just as he done earlier with Dan.

Monty seemed to be a nice guy, a little shy, but he was happy working there and spoke how he liked his manager Dan. After another couple of minutes talking to him, Alex invited him to walk with him as he visited someone else. At first Monty thanked him for the invitation, but he also had a new project that he was starting and didn't feel right just walking around when he should be working. Alex explained that he worked for him, so if it was ok with him then it would be ok with Dan too. Finally, agreeing to accompany him, Monty followed Alex all the way to Timothy Hardy's office. Alex introduced Monty,

Hardy invited them both in and soon as they were seated, Hardy closed the door.

"Well gentlemen, what can I do for you this morning?" Hardy asked in his most pleasant voice.

"Well Hardy, I have an issue and since I was in Monty's area I asked him to come and walk with me, because I know he could share some light on it for the both of us," Alex replied.

Monty at that point became nervous and explained that he was just a programmer, so if it wasn't a coding issue, he couldn't help.

"Actually you can help Monty, because you are a major player in this issue," Hardy told him.

"See Monty, I have proof beyond the shadow of a doubt that you modified some data in our Accounts Payable System and I need to know why," Alex told him.

"Sir there has to be some mistake, because that system is in production, so no one can get to the data."

"That is true and false Monty. You can't get to it the conventional way, but if you have access to the backdoor that is where you can. Also, that is how you did it," Alex said. One thing that Alex hated the most was to be lied to.

"I don't know of a backdoor. Maybe somebody used my id and did it?"

"Monty, like I said before, I have the proof. We need to know why you did it. Did you do this by yourself or did someone ask you to do it?"

"Look, I don't know what you are talking about, so you can keep on asking me questions from now until tomorrow, but the answer is still is going to be the same."

Hardy spoke at that moment. "Gentlemen, could you stop for a moment, I need to place one quick call, thanks"

Hardy went into his address book in his cell phone located a number and dialed.

"Emily Simmons," the voice on the other end said

"Emily, Timothy Hardy here. Could you do me a quick favor in the next ten minutes or so?"

"Sure Hardy, what do you need?"

"I need you to cut a final paycheck for a Monty Cooper, employee badge number, could you hold Emily? Monty what is your employee number please?"

Monty became red as a beet when he heard Hardy talking to somebody named Emily.

"My badge number is 56122, sir," Monty was almost in tears knowing that he was about to be fired in ten minutes from now.

"Sorry Emily, Monty's badge number is 56122. Could you personally deliver that check to me? Thanks. Sorry, where were we?" Hardy said as if he had just called the weather to check the temperature.

"Monty was explaining no matter how much we ask him, he doesn't know anything about the matter in question," Alex replied.

"Monty, as my kids would say, is that your final answer?" Hardy interjected

"Look, I am just a programmer, and I only do what my manager tells me to do. Nothing else," Monty's voice was cracking as he spoke.

"We know that, so who told you to change data on the AP system."

"Paul!" Monty was losing his composure.

"Paul Copeland told you to change some data on the AP system?" Hardy asked.

"Yes."

"Did he tell you why?" Alex asked.

"He said he needed some hard proof against someone he wanted out of the company. Said this person was nothing but trouble but he stayed just below the radar to ever being caught. You know the type, talked a great game, did just enough, but wasn't an asset to the company," Monty spoke.

"So, Paul asked you to change the files, so the person would look guilty?"

"Yeah and I changed the supporting files too," Monty told them.

Thinking that since he is telling them exactly what he had done and the person who wanted it done, just maybe he wouldn't lose his job. See, in the big scheme of things he was a small fish playing in the big guy's lake.

They continued to ask Monty the details on when he did this, if he saved any files or backed up the data. Was Josh the only person that he changed? Monty told them everything that he had done, including telling Paul how Alex had been in the system the last couple of weeks.

Just then someone knocked on Hardy's door. Hardy got up opened it and stepped outside into the hallway.

"Are you really going to fire me, Mr. Mann? My wife is pregnant and I need my job and benefits," almost in tears while he was speaking.

"Monty, I don't think we should fire you, because you said it just as it is. Your manager asked or instructed you to do something and you did it. It was a bad decision on your part, because you should have informed someone higher that this guy was asking you to do something both illegal and unethical. I think the best course of action would be something permanent in you personnel file and a written warning.

Hardy was still out of the room for several more minutes, but then the door did open. Standing with Hardy were two members of the Security team and Emily Simmons.

"Monty, these gentlemen will escort you to your office, help you pack your personal belonging and ensure that you out of the building. Ms. Simmons does have your final check, and your separation papers. Good day."

"Don't I get some type of severance? Everybody I know has gotten one." Monty asked.

"Monty for the liability that you have placed this company in, that would be a crime for me to even consider giving you severance it is against my better judgment. Gentlemen, get this person out of my office and out of this company as quickly as you can," Hardy was red from anger.

Monty left with Security and Hardy was trying to regain his composure. After a couple of minutes he did say, "Now we know who but I really want to know why."

Meeting with Kay and Nicole for the first time Josh was seeing proof that he was innocent. These were more than just his words against his former company.

"With this can't you walk in there, show them the evidence and then they would have to settle this?" Josh posed the question to Nicole.

"Well, even though it proves our theory and supports your case it isn't quite enough for them to open up their wallets." Nicole replied.

"Then what is next?"

"We are going to court to pick a jury."

"But we still don't know who is behind this and why," Josh said.

"I know that, but we will still be looking for evidence to win the case even while we are in court. Since Kay's documents prove what was done, then we will get some computer people in to see if they can tell us how. I know of a firm in KC, the guy Sawyer is one of the best in the country getting into people's systems."

"Oh, I always see on TV, that when they go to court they already have everything."

"You got to remember they only have an hour too," Nicole laughed.

"I guess I was starting again, trying to tell you how to do this."

"Exactly, so let me be the lawyer, ok."

She then explained to him what would be happening the first few days in court. Nothing real exciting like he had seen on TV, just lawyers being explained the rules of engagement by the judge, picking a jury and just maybe on the third or fourth day, opening statements. She reminded him to dress professionally, but not flashy when he came to court. Remember, most people on the jury make about third of what you used to make and have a family of four to provide for.

Directly after her meeting with Kay and Josh, Nicole asked Taquitha to find the number for Sawyer Kelly.

"Sawyer, this is Nicole Singleton. How are you?"

"Nicole, long time, so you must have some work for us because you never call unless it is business?"

"Actually, I do and I need some of your people like yesterday. I got a case, where someone is changing data on a computer system and making my client look guilty as hell."

Sawyer thinking, this can't be happening, Nicole's client couldn't be going after Cavanaugh?

"So, you want us to find out who is doing this?"

"That is what you do best."

"Nicole, and I know this is going to sound at first as heaven sent, but it isn't.

Let me ask you one question, first. By chance is your client suing Cavanaugh Industries?"

"Yeah, and how do you know that? Better yet, are you working for them right now?"

"Nicole, you know I can't tell you one way or the other if I am or not. I really would like to help you, but I got to pass on ethical grounds. You do understand?"

"Sawyer, that is what I loved about you from the day I met you, you are totally honest which is a rare quality these days. Could you recommend another firm just as good as you guys are?"

"Yeah, there is a firm in Oakland, the firm is Security Facts. The guy who started it actually worked for me, but moved to the west coast because of his children. He is good."

"Thanks, I will give them a call."

After hanging up with Sawyer, she wondered how long has Cavanaugh had Sawyer in and most importantly, what had he found? Quickly, she called Security Facts and hired them. They would be in Dallas by the end of the week.

Meanwhile Hardy and Alex were trying to figure out what to do with the mess that Paul Copeland had gotten the company into. Hardy's impression was Paul wasn't sharp enough to think of this, oh he could make it happen, Paul's mentality to Hardy was more of an in your face type of person.

"So now we know one clog of this wheel, but we don't know how many spokes there are," Hardy told Alex.

"Do we do Paul the same way we just did with that Cooper guy?"

"Not quite, I think I may call in a friend of mine to meet with us when we talk to Paul. With him or a representative from his office present, I think Mr. Copeland will be more than willing to tell us everyone involved."

With that out of the way, Hardy changed gears and asked if Alex had any more information on the actual theft using the Accounts Receivable system.

"How many people are we looking for? Are the two incidents separate or are they connected?" Hardy asked.

"Well, they got to be connected some type of way is my thinking." Alex answered.

39

August 27th, the first day of the trial in the 256th District Federal Court. Timothy Hardy and his assistant Kenneth Walton were seated when Nicole, Kathleen Sullivan, and Robert Howard entered the courtroom. After Judge Hathcock had sworn in the jury pool, and explained to them the merits of the case that they were going to hear, the *voir dire* process began.

Robert Howard interviewed the potential jurors for the plaintiff, and Kenneth Walton was interviewing for defense. The potential jury panel was seventy-five citizens and each had filled out a pre-trail questionnaire that each side had approved. The selection of a jury took three days, just as Nicole had estimated in her office with Josh. The panel was seated on Thursday and opening arguments were to begin the following Monday morning.

Josh was surprised when the panel was called and only six people were selected. Kathleen explained to him this was a civil matter and in most civil cases the jury is normally made up of six individuals instead of twelve, which he was accustomed to seeing on TV.

Judge Hathcock informed the lawyers for both sides that all final motions and briefs had to be logged by the court's clerk no later than the close of business that Friday. She instructed the jury, just as with any legal proceeding, that they should not discuss with anyone the case, read or watch any news coverage concerning the case, and if they suspected any member of the jury having done so, they needed to immediately notify the court. With that she excused the jury for the remainder of that afternoon and wished them well for their extended weekend. The lawyers in the case remained to clarify or challenge different motions that were already before the court.

Josh left the courtroom and going to his car called Keith, his best friend.

"Keith, man it is finally here and even though Nicole and the team say that they are ready, I still don't know where this is going."

"Man, from what you have been telling me the last few weeks, you have Cavanaugh scrambling just to make sure that the name doesn't change when this is over. Relax and just let your law team handle this," Keith told him.

"I know, but even knowing how they did it, Nicole still doesn't know why."

"Are they still trying to back track everything?"

"Yeah, but so far nothing. It's like we see the gun, hear the sound, but we can't identify who is shooting at us."

"Josh, you are at the finishing line of the race and you are thinking, I don't know how to cross and win. Just let the race come to you," Keith told him knowing that his friend was just being anxious.

"I am trying to, but I have no say in this matter, none whatsoever. It looks like I go where they tell me to go and that is it."

"Man, when they figured out how they did it, a lot of pressure should have been taken off your shoulders then?"

"You're right, now I wonder what this jury is going to decide."

"What's the makeup of the twelve?" Keith asked.

"See, you of all people, a college professor, doesn't know that in most civil matters there normally is just six people on a jury," said Josh laughing because up until two hours ago he too was looking for twelve of his peers.

"Alright, what is the makeup of the six?"

"Four women, two men, three white, two blacks, and I think Asian?"

"More women than men. That might work in your favor too. See women listen harder than men, corporations don't intimidate them easily and most are more liberal than us."

"Really, I didn't know that."

"I see a lot of Court-TV between classes and there is always someone talking about the jury for some trail or another," Keith explained.

"Look, I am tired. I don't know from what, I guess it is the strangeness of all of this that is beating me down."

"Don't forget to keep me posted, and I am praying for you every morning."

"Thanks, I call you when something breaks, ok"

Getting into his car, Josh lowers his head and asks "Lord am I close to finishing this test? It has been six months and I really would like to know if I am passing. If I am not passing, then help me cram for the final. I truly don't want to repeat this course ever. Amen."

After court, Tim Hardy and Kenneth rushed back to campus for a six o'clock meeting with Paul Copeland. Paul wasn't even aware that Monty Cooper had been fired, because Alex instructed Dan not to tell him and as part of Monty's three months severance agreement he was not to contact Paul by any means.

True, a severance package was not the deciding factor in Monty agreeing not to contact Paul; it was the possible criminal charges that he was facing. Falsifying documents in a company that is publicly traded is a Federal crime. Hardy told Monty that if he did not try to warn Paul or anyone else connected to this case then he would not pursue charges against him. Monty agreed to Hardy's terms.

Paul was caught totally off guard when he received a meeting invitation for a last minute afternoon meeting with Alex and CCDA. Walking into the conference room that had been reserved, Paul was in shock when he entered the room. In the room were Alex, Hardy, Kenneth Walton, and the Collin County District Attorney, Daniel Davis.

"Ok. Alex what is going on here? Your request said that you and I were meeting with some clients from CCDA and in I walk and I am seeing our legal staff," Paul asked and you could tell that he was upset.

"Paul my request said that we were meeting with CCDA and we are. Let me introduce Daniel Davis, the District Attorney for Collin County," Alex replied.

"So, why are we meeting with the DA, if I may ask?"

Hardy took over at that moment.

"Paul, you and whoever else is involved in this has placed the corporation in the middle of something that could ruin this company and we need the truth. We know through our own internal investigation that you had an employee under your direction falsify documents. Those documents were used against Josh Harrington and because of the surrounding allegations Mr. Harrington was arrested and charged with felony theft. Those two charges alone could get you five years in a Federal prison and cost you up to a hundred thousand dollars in fines. What we are seeking here today is who else is involved this."

"First, you can't prove any of the stuff you just said. Secondly, there aren't any records of me or anyone else of tampering with any data. So what you are doing is fishing and I am not biting," Paul said, hoping that what he said would not be challenged.

"We have the proof and a witness to the tampering with the data, but I also know you would not have done this without someone else's approval. So, be stupid and take the fall by yourself or tell us who else is involved," Hardy shot back.

"Mr. Copeland, my name is Daniel Davis and I am the DA for Collin County. Before we go any further let me clear up some things for you. (1) All that Hardy told you was the truth, (2) you have broken some State of Texas laws in this matter (3) State and Federal are still separate even in criminal matters. So, if you were convicted of both a Federal and State crime, you don't serve the two sentences together or at one time and what I mean by that is, when you are released, paroled or pardoned from one facility you then begin serving your other sentence at that time, and (4) my office is prepared to prosecute you to the full extent of the law."

Paul just sat there for a moment, hearing the words of the DA ring inside of his head. Was he prepared to go to jail by himself? What kind of deal are they offering him? They hadn't offered anything at this point, so are they willing to deal. This was just like he thought before he gave that deposition, this was totally beyond what he had bargained for and he wasn't prepared to take the full blame by himself.

"What is the point of this? If you really have a case against me, then you wouldn't be here now," he said bluffing. He hoped he hadn't shown his hand before he called theirs.

"Paul we have a case against you and I think you already know that. What we are hoping is that you aren't stupid and take all of the blame alone if others are involved. See this is corporate America, not the mafia, so whoever else is involved is not going to kill you or your family. No, what happens is their lives and careers will continue while yours is ruined forever, simple," Hardy spoke up and told him.

"So, what if I gave you the names of the others, what happens to me then? You can still prosecute me, my life is still over, and so what is in it for me, Paul Copeland?"

"What is in for you? You tell us who all is involved and I guarantee that you won't be prosecuted for what you did to Harrington by us." Hardy states

"If you give us everyone who is involved that is it," the DA states.

"And I also want to know why? What did this guy do that you and whoever else involved would take such a risk? That is what's so damn puzzling?" Hardy could not imagine anything that could cause this type of behavior. From that point forward, Hardy asked all of the questions to Paul.

Still not ready to name names, Paul figured if he gave the reason that started this, then maybe he wouldn't have to give names. "Josh Harrington tried to rape another employee."

"Paul, if you are going to continue to lie then don't say another word. Why are you still trying to slander this guy?" Alex asked.

"I am telling the truth! Harrington tried to rape a woman that works here in corporation. You've got to believe me!"

"Then if he tried to rape this woman, why weren't the police involved?" Alex asked.

"Why didn't they arrest him?" Hardy chimed in.

"I don't know. I wasn't there that night."

"Who is the woman?"

"I'd rather not say."

"Look if this is the truth, then I may understand the motive, but I need to know who this woman is," Hardy says.

"Lori Greenspan."

"Who all knew about this attempted rape, Paul?" Hardy asked.

"Myself, Russell Smiley and his boss Michael Jefferson."

"Is it just you three or four people in this?"

"I didn't say they were involved."

"However, you didn't say that they weren't either. So is this the group who master minded this plot to get Josh Harrington out of here?"

"Yes, I met with Russell and he told me that Josh needed to leave the company, and it didn't make him any difference how he left."

"Ok, I understand Michael and Russell. I understand you and Monty Cooper, but I don't see the connection between Russell and you. How did that happen?"

"Lori must have given him my name?"

"So how long have you and Lori been let us call it, been friends?"

"About three years."

"Paul, you now know what we know, plus you filled in the blanks on the missing pieces and you also know DA Davis will not prosecute you, correct? So, this meeting tonight never took place, you understand. Not a word to the others that we know what y'all have done, not that we are investigating this or anything. Now if you leak this I promise you two officers will pick you up and DA Davis will start the process of prosecuting you, understood?"

"Yeah, I got it. What's next?" Paul asked in a somewhat daze.

"Be in my office at 9:00 am sharp and I will tell you. Have a good evening."

Paul excused himself, stopped in his office, got his keys only and left the building. Stopping at the first bar that he came to, he reached into his wallet and handed the bartender his corporate credit card. Told the bartender, "You know what about that card I love, the slogan, yeah the slogan. If you feel you can afford it, then the card can hold it. So, keep pouring until either I am too drunk to drive or pass out. In either case, here is my address for the cab driver. Tell him just leave me on the curve, with the rest of the trash. If he follows my instructions, tell him to write him self a $100 tip. Ok then, double whiskey neat, with a beer chaser and keep them coming," Paul instructed the bartender.

After Paul had left the three men pondered was he telling the truth? There are four people in on this, two top executives and two managers. Well that would explain how they got rid of him, but what was the reason that Harrington tried to rape this woman. Only Alex knew Josh and he felt that was a lie too, but for whatever reason, the company was standing to lose if this became public.

Hardy spoke first. "Well first thing, I've got to call Serif in London and bring him up-to-date. That is going to be an ugly conversation. Then we got to find a way to make this lawsuit go away."

"Gentlemen, it seems that you have a couple of choices here. Actually, neither one of them are good. (a) Fire the whole damn bunch involved, then prosecute them on fraud. Harrington would surely win his lawsuit and you better pray the judge set limits on the company's liability, (b) settle this lawsuit out of court, then drop the criminal charges against Harrington, then fire that bunch," DA Davis spoke from his viewpoint.

"Well, it seems that I have done all that I was asked, so I will leave you gentlemen to deal with your dilemma." Davis said, while picking up his briefcase and leaving.

"I wonder just how much Harrington would take to end this," Hardy said out loud.

"Kenneth, please make sure you set-up a meeting with Harrington's attorney as quickly as possible," Hardy instructed his assistant.

40

Nicole received the call around 9:00 pm from Kenneth Walton.

"Ms.Singleton, Kenneth Walton here, are you available to talk for a moment?"

"Mr. Walton, how may I help you?" Nicole asked.

"Mr. Hardy would like to meet with you and your team tomorrow afternoon at 2:00 if possible?"

"And where are we meeting at Cavaungh?"

"At the Crowne Plaza, Presidential Suite."

"The Presidential Suite at 2:00 tomorrow, make it 3:00 and we will be able to attend."

"3:00 pm tomorrow; thanks for your time, Ms. Singleton. Have an enjoyable evening."

Getting off the phone with Kenneth, Nicole ran to her spare bedroom and knocked on the door.

"Kathleen, slip on some jeans, while I call Robert. Hardy wants to have a sit down tomorrow at 3:00 at the Crown Plaza."

Nicole called Robert Howard and he told her he would be there in fifteen minutes. Nicole put on some coffee, turned on her laptop, and slipped some jeans on herself.

Fifteen minutes later, her doorbell rang and Robert walked in with a cheap bottle of wine. "What in the world is the wine for? I called you to come to work and you show up like I have invited you to a dinner party."

"My dear, when you are about to roast a chicken, always marinate it first in wine," Robert joked.

Sitting in her den, she wanted to see how everyone stood on the critical points of talking with Hardy on tomorrow.

Kathleen spoke up first, "Why does he want to sit and talk now? The trail is only four days old, we only sat the jury, and Judge Hathcock still has five motions to rule on. So at this point, the game has not even started."

"Maybe he or someone higher than him, doesn't want the media backlash from this to hit the papers?" Robert said.

"I don't agree with you Robert, Hardy is up to something? I am betting that he has been doing his own internal investigation and he doesn't like what he seeing. So not to get caught in the fire, he thinks it is better to settle now than later. Think about it, just as Kathleen said, it's way too early to throw in the towel. So if you are willing to do so, then they must have found the same evidence that Kay found and they don't want us to know that."

"To keep us from discovering their little secret, how much is it going to cost them?" Kathleen asked.

"How much are our expenses and fees to-date, Robert?" Nicole asked.

"As of Monday, and this doesn't take into account having those depositions transcripts, our expenses were $289,290.02. I am estimating on the high side the deposition work will be another $25,000, so roughly and I mean roughly an estimate of $320,000 and some change," Robert informed them.

"So, even before we start talking settlement for Josh, Cavanaugh owes us about $500,000, right?" Kathleen asked.

"Make that $600,000 and we know all of our expenses will be taken care of," Nicole said.

"Now from Josh's original suit, what was the bare minimum?" Robert asked.

"Well guys remember in our first meeting, the group wanted each partner to come away from this with a minimum of $75,000. Anything less and we have failed," Kathleen said.

Corporate Deceit

"Then the minimum we should take is $4,000,000," Robert said.

"Look, since I brought this case to the group, I need a little bit more. So I am saying we don't entertain and offer less than $8,000,000," said Nicole making her wishes known.

"That would be around $100,0000 for each partner. Now those types of numbers work for me," Robert said.

"Nicole, do you really think Hardy is going to let us walk out of our first meeting with $8 million dollars? Kathleen asked. Even though the number sounded great, no good lawyer is just going to hand over the farm to the first person that walks by," Kathleen retorted.

"No, that's for just that suit, we still haven't addressed the malicious prosecution case and that was for another $5 million. What they did there should cost them at least three million alone. We can stress the humiliation, the trauma, and wrongful incarceration of our client there. So with both suits, if Hardy isn't ready to write a check for $12 million, he is wasting our time," Nicole said.

"Now, you are talking. That would mean we each would get something over $150,000 each ourselves," Robert says, and he was visually excited.

"Nicole, has Josh ever said what he wanted out of this?" Robert asked.

"Not really. He wants to be compensated for sure, but has he put a number to it, no. You know, he would probably walk away from this happy with five or six hundred thousand maybe even less, but he doesn't understand his own self worth. What that company did to him, it needs to step up to the plate and compensate him. Also, since he stepped out on faith with us, we owe him the very best of our abilities too. Why not $12 million?" Nicole was on her soapbox.

"12 million, Hardy is going to choke when he hears that," Kathleen said.

"No, Mr. Hardy will not choke or turn blue when he hears $12 million because $15 million will come out of his mouth not ours. Our number will be $20 million with the option to negotiate the first installment, with the remaining balance paid out over 10 years. What Mr. Hardy is going to do is this: put Cavanaugh Industries freedom on a lay-away plan for the next ten years," Nicole said.

41

7:00 am, Friday morning standing outside of Terminal E, Alex Mann is waiting for the red-eye from the west cost to arrive with Sawyer Kelly aboard. Alex had spoken to him briefly on Thursday night and since Sawyer had a layover in Dallas, Alex agreed to meet him for breakfast. Sawyer's plane was on schedule and the two sat down at Donna's Cafe that was in the airport to have breakfast.

After they had placed their orders with their waitress, Sawyer said he not only knew who was stealing the money, but also where the money was.

"Ok Alex, here is the short version of what is happening. Your theft is actually working with two other people and these boys are good. First, they are changing the data in your billing system and reporting one thing to Cavanaugh and another to your clients. Then when your clients pay the invoice, their program takes what it wants and transfers it to their bank, simple."

"So, they create this great scheme, and then turned stupid. So, all the FBI has to do is find out who the owners are of that account?"

"No my boy, like I said these guys are good. When the money hits the first bank, it is then transferred to several other banks here and in Canada before it land in their real account. And of course, their real account is in the Cayman's."

"Damn, with their banking laws, it may take years to find out who they are." Alex was now frustrated.

"Normally, that would be true, but here are the names of your thieves," Sawyer says while handing Alex a piece of paper. Michael Jefferson, Russell Smiley and Paul Copeland were the names that he saw.

"What, these three are the ones stealing? Sawyer, you won't believe the lies these three have told. They apparently had one of my managers fired as if he was the one that stealing from the company. They were doing it to protect a woman that they claim he tried to rape. So, all along they had Josh fired to take the heat off them. You know it would have worked if Josh was the type to just take what is given to him, but since he felt we were firing him for no reason, he fought back."

"I bet those three hated that. Are you telling me, well why would you look into someone being fired if the evidence looks as if he did? Then when this guy fought back, he actually helped you guys in the process. Just think, this guy should be the employee of the year, but he is suing you for terminating him."

"Sawyer, how do you know that Josh is suing us? I never mentioned a lawsuit to you."

"Oh, his lawyer Nicole Singleton called last week and wanted to hire me. Actually, she wanted me to do exactly what I was doing for you. See, it is so hard being ethical, because I explained that I couldn't take the job and gave her the name of another company. Actually, I could have been paid by both sides for during the same job."

"I wonder if she knows about these three stealing and setting up her client to take the blame?"

"Alex, I think she only knows that his data was changed, this other part unless you know what you are looking for, that could have gone on forever."

"Speaking of that, what kind of proof do you have to say that Paul and that bunch actually are stealing?"

"As much information that you need. From the time the program was first installed, the first transfer, the routing of the money, even a photo-stat of the signature cards in the Cayman's. The works!"

"Good, get all of that together, because either the DA and the FBI will want that."

Leaving the airport shortly after 8:00, he was hoping the traffic between there and his office would be light. He didn't want Hardy's meeting to start without him. Worst case if the traffic was too heavy, he would conference in from his car. Calling Hardy from his car, he wanted to bring him up-to-date about what Sawyer had found.

"Hardy, would you believe that Paul, Russell and Michael Jefferson are the ones that are stealing? My guy has traced the money to the Caymans and he also has the proof on how they are doing it. So are we going to have those three arrested this morning?"

"Alex, actually no we aren't. What I think I will do is fire the bunch, making them believe that their other crime has not been found out. I don't want to have them arrested until the Feds can assure us that they can recover the money. This is a white collar crime, so I don't want them to go to jail for a couple of years and still have twelve million or so to look forward to when they are released," Hardy explained.

"So, when the Feds get the money, then we send that bunch to jail? Then they go to prison, serve their time, and be ruined. That makes a much nicer picture in my mind. Question, how long does it take the Feds to say if the money can be returned?" Alex asked.

"Well, that could take a couple of months, depending on who is putting pressure on them to work the case. If I call Serif today, our political people could get the ball rolling as quickly as a day or two.

Since you are calling me from your cell, then are you going to make this meeting?" Hardy asked.

"Depending on traffic, I should be there. But, if I get stuck in traffic, start without me."

First thing Nicole did that same morning was to call Josh and tell him about her meeting that afternoon.

"Good morning Josh, did I awaken you?" She asked.

"No, I have always been one of those people who, regardless of what time they go to bed, still rise early. Since we don't have to be in court this morning, why is my lawyer calling so early, is the question?"

"Truth be told I am an early riser too, but the reason I am calling is because I have some news for you and a question as well."

"Let's see, do I want the news first or the question?" Josh says jokingly.

"Well, the news is we are having a meeting today at 3:00 with Cavanaugh."

"So, where is this meeting and what is the purpose of it? Did we call them or did they call us?" Josh was excited. For the first time in months, this thing was beginning to sound and act like those TV law shows that he watched. There was always a meeting.

"The meeting is at the Crowne Plaza, and they called us," Nicole told him answering his question.

"That means they want to settle this thing and get on with their lives, right?" Josh asked.

"At this point I would say they are fishing and they want an idea on the bait they need to buy, is my guess."

"Well they need at least to buy $8 million dollars of worms for this fishing trip," Josh said laughing.

"Josh, Kathleen, Robert and I ran the numbers last night here and we came up with another number which included our expenses.

Josh's mind said to him, *$8 million was high I really thought that would be just about right.* Holding his breath, he was waiting to hear Nicole's answer.

"Josh, we are thinking more like $15 million ballpark."

Josh was drinking coffee and he almost missed his mouth completely when he heard her number.

"You got to be kidding me? When we filed the original suit, you said that was for shock value more than anything else," Josh reminded her.

"Josh, I said we think $15 million was a good number. The real question is what is a fair number to Josh Harrington? If we could have our way, the full $20 million plus would be our target, nothing less. But this is your case, so I need to know what amount could you walk-away from this with and feel really good about yourself?" Nicole asked, believing she already knew his answer.

"Nicole, $15 million, wow! That is a number. Do you really believe Cavanaugh would pay that kind of money as a settlement?" Josh asked.

"No one or any company is willing to pay out that type of money, but because of what they did, they would have to if they lose the case."

"What could I walk-away from this nightmare with and feel good with myself? This is really a tough one because I never really did believe that I or rather we would get to this point. See fighting a corporation to me is like going into the jungle, looking for a lion and the only thing you have to fight with is a stick. Then to get where we are in court, with a jury and you have the proof that they lied and must pay, that blows my mind. How much? Nicole, to be honest I really don't have a number. I have cried, prayed and wished that I was having the worst nightmare of my life and would roll over and my life that I thought I was living would still be there. Can I say you go for it and roll the dice? No because I need to know something for me. I need to know for the first time in my life what the value of Joshua Alexander Harrington is worth to me."

"That's right Josh; you've got to set the price for you. And when you figure out what you think you are worth, I have found out, then you are not only happy with yourself externally but internally as well."

Remembering a poem he had read in the book "Think and Grow Rich" by Napoleon Hill:

> I bargained with Life for a penny
> And Life would pay no more
> However I begged at evening
> When I counted my scanty store
>
> For Life is a just employer
> He gives you what you ask
> But once you have set the wages
> Why, you must bear the task.
>
> I worked for a menial's hire
> Only to learn, dismayed
> That any wage I had asked of Life
> Life would have willingly paid.

"Nicole, I think I have an answer for you. No, that is incorrect. I know that I have an answer for you and this is it. Josh Harrington wants $12 million dollars, minimum."

"That is what I needed to know."

"So am I going to this meeting or is this just a lawyer's thing?" he inquired.

"Lawyers only today, but I will call you as soon as we leave. Should I try your cell first?"

"Yeah, and that reminds me, I better go online and pay the damn bill as soon as we finish."

"Josh, don't get your hopes up that this is going to end today. This may happen several more times before we are through, ok?"

"Got you."

42

Sitting in his office that Friday morning, Tim Hardy was sizing up his day. First, he had his meeting with Paul Copeland, then he had scheduled a meeting with Michael Jefferson and directly after lunch he was meeting with Russell Smiley. Those three meetings alone were a full day at the office, but then at 3:00 pm off to the Crowne Plaza to meet with Harrington's attorneys. What to expect out of that meeting would dictate if he ate dinner or had a liquid meal of scotch and sodas that night.

Well, Serif either was too tired from his flight to London to yell or he was trying to understand what the company could do to minimize this. He was surprised at how well the CEO had taken the facts, but the ball was still in his court to find a solution to this mess.

Promptly at 9:00 am, Paul knocked on his door with a visitor with him. Looking at Paul, you knew either he had been up all night worrying about his future or he had spent most of the night before drinking.

"Mr. Hardy, this is my personal attorney William Bradshaw. I asked Bill to join us this morning to make sure I understand my rights and options in this," Paul said.

"Mr. Bradshaw, actually Paul has taken this whole matter out of proportion and he really doesn't need a lawyer for this matter. This is strictly an internal business matter." Hardy had not foreseen Paul walking into his office with his own attorney.

"Thanks Mr. Hardy, but if you don't mind, I would like to stay and advise my client," Bradshaw replied.

Hardy was thinking *this guy really knows how to screw up things. The last thing I need this morning is another lawyer present. What can I say? I just got to change my directions and make the best of it.*

"That's fine, would you care for some water, coffee or a soda?" Hardy asked
They both declined his offer.

Alex walked into Hardy's office, saw the guy sitting next to Paul and was surprised as well that Paul had invited his own attorney to this meeting. After everyone was introduced and seated, Hardy closed the door. As he was walking back to his desk he begins

"Well, it appears that your client and several other individuals have created a situation that we are now in Federal Court fighting. The truth of the matter is not how this got started, but how does the corporation come out of this without losing its shirt because of their actions? The logical course would be to sue your client for whatever damages that the corporation is being sued for and recoup our liability from him. The problem there is it would only mean a worthless judgment, because your client doesn't have the ability to pay that sum of money, correct?"

"Mr. Hardy, my client last night was coerced by you, the DA, and whoever else was present to divulge his involvement, so those statements are invalid in my opinion," Bradshaw said.

"Mr. Bradshaw, may I call you Bill?" Hardy asked.

"Bill is fine."

"Bill, what your client did was wrong, morally, ethically and against the law. The corporation has proof of his involvement so that is a moot point. Our challenge is and the purpose of this meeting is to minimize the monetary impact of their actions."

"And how are you proposing to do that?" Bradshaw asked.

"That's the problem. I don't have a viable solution for that," Hardy shot back.

"Then what did you expect of my client this morning?"

"I guess first I needed the whole time scale, what was really discussed by all parties, what was only implied and who authorized this so called scheme to take place."

"Here are the provisions; my client will tell you everything he knows under the following conditions. First, you nor any member of this corporation files criminal charges against him; secondly there will be no documentation showing his involvement in this matter; and third no member of this company will use his or her power to retaliate against my client, clear?" Bradshaw states the terms that he felt that would protect Paul Copeland from going to jail.

"Agreed," Hardy replied.

For the next hour, Paul Copeland gave Hardy and Alex Mann details of how he, Russell Smiley and Michael Jefferson masterminded the termination of one Josh Harrington. At the conclusion of this meeting Hardy had enough information for his meeting with Michael and Russell, so neither person could deny his involvement.

Following his meeting with Paul, Paul's attorney and Alex, Hardy started his way to Michael Jefferson's office, which was in the executive wing of the building. Stopping and purchasing a cup of coffee, he bumped into Russell in the coffee shop.

"Good morning Hardy and how are we today if I may ask?" Russell was his usual jovial self.

"I am fine, just a busy day; too many meetings on my plate," Hardy answered.

"I see, well if I may help, I saw on my calendar that we are scheduled today for 1:00 pm. So to ease your day, if the matter can wait for another day or so, we can always reschedule it to sometime next week," Russell said always trying to be the good corporate citizen.

"Thanks for the offer, but next week is just as bad as this one has been. So, I would say we are still on for 1:00 pm," Hardy replied.

"I saw the subject was titled 'Personal Issues', so should I have Emily Simmons to join us?" Russell wanted to be sure the right people were in all meetings.

"I think you and I can handle this one. See you at 1:00," Hardy said walking off. He didn't want Russell to catch wind of what they were going to discuss until then.

Michael Jefferson met Hardy as he entered the Executive Wing and they went directly to Michael's office.

"Well, Hardy what have I or someone who reports to me done, that you needed to speak to me this morning?" Michael inquired while leaning back in his chair in a very relaxed posture.

"Michael, I don't have the time or the energy this morning for a cute game of wits, so I am going to cut to the chase and we will start from there, agreed?" Hardy wanted to set the tone early.

"Since I don't know the extent of what the possible problem is, but trusting you, ok," Michael replied.

"Russell, Paul Copeland and you have put this corporation in a Federal lawsuit that could ruin this company. Moreover, those actions by you and your group were illegal, and I should have all of you arrested and sent to jail."

"How in the hell do you have the nerve to walk into my office with such accusations like that?" Michael asked angrily back to Hardy.

"I have the proof of your involvement, and I have also talked to Serif in London. Do not insult my intelligence with a bunch of lies. So here is the deal; Serif wants your resignation on his desk by the close of business today. I have been authorized by Serif that you will be allowed one year of compensation, fifty percent of all options that are currently owned by you, and you must obtain financing for your home with another institution within sixty days from now. Those are the terms and they are non-negotiable," Hardy told him.

Michael looked at him for several minutes.

"Hardy, do you know what you are saying? You just fired me," Michael stated.

"Yeah, that is what I just did," Hardy acknowledged that he had heard him correctly.

"Hardy, whatever so called evidence that involves me is inaccurate. I would never do anything that would jeopardize the company. You've got to believe me," Michael said visibly shaken by Hardy's demands.

"Michael, I understand what you are saying, but the truth of the matter is you are guilty, so this is it. Serif doesn't want anyone in his inner circle that he can't trust and he can't trust you. The Board of Directors can't trust you or the twenty-four hundred employees of this company can't either for that matter. So the announcement will be released today at 4:00 pm our time that you are stepping down because of health issues," Hardy told him.

"What if I don't agree? What if I say that this is a bunch of lies, and I am going to fight?" Michael asked.

"Then in the morning, around 7:00 am, officers from the Murphy Police Department will be ringing your doorbell with a warrant for your arrest issued by the Collin County District Attorney's Office. So, either resign or go to jail. I don't care which you choose, actually I'd rather see you fight and lose," Hardy replied.

With no words to change the tone or the outcome of this meeting, Michael asked if his personal attorney could draw up his compensation package. Hardy reiterated the terms of his resignation was non-negotiable, so the terms that he had laid out were final.

"When do I leave, if I my ask?" Michael was devastated.

"Today!"

Hardy then got up and walked out of the former office of Michael Jefferson. Leaving Jefferson's office, he called head of security to terminate all access including network and email of Michael Jefferson immediately. He then called corporate accounting terminating all credit cards that had been issued to Jefferson.

His next call was to London to inform Serif that Michael's resignation was forth coming. His next call was to media relations, giving them the details and the release time announcing Michael Jefferson's decision to resign that day.

When he got back to his office, he called Dan Davis, the district attorney for Collins County and asked him could he get the police report for Lori Greenspan's attempted rape complaint. Davis told him that it shouldn't be a problem and someone would fax the report to him within the hour. After that Hardy and Kenneth Walton went to lunch so they could discuss the strategy for the meeting they were having at 3:00 at the Crowne Plaza.

Corporate Deceit

At noon Paul Copeland left the building to meet his wife for lunch. About a block from the office, the police pulled him over. Reaching in his glove compartment he searched and found his current insurance card and then he reached and got his driver's license while the officer, it appeared, was running his plates for outstanding tickets or something.

"Good afternoon sir, may I see your license and insurance cards please?"

"What is the problem officer, I don't believe I was speeding?"

"Just a moment sir, I will be right back."

The officer again got into his car and called the station. While he was waiting, he phoned his wife, informing her he would be late because the police had pulled him over. Just as he was finishing his conversation, he looked into his mirror, ok the policeman was returning, but he had unbuckled his gun. What in the world was that about?

"Sir, could you please step out of the vehicle with your hands visible at all times where they can be seen?"

"What is this about?" Paul asked as he stepped out of his truck.

"Sir, I am placing you under arrest because of a warrant issued by the Collin County District Attorney office."

"What in the hell are you saying? What warrant, and what are the charges?"

"Sir, the warrant is first degree felony theft. You have the right to remain silent and refuse to answer questions. Anything you say may be used against you in a court of law. You have the right to consult an attorney before speaking to the police and to have an attorney present during questioning now or in the future............................" Paul was read his Miranda rights and was taken to jail.

Returning from lunch Hardy finds a fax on his desk:

Tim,
There is no record of any police reports filed under the name of Greenspan.
Dan

At 1:00 pm Hardy walked into Russell Smiley office. "Ok Hardy how can I help you today?" Russell smiled broadly.

"If you haven't heard yet, Michael Jefferson is resigning from the corporation today effective immediately for health issues," Hardy began the conversation.

Since Russell reported to Michael directly, he was overtaken upon learning this. Michael hadn't said anything about having any health issues. Then he began thinking this is the official story that would be told, so why is Michael out?

"Really, I have been meeting with him regularly and he didn't mention that he was under a doctor's care. I pray that everything works out for him," Russell said with a voice of concern.

"So, who will be assuming his duties?" Russell asked. *Is this the reason, I am being promoted to Sr. Vice President and assuming all of Michael's duties? Who will I promote to my job?"*

"Actually, this happened so suddenly, that who will take such a valuable role hasn't been thought out yet," Hardy replied.

His answer took some of the wind out of Russell's sails, but if he was the best qualified for the position Serif would do the right thing and promote him.

"Michael's leaving; is he just out on disability?" Russell asked.

"Leaving the organization. The press announcement will be released at 4:00 pm our time today. But again, I thought you may not have heard so I am sharing that with you as well," Hardy said.

"As well, so what other information are you sharing?" Russell asked.

"That you are also leaving the company today, Russell," Hardy told him.

"What? Hardy, this isn't the damn movie 'The Godfather', where you eliminate all of your enemies in one day. What on earth have I done to be fired? Name one thing?" Russell was demanding an answer.

"I had never thought of it that way. In a way you are right, Cavanaugh Industries is cleaning house all in one day. You are being fired because you have placed this whole company in jeopardy when you went after a guy for no apparent reason," Hardy told him.

"Look, it was Michael's idea to fire the guy. I did the right thing from the beginning. When she called, I went over and I made her call the police and file a report." Russell was recalling all of the events of that night.

"The police have no report on file, so you are still lying even now." Hardy was getting very angry.

Corporate Deceit

"Believe me, she called them and they came out and took her statement," Russell said.

"It doesn't matter at this point. You may have tried to do all of the right things when she called, you may have gone to Jefferson for directions on how to handle this, but that's where your judgment made the wrong choice. When you entered into the conspiracy to falsify data to wrongfully terminate an employee that was your biggest mistake. You had multiple options at your disposal, but you placed your own self-interest above Harrington's and this corporation. Personally, I am embarrassed to know that this company has individuals at this level with little or no moral fiber. To think we have allowed a person such as you to dictate policy and procedures for us. I have spoken to Serif and here are the details:

Your resignation will become effective immediately.
You will be allowed to receive three months of your current compensation including health benefits.
All current options that were granted to you and are not vested will be retired back to Cavanaugh Industry.
All vested options will be returned to Cavanaugh Industries.
You will be given the option to purchase your company vehicle at the fair market value.

Those are the terms and just as in Jefferson's case, they are not negotiable, understood?" Hardy stated.

"Is there anything that I can do? Look Hardy, I am 57 years old, the current market is extremely soft, and if I leave here then the chances of me finding another position comfortable to this one is almost impossible. Look, I will take a demotion, cut in pay, hell take the company stock away, but don't fire me." Russell was pleading for his job.

"Russell, the same way that you feel that you need your job, what about that Harrington guy? Didn't you think that he needed his? The difference in your heart is, you know why you are being fired and you understood there was a chance that this scheme could be found out. You actually know that firing you is the better of two options, because you should go to jail. So, here you are telling me all of the reasons on why you still need to work and you didn't give that guy a second thought. You know, people like you make me want to throw up! Please have all of your personal possessions off the premises by 6:00 pm on Sunday, or we will do what you instructed your subordinate to do with Harrington's things, we will dispose of them," Hardy stated.

Hardy left Russell Smiley sitting in his chair, elbows on his desk, with his head buried in his hands, contemplating his future. Leaving him, he called Emily Simmons congratulating her on her promotion as the new Assistant Vice President of Human Relations.

"What are your saying Hardy? I am the what, new Assistant Vice President?" Emily said so loudly that several members of her team that were close by stood and listened outside her doorway.

"That is exactly what I said. Congratulations! Couldn't happen to a nicer person," Hardy told her.

"When, what happened, who do I report to, has Russell been promoted as well?" she asked because this was totally out of the blue.

"No, Russell hasn't been promoted. The only promotion that I know of today is yours. So enjoy. Look there are several things such as compensation, fringe benefits, options, you know the normal stuff, that either Serif or myself will talk to you about in a couple of days. Why don't you take the afternoon off and share the news with your family? Look I got to run, schedule a meeting with me for next week. Congratulations."

With that he hung-up and then made the same call to Security concerning Russell Smiley as he did for Michael Jefferson. While he was talking his phone beeped, asking the person to hold for a moment, he answered the incoming call.

"We have him incarcerated," Daniel Davis told him.

"Then pick up the other two. If you could, be sure that their wives and kids are home when it happens. Thanks, oh what time is our tee time tomorrow?" Hardy asked.

"11:16 am at Tour 18. Why don't we send at least three cars to each address? That way all of the neighbors will be outside wondering and watching." .

"Fine and thanks. See you tomorrow."

Clicking back over, he instructed the security person to do the same things for Paul Copeland. Checking his watch at 2:30 pm, he rushed to his office, threw papers into his brief case, and left.

43

Lori Greenspan was sitting by the pool at the Westin Galleria Hotel in Houston waiting for a call from Paul Copeland about how his meeting had gone that morning. Surely, she thought, everything must be fine but his call last night really did worry her. She knew right from the beginning of the conversation that he either was still drinking or he had just finished because at first she didn't understand what he was saying.

As she recalled the conversation in her head, he was saying that the DA, Hardy and Alex Mann not only told him what he had done, but also wanted the names of everybody who was involved. She was sure it had been the liquor because he said they all would go to jail behind this. How could she lose her job, her career and possibly go to jail because Jefferson, Smiley and Paul figured out a way to fire Josh Harrington and not her? She wasn't even present when that scheme was planned, nor was she in on it when Paul took those fake documents to Human Resources. Until Paul mentioned the entire scheme one Saturday morning lying in bed, she wasn't a part of anything. Those dumb bastards took it too far; all she ever wanted was Josh to be taken off the committee that they were on.

When she learned of what they were doing, it was too late for the truth. Instead of firing him, all chances were she would have been fired. She had done everything to get him out of her life. She called Russell repeatedly and complained of his treatment to her, but Russell was such a weak manager. Every week he would say he was taking care of it but then Josh would walk in, cockier than ever, putting her and her ideas down in front of everyone. Instead of removing him, what did Russell do? He asked Josh and me to put together a presentation for the Executive Steering Committee. When he told us that, I was thinking that day: "Brilliant idea, you idiot. Why don't you just ask me to marry this egotistical, I walk on water; I know everything, SOB?" What a waste of my time. No matter how hard I tried to see his point, he never acknowledged that I had a brain in my head. Then when I make a complete fool of myself, he just says, "Thanks, but no thanks to me."

Sitting there drinking some type of frozen thing from the bar, she started to replay the night she called Russell, but between the drinks and the Sun, her memory took her to the early part of the evening leading up to the phone call to Russell.

Yes, they were working late, just as she had told Russell, but there wasn't a power outage at the building. Around 7:00 that night, she suggested that they grab a quick bite of dinner since they were almost through with their presentation. Apparently he was hungry as well, so they left in his car and drove to a nearby Italian restaurant. When they arrived, she noticed that other couples, either walking or entering the restaurant, were noticing them. It was a different type of notice, one that she couldn't explain, and the stares were mostly coming from other women. At first she tried to ignore them, but as each couple either passed them or glanced their way, instead of becoming uneasy, she was enjoying the envy that she was feeling from those other women.

At dinner she saw another side of Josh Harrington that she had never seen before. Oh, she knew that he was articulate, smart and self confident, but this other side of him was warm, caring and quite charming. At dinner she wanted wine; he didn't object and actually ordered a bottle instead of a glass. If he was going to drink wine, he preferred it from a bottle rather than from a box under the bar. That made her laugh and it had been a long time since she had been at dinner with a man that made her laugh. During dinner he made sure that she was taken care of and even at one point when she had extra sauce on the bridge of her nose, he leaned over very gently and removed it. Was the wine going to her head or was this guy the real McCoy and knew how to treat a lady? Several times during dinner she reminded herself that he was a co-worker not Mr. Right.

Finishing dinner, they decided to walk the strip mall for a moment, because it was a beautiful Indian summer night; the stars were shinning brightly in the sky and the moon was too. Even Josh commented how bright the moon appeared to him and he could not remember when he had seen it like that except when he was in the Islands. As they walked, he told her that often he would dominate a conversation, but instead he wanted to know more about Lori Greenspan. Maybe she shouldn't have had that third glass of wine because she talked and shared too much information that night.

Of course there were the usual things: where she had gone to school, her ambitions goals and her marriage. Wine or not she didn't share that she was having an affair with a married man. That she knew that she had not done. But she did tell him her legal name, the one she only signed on legal documents, not even her checkbook had that name.

"So, Lori Greenspan is not your legal name?" he inquired.

"No, Lori is part of my middle name, my first name is Bryce," she replied.

"Okay, so what was so awful with Bryce Greenspan? The middle names that parents give usually traumatize the individual." They laughed and agreed on that point.

"Well, Lori is just part of my middle name. My full legal name is Bryce Lori-Beth Greenspan."

"Wow, but Bryce is kind of nice."

"Well, you can have it! I hated it because as I was growing up I never heard Bryce by itself, I heard Bryce Lori-Beth. That is how my family called me—everybody: mom, dad, aunts, uncles cousins and even in school."

"Now I understand, but we'd better get back and finish this so we will at least be fresh on tomorrow," Josh said.

"Josh, we can't finish at the office because we have been drinking. My house is about five minutes from the office; we can finish there."

"Great idea, but that won't work. Both of our laptops are in your office, and our document is on your PC."

"Not a problem; all I have to do is VPN, and I can start exactly where we left off."

"What about your car?"

"We will drive back, I'll pick up my SUV and you follow me."

"Let's do it."

Arriving home it took maybe an hour to finish and send the document to a printer close to the office to generate twenty copies. Still wanting to know more about the person that she had dinner with, Lori opened a bottle of wine and we continued the conversation.

She was fascinated with him and the more they sat there and talked, the more she wanted him. What was she thinking? Lori wanted Josh Harrington not for the moment, but she wanted him. So just as everything else in life that she wanted, Lori told him.

"Lori, it may be the wine, but I think I'd better leave."

"Why, we are two individuals and maybe the wine helped me to see another side of you, but I know what I want at this moment and if what I am thinking is right, this could be a very long, rewarding relationship for us."

"The idea is very appealing; you are a beautiful woman, but I am already in a relationship, so as hard as it is for me to say it, the timing is totally wrong."

Then he just picked up his keys and left. Lori was furious not just at him but also at herself too for basically throwing herself at him and him refusing her. She was hurt. How could she get back at him was her forethought? How could he not see that she honestly wanted to have a relationship with him and just walk out on her? That was so baffling to her.

Before she knew it, she was crying. Lori needed to talk to someone and she called Russell and t said, without thinking, that Josh tried to rape me. Then when Russell was not only concerned but came over, she didn't have the nerve to tell the truth. How could she, at her weakest moment of wanting to be cared for and to be loved destroy a person's life because his feelings were not the same as her?

Lori even told Paul that same lie that she had given Russell about Josh. Paul was furious and at first wanted to go to his house with one of his rifles and kill him. So, when Russell mentioned that they needed someone set Josh up, Paul was the logical choice. From the moment she told Paul that story, he was eager to help her, and it didn't take much to get him to buy-in on the scheme to destroy Josh's career.

She ordered another drink and weighed her options. If Paul was correct, everyone would be fired and just as it had happened to Josh, no one in this city would hire them. Okay, what about relocating? But where was the question? Then there is the possibility of being sued by Josh. Cavanaugh could press criminal charges against them all and there were SEC violations when Paul changed those financial documents.

Reaching into her robe that was draped over the back of her chair, she removed a small piece of paper with an account number on it. Studying the number for several minutes, she concluded that Paul owed her. She had known for months that Paul, Russell and Michael were stealing. She ordered another drink, took a couple of sips and laid back and enjoyed the sun. Thinking to herself, at least if her career in corporate America was over she didn't have to be broke. She transferred a third of the balance to her personal account that she had opened in the Caymans two months earlier.

Checking her balance a few moments later, her account had a balance of $4,500,000. She then made another transfer to a numbered account in Switzerland. She knew Switzerland's banking laws would not allow even the FBI to learn the identity of the owner. With that complete, let them do whatever they wished; she was now financially stable to weather any storm.

What she didn't know, Paul Copeland had only identified her as the victim. He never implicated her in the scheme to get Harrington fired.

44

Kenneth Walton had everything ready when his boss arrived at the Crowne Plaza. Going up on the private elevator, Hardy told Kenneth that before he had left the office, he had fired Russell Smiley, Paul Copeland and Michael Jefferson. Kenneth then said the only one left was Lori Greenspan. Hardy said that they could not touch her even though it was her who started this train wreck. She was in the clear from this mess, but her career with the company was dead because of this. The best thing she could do was resign and go somewhere else. Since she was smart, had multiple degrees, and an excellent job history, she would be able to find something within a couple of weeks. Because she was cute and smart, Hardy felt she probably would get more money in the process.

The first order of business was to make sure that the conference call number to London was correct. Serif wanted to make a brief statement to Josh's lawyers insuring them that the company wanted to be fair and would prosecute all responsible parties to the full extent of the law. He also wanted them to know that these were the acts of several individuals and not Cavanaugh Industry.

Promptly at 3:00 P.M., Nicole Singleton, Robert Howard and Kathleen Sullivan arrived. Hardy informed them that Serif wished to make a statement on the behalf of the corporation; after that they could get down to the business at hand.

"Mr. Hardy, since you called this meeting, what are your expectations of this meeting today? Kathleen Sullivan asked.

"Ms. Sullivan, my intention today is to find out how close we are in settling this matter without tying up the judicial system and to let everyone in this room have the opportunity to focus on other matters beside this one," Hardy replied.

"So, only after four months, twenty-three motions, eleven briefs and countless hours of our company, you are tired of us, Mr. Hardy?" Nicole said smiling broadly.

"Ms. Singleton, your beauty and grace I will always treasure, but the motions, briefs and hearings on this one subject have begun to bore me."

Quoting Judge Hathcock, "So noted." Everyone in the room found that amusing and laughed.

The phone rang and the overseas operator informed Kenneth that his party was on the line and waiting. Kenneth placed the call on speaker and the next voice that they heard was Serif.

"Good afternoon, ladies and gentlemen. I believe it's afternoon there, correct?"

"Correct." someone said.

"My name is Serif Wali, I am the Chief Executive Officer of Cavanaugh Industries and Cavanaugh's Consulting Inc. I first just wanted to first introduce myself and take a brief moment of your time and express the sentiments of the Board of Directors, the shareholders and of the Executive Management Team. First, the Board of Directors, the Shareholders, the Executive Management Team, and all employees of Cavanaugh Industries believe in the Standard of Ethical Behavior Policy of this company and at no time would promote any

Corporate Deceit

actions that did not follow those guidelines.

As the CEO it is my responsibility to address all situations and I wanted to assure you that the entire Executive Management team, the Board of Directors and I take very seriously the accusations of your client concerning the practices and policies of the corporation. I would like to also assure you those accusations about any member of the Executive Staff's involvement in this matter are unfounded and untrue.

Secondly, we do not nor ever have condoned the practice of discrimination on any level. Cavanaugh Industries believes in the Fair Employment Act, and does everything within the corporation's power to exceed those guidelines. Our policies and procedures state clearly how the corporation and those representing the corporation will conduct themselves in the treatment and employment of all individuals.

Cavanaugh Industries vigorously investigates all allegations that the corporation or its representatives are not following those principles of ethical behavior. Every employee, regardless of position within the corporation, is encouraged to report all actions or violations without fear of retaliation. It is his or her responsibility to report such acts in a timely manner to the appropriate representatives of the company. Furthermore, it is also the right of an employee of this corporation to escalate the perceived infraction or infractions to the next level of management if he or she feels that the matter has not been taken seriously or no action was instituted to correct the perceived violation.

I just wanted to take this time to assure you that I am aware of your concerns, and that Cavanaugh Industries will not tolerate or promote any actions that are not in accordance to either the policies of the corporation or violate any law, be it state or federal, concerning the employment rights of an individual.

Thanking you again for allowing me to take this brief moment to express my sincere stance on this matter."

Hardy spoke first: "As Serif stated, the corporation does take the accusations of your client seriously; however, as an officer of the corporation he does have the responsibility to protect the rights of the shareholders as well. If the allegations of your clients are true, then he should be compensated, but that compensation should not be based on emotions or the perceived ability to pay of the defendant. The intent of the law was not to enrich the quality of life of the injured party, but to ratify the wrong and harm of said individual.

Cavanaugh Industries today does not acknowledge any guilt by any member of the Executive Management Team or any employee of the corporation. The intent of this meeting is to find an equitable solution between parties and end the expense, time and effort that has been devoted to this matter."

"Mr. Hardy, as lead counsel, I am appalled to hear from your CEO that Cavanaugh Industries does not share any responsibility of guilt in the actions of those within the employment of your corporation in the wrongful and malicious acts toward my client. That neither you nor the corporation that you represent feels that our client should be awarded for those acts, and the emotional traumas of said acts are not quantifiable in a monetary sense," Nicole responded to Hardy's statement.

"Ms. Singleton, before you take my comments out of context, the corporation does feel that your client is entitled to some type of retribution if his allegations are proven to be true."

"It's just that the corporation does not agree with our client what that monetary value should be. Is that what I am hearing?" Kathleen asked.

"Precisely. The corporation wishes to end this matter because Cavanaugh is a responsible corporate citizen and because the corporation values its conduct in its treatment of its employees."

"Then apparently Cavanaugh, as a good corporate citizen, wishes to end this matter solely because of its negative impact to its image. It does not share or acknowledge the corporation's guilt in allowing those types of behavior to happen?" Nicole interjected.

"You may state it that way. The corporation's goal is to find closure to this. The corporation is willing to step up to the plate and bring all parties together to find the right solution. Does your client or the corporation really want six citizens to decide, based on the evidence that each side presents, painting a picture that may or may not be true? What we have today is the opportunity to not only resolve this matter but also to institute the proper policies and procedures to ensure this situation does not happen to anyone else," said Hardy trying to paint a positive spin on the matter.

"Our client for the last seven months has been subjected to public humiliation, falsely accused of a crime, wrongfully terminated and subjected to emotional stress. Our client believed in the ethical policies of your organization, lived those qualities, supported them; to have that trust violated is a miscarriage of justice in itself."

"Ms. Singleton, the Board of Directors, the Executives and management agree that Mr. Harrington is a victim here, ok, if what he perceives as truth is true. But the question on the table before you is not guilt or innocence; the question is how do we resolve those issues fairly? Kenneth will pass out our proposal of what Cavanaugh believes is a fair settlement to this matter, and we can discuss those items that are not agreeable."

Kenneth handed Nicole, Kathleen and Robert copies of what Hardy had drafted out as a possible settlement offer from Cavanaugh Industries. Hardy had faxed a copy to Serif in London and Serif had challenged him on several points but trusted his judgment.

The offer before Josh's attorneys listed ten items of consideration:

1) Cavanaugh Industries or any subsidiary of Cavanaugh Industries does not acknowledge any guilt or innocence concerning this matter.

2) Cavanaugh is willing to pay all incurred expenses surrounding the investigation for discovery of said matter by the plaintiff up to and not to exceed $100,000 US.

3) Cavanaugh is willing to pay all attorney fees of the plaintiff up to and not to exceed $250,000.00 US

4) Cavanaugh is willing to pay all wages that the plaintiff has been denied because of such action up to and not to exceed $65,000.00 US.

5) Cavanaugh is willing to pay all associated court costs because of this action not to exceed $10,000.00 (this includes depositions).

6) Cavanaugh is willing to pay up to and not to exceed $50,000 US for the restoration of the plaintiff's emotional health by a qualified physician.

7) Cavanaugh is willing to pay punitive damages to the Plaintiff for duress up to and not to exceed $350,000.00 US.

8) Cavanaugh will reinstate the plaintiff in its employment as a Division Manager with an annual compensation base of $250,000.00 US with the right to increase his annual compensation with the inclusion of bonuses based on the performance of his organization.

9) Cavanaugh will reinstate the plaintiff without penalty of tenure, retirement benefits or health coverage during his absence from the corporation.

10) Cavanaugh will compensate the plaintiff's personal 401K-retirement account of lost benefits, penalties and interest during the plaintiff's absence from the corporation not to exceed $25,000.00 US.

Quickly the attorneys for Josh reached for calculators to see the overall monetary proposal before them. As they read the proposal, they recognized that this was nowhere close to the estimation of damages; each wanted to know what Hardy felt was fair and equitable. Taking into account Josh's age and the potential of income from returning to work; Hardy's proposal at best was around $2 million dollars.

"Mr. Hardy, not bad for the first try out of the box. From this list, six of the ten items listed are workable; however, the four items in question that we are apart on are show stoppers. Items 1, 3,6,8,9 and 10 are workable with minor modifications, but items 2, 4, 5, and 7—at this point we would agree as the attorneys for our client— were not given in good faith," Nicole told them.

"Ms. Singleton, I never said that what we were proposing was non-negotiable. And since we do have this suite as long as we wish, we could discuss each point in question at great length."

Hardy, Kenneth and Robert all still wearing their jackets to their suits, stood and placed them on the back of their chairs. Nicole and Kathleen poured water for themselves. After everyone was comfortable, Hardy asked the question, "Which item number will we address first?"

45

Around 7:00 Josh still hadn't heard from Nicole concerning how her meeting had gone that afternoon. He wanted to know the details of what the meeting was really about and what were the next steps. The feeling of having others control his life was driving him crazy, but he knew this was a process that he had to go through. Sitting in his den he wondered how much longer, and after it was over, what would he do? If he wins and the award is somewhere in the neighborhood of what they were asking, then he was financially set. But would money really give him back what he had lost?

Quietly, he sat thinking, trying to define himself and his purpose in life, but he just could not put a definitive answer to who Joshua Harrington was. He thought he knew who he was, but was that truly him? Had he defined himself by what he did for a living and his perceived standing among his peers? Was he just average, nothing special, no real traits or talents that others would admire him for? Was he just like everyone else—trying as hard as they could to carve out a piece of existence while here and enjoy a few of the fringe benefits of their labor?

No, I am more than that. I have the ability to be whatever I choose to be if I am willing to make the sacrifices for those goals. I can be whomever I choose to be if I am making those choices and not letting others define my limitations. Thinking to himself, he decided that when this was over, he would be more than someone with unlimited resources; he would create for others the opportunity to reach their full potential in life. What that would be he didn't know, but he wanted to do something.

He tried to watch TV and take his mind off what may or may not have happened that afternoon. Soon he had fallen asleep, and thought he was dreaming when the phone woke him up.

"Josh, were you asleep?" The voice on the other end of the line asked.

"I guess I had drifted off."

Recognizing Kathleen's voice, he checked his watch. It was 2:30 AM, "Kathleen, is there a problem?" He inquired.

"No, we just wanted to give you an update on today. We are still at the hotel and it appears we might never leave," She told him.

"Hotel! What hotel?"

"We are still at the Crowne Plaza with the Cavanaugh group."

"What? You are telling me that all of you have been there since three, yesterday?"

"Well, that really isn't that unusual when you are trying to put closure to a case. Cavanaugh walked in with ten points for us to consider; only four of those worked, so we are hammering out a deal, we think. So we wanted to call you, but this is the first breaking point that we have had," Kathleen said.

"Where are we, winning, losing what…?" Josh was anxious to know where they were in the negotiations.

"Well, we haven't won. But I can tell you we aren't losing either."

"So do you have an idea of how much longer?"

"Not really; it could end in the next hour or two weeks from now. When you get to this stage, everybody circles his own wagon and fights to the end. Anyway, I got to get back. We will call with more updates later, so go back to sleep. Bye."

After Kathleen got off the phone, he sat there thinking. *How in the world does she expect me to sleep now?* He thought about calling Ronnie, but changed his mind. What could he do? Nothing feasible but going for a drive, so he picked up his keys and left the house.

Driving without a destination, Josh quietly prayed for Nicole and the rest to be successful. He thanked God for this moment because if it had not been for Him in his life, he really had no idea what he would have done. But because of his faith, He knew that what was done to harm him was now being used to benefit his life. The most important thing he knew was that it was not by his hand, but the God that he served had provided him the resources that he needed. When he finished thanking God, he was so overwhelmed with a sense of praise for his Heavenly Father that he had to pull his car to the shoulder of the road. Stopping there for a few minutes, he had his own private PRAISE PARTY, as his pastor Karry Wesley, called them, just acknowledging what an AWESOME GOD he served.

Returning to the Presidential Suite, Kathleen told Nicole that she had talked to Josh and brought him up-to-date.

Room service during their break had brought fresh coffee, a fruit tray and an assortment of sandwiches. Prior to starting up again, everyone surveyed the trays, picking what they wished, and got ready for round seven. As they worked their way around the table there was conversation but not on the case, but about things that still were happening in the world besides this matter. Hardy, being a huge basketball fan, was in deep discussions with Robert explaining how the Mavericks with the addition of their new center, now would challenge Robert's Spurs for the Western Conference title. Kathleen jumped into the middle of their conversation: "Don't count my Rockets out of this race." Both Hardy and Robert laughed at her comment because they thought the Rockets were a one-dimensional team.

When everyone was seated, Robert Howard asked were they ready to continue.

"So, where are we? Kenneth, since you have been our recording secretary please give us an update," Nicole said.

As he told the status of each point, each person placed either a check or X by the particular point.

"Point 1 is acceptable.

Point 2 will be ratified to a sum of $750,000 and will cap at $2 million.

Point 3 will be removed and replaced with wording indicating the plaintiff will be responsible for all attorney fees that were incurred by the plaintiff.

Point 4 will be modified to the proposed rate of pay for the plaintiff outlined in point 8 and that will reflect a maximum amount of $175,000 US.

Point 5 is acceptable

Point 6 is acceptable.

Point 7 is still in question,

Point 8 will be ratified to include stock options to the plaintiff that will have exercisable price for the first five years reduced 40% below the market price per share of said stock. And that stock will be given as preferred stock instead of common stock. It will also contain a provision that for years six through ten, regardless of the employment status of the plaintiff, the plaintiff will be given options equal to and not to exceed the current market value divided by his last year's income with a multiplier of 3.5.

Point 9 is acceptable, and

Point 10 is acceptable."

"From Mr. Walton's recap we are about half way with modifying this to an actual document to start from. Let's begin this round of conversation with Point 7," Nicole suggested.

"Ms. Singleton, are you still suggesting that Harrington is entitled to punitive relief in this? What we have already agreed upon, at this very moment Harrington has a net worth of $15 million dollars. Using that as a basis by the time we finish, Harrington's net worth may increase another three to five million. Don't you think that $20 million is relief? Hardy said.

"Mr. Hardy, because of the gravity of the injustice, not only is he entitled to punitive damages, but those damages should send a message not only to Cavanaugh Industries, but also to your management teams concerning wrongfully terminating someone. Kathleen, do you have copies of the Enforcement Guidance: Compensatory and Punitive Damages Available under § 102 of the

Civil Rights Act of 1991? If you do, could you please give everyone a copy?" Nicole asked. Kathleen handed everyone a copy of the Civil Rights Act of 1991.

   The award should be considered in the context of the respondent's monetary resources. The amount of punitive damages should "sting," but not "destroy" the respondent. Keenan v. City of Philadelphia, 55 FEP Cases at 944-45. The factors are relevant in determining a respondent's financial position. Note, however, that this list is not exclusive and other relevant factors may also be considered:

A) The revenues and liabilities of the business.

B) The fair market value of the respondent's assets.

C) The amount of liquid assets on hand, which includes amounts that they can reasonably borrow.

D) The respondent's propensity to generate income in the future — projected earnings.

E) The resale value of the business. This is particularly useful where the business has a unique spot in the market. For instance, large companies may be seeking to buy the business.

F) Consider whether the respondent is affiliated with a larger entity that could provide additional financial resources to the respondent.

   "Everyone, please note the first criteria of what punitive damages should do. "The award should be considered in the context of the respondent's monetary resources. The amount of punitive damages should "sting," but not "destroy," and now focus your attention to item "F," Nicole directed everyone to read.

   Nicole continued, "By the definition of the Civil Rights Act of 1991, the amount suggested by Cavanaugh does not satisfy those conditions."

   "Everyone, these are only guidelines and not law. What responsible individuals must also take into consideration is the total package that is before them," Hardy responded.

   "Mr. Hardy, but I must strongly disagree, and based on the financial record from the Cavanaugh Industries Annual Report that was published this past April, Cavanaugh's total worth is $9.5 Billion Dollars US. The punitive damage settlement of $350,000 is not a string and does not support the intent of the Civil Rights Act of 1991. Using the guidelines, our suggested punitive award should be no lower than $65 Million Dollars, Mr. Hardy. Don't you agree, since you now have read the law?" Nicole asked.

Hardy was red and angry. No way could he even suggest to the Board of Directors that because of the act of three people that the company was now liable for $80 million dollars because of a wrongful termination suit.

"Ms. Singleton, if this is where you wish to begin, then these conversations are at a point that a reasonable solution can never be reached," Hardy said.

"Mr. Hardy, Mr. Harrington is not trying to put Cavanaugh Industries out of business, but your offer of $350,000 is totally unacceptable. Now that is settled, Mr. Hardy; what is the true offer that Cavanaugh would like to place on the table for consideration?"

46

Arriving home around 6:30 A.M., Nicole and Kathleen each found a recliner in Nicole's den and just sat for a moment. Nicole, wishing that the answer would be no, asked Kathleen did she need some breakfast or anything before they were due in court? Kathleen understood the condition that Nicole was in and declined the offer. Both just sat and tried to regain their strength to shower and be prepared for what was going to be a very long day.

Nicole reflected that she hadn't been up that many hours straight since she was preparing for the Bar exam and that had been seven years ago. Kathleen also was trying to remember the last time she too had gone that many hours without sleep. Oh, last month when she was in Boston. Different reason so she just smiled and made a note she should give him a call.

Hardy, even though he may have been tired, had several calls that he had to make. First, he had to call Serif and give him an update. Second, he called his administrative assistant and informed her that there were some items by his desk that she needed to handle first thing that morning and that she would be receiving several faxes from Howard & Howard.

Arriving at the courthouse shortly before 9:00 that Monday, Josh was met at the elevators by Robert Howard. Robert informed him that before going into court, they wanted to speak with him privately. Nicole and Kathleen had found a conference room on the floor below and called Robert with the location. Josh and Robert took the emergency stairwell to the floor below and found Nicole and Kathleen looking at the view of the city from the 32nd floor of the Federal Building. Hearing Josh and Robert enter, the ladies took their seats at the conference table.

"Josh, first let me explain something here and I want you to be very clear on this, ok? We do have a proposal from Cavanaugh; however, no matter what we think it is this is your decision. You understand? It is yours to say yeah or nay to—no one else." Nicole told him.

"So what is their offer?" Josh asked.

"The total offer is broken into points," Robert informed him.

"Okay, what are the points?" Josh asked.

Handing him a copy of what Robert had typed that morning, Nicole began going over each point:

1) Cavanaugh Industries or any subsidiaries of Cavanaugh Industries do not acknowledge any guilt or innocence concerning this matter.

2) Cavanaugh is willing to pay all incurred expenses surrounding the investigation for discovery of said matter by the plaintiff up to and not to exceed $2,200,000.00 US.

3) Cavanaugh is willing to pay all attorney fees of the plaintiff up to and not to exceed $1,250,000.00 US.

4) Cavanaugh is willing to pay all wages that the plaintiff has been denied because of such action up to and not to exceed $165,000.00 US.

5) Cavanaugh is willing to pay all associated court costs because of this action not to exceed $50,000.00 (this includes depositions).

6) Cavanaugh is willing to pay up to and not to exceed $50,000 US for the restoration of the plaintiff's emotional health by a qualified physician, and will pay the plaintiff directly for such hardship a sum of $150,000.00 US.

7) Cavanaugh is willing to pay punitive damages to the Plaintiff for duress in the sum of $3,500,000.00 US.

8) Cavanaugh will reinstate the plaintiff in its employment as a Division Manager with an annual compensation base of $250,000.00 US, with the right to increase his annual compensation with the inclusion of bonuses based on the performance of his organization.

9) Cavanaugh will reinstate the plaintiff without penalty of tenure, retirement benefits or health coverage during his absence from the corporation.

10) Cavanaugh will compensate the plaintiff's personal 401K-retirement account of lost benefits, penalties and interest during the plaintiff's termination from the corporation up to and not to exceed $125,000.00 US.

11) Cavanaugh will dismiss all criminal charges against the plaintiff and will pay the plaintiff restitution of $2,500,000 US.

12) Cavanaugh will submit a motion to the Collin County District Attorney's Office to have all police and criminal records of the plaintiff expunged.

13) Cavanaugh Industries, its subsidiaries or agencies representing the corporation renounces all rights to appeal this agreement or sustenance agreements concerning this matter.

14) This agreement can be challenged and become void if either the plaintiff or the respondent in this matter divulge the contents and conditions of said order. This non-disclosure extends its boundaries to those who represent either the plaintiff or the respondent in said matter.

The total award based on one year of employment alone is $19,850,000 and if you decide to go back and work, the total package exceeds $23,500,000 and some change."

Josh was breathless; not only had he won, but he was a multi-millionaire. Did he hear her right? The total award exceeded $19,850,000? He was overwhelmed and began to cry tears of joy and thanksgiving. Here he was six months earlier unemployed, jailed for a crime that he did not commit, possibly denied his unemployment benefits, and saw no future at hand. Not only had he won an uphill battle but also his faith in both God and the U. S. legal system had been restored. He had multiple questions for Nicole, Kathleen and Robert, but first things first:

"There is one thing I don't agree with, so can we change it?" Josh asked.

"Josh, we can change the whole thing if that is what you want. This is a combination of both sides working around the clock to hammer this out, so think carefully of what you want to change," Nicole asked of him.

"I don't think I want to work for them, so that job that they are offering is not being given on my merit, but to keep money in their pockets."

"You know that could affect the stock options as well?" Kathleen pointed out.

"Yeah, I know that. What is the impact of me turning them down on those two issues? Josh wanted to know.

Robert as usual ran the numbers quickly and replied, "Somewhere between 1.2 and 2 million, give or take a couple of hundred grand."

"Take those points out and they got a deal," Josh told them.

Thinking for another moment, Josh had another question. "When am I truly going to start to see some of this?"

"In about a month is my best estimate," Nicole stated.

"Okay, take those two things out, and you can tell them we have a deal," Josh told his attorneys.

They all took the stairs to the 33rd floor. Standing in the hallway was Kenneth Walton. Robert walked over to him, explaining the changes needed and rejoined the group. Kenneth quickly dialed Hardy on his cell and gave him an update on what must have happened when they went over the terms with Josh. Kenneth made another call to the clerk in the 256th to schedule an in-chamber meeting with Judge Hathcock. Calling Robert on his cell, he informed him that they would meet in the judge's chamber in about fifteen minutes.

Josh called Veronica and told her that this whole matter might be over today. Of course, she wanted details, but he explained he had to go into the judge's chamber so he would have to get back to her later. Calling Keith, he told him in about a month they would be going deep sea fishing, instead of fishing at the lake close to Keith's house. Keith asked what had happen? Josh explained that he would have to tell him later too, because everything was moving faster than he could handled at the moment. Promising to call his friend later, Josh ended their conversation.

Entering Judge Hathcock's chambers, the Judge asked if they needed a court reporter present. Nicole acknowledged that they would, and Judge Hathcock sent for her court reporter. While they were waiting for the reporter, Judge Hathcock put on her robe and when the reporter arrived and was set up, Judge Hathcock began:

"This is in the matter of case number 7820-781784-90782 docket number 1902-2005-1122 in the civil matter of Joshua Alexander Harrington v. Cavanaugh Industries and its subsidiary Cavanaugh's Consulting Inc. What matter are the attorneys for the plaintiff and the respondents bringing before the court this morning?"

"If it pleases the court, Your Honor, the plaintiff and the respondents in this matter have reached an agreement that both parties wish to present to the court for consideration." Timothy Hardy stated.

"Is Mr. Harrington aware that he is fully within his rights to refuse such agreement, and his attorneys are duly bond to represent him to full extent of their capacities if he chooses to refuse such agreement?" Judge Hathcock asked.

"Your Honor, our client has been informed of his rights and understands that he has the right of refusal. Our client has gone over the agreement and those areas in question that he wishes to ratify are noted and those modifications will be reflected in the final order that will be presented to the court," Nicole informed Judge Hathcock.

"So noted."

Checking her calendar, "I would like to have the final agreement of this matter ready for my signature on on September 12th. Does that pose a problem to the attorneys?" Judge Hathcock asked.

"No, Your Honor," Hardy answered.

"So ordered. Okay, then, let's send this jury home."

Walking out of the Judge's chamber, Josh asked what was next. Kathleen explained that someone from their side and Hardy's office would prepare the final draft of the agreement; then Nicole would have him sign it similar to the original complaint that he had done, and then they would wait for a check. Oh, there was one other matter; he should be receiving in the mail in about a week a bill for their services.

"Don't faint when Cavanaugh sends their check to Nicole's office, we will take ours off the top," Kathleen informed him laughing.

Josh stopped for a moment in the hall sat on one of the benches by another courtroom. Court was already in session, so the hallway was empty; he just sat there and offered a prayer to God for supplying him all of his needs.

Calling Veronica back, "Veronica how is your day, and what does your afternoon look like?" He asked.

"Light! Would you believe it? And what about yours?" she asked.

"Mine too. I will pick you up in about an hour."

"In an hour?"

"Yes, and I will tell you about my day then."

About six weeks later, Josh was standing in Nicole's office waiting for her to finish with another client. Finally, her office door opened and after telling her other client "good-bye" and wishing them well, she invited him into her office.

"Good morning, Mr. Harrington, and how are you today?" Nicole asked.

"Nicole, I am fine. Don't tell me you have more documents for me to sign." He stated.

"Actually, Josh, I do. Sorry, but you know how lawyers are; we want to make sure everything is documented. So this should be the last one for a while, I promise."

Over the last several weeks he had gone to Nicole's office signing each point and often multiple copies. So one more call from her concerning his signature wasn't unusual, but this time she didn't mention what this meeting was for. Well, since he always gives her the same answer maybe she felt she didn't have to explain.

"Josh, there are two forms to sign today and this really should take care of everything for a while. The first is a release form from Cavanaugh stating that you received the second document, ok?" Nicole asked.

He was about to begin writing his name, but he glanced at the top of the form to see what he was signing and it read **CHECK RELEASE**. His eyes lit up; he quickly signed and handed the form to Nicole.

"Did you see the game last night on ESPN. Boy those Rams are……."

Josh cuts her off in mid-sentence

"Nicole, don't play with me today. I don't care about the Rams, the Dolphins, or the NFL, NBA, or the WNBA; let me see that other document that you said I had to sign."

"Oh. That! Where did I put it?"

"Nicole, I am not playing with you!"

"Here! You are not any fun today, Mr. Harrington," she said handing him a check. The check was paid to the order to Joshua Harrington in the sum of $16,678,879.49. He just looked at it for a moment. "Is this it?"

"No, they will send another check in about ninety days directly to you. That check will be for $1.2 Million; then for the next five years you will have to save and use coupons because those checks probably won't be no more than $200,000."

"Now, with this, I've got to write you guys a check for your bill. Right?" He asked. The bill from Nicole and her team was just shy of $1,650,000, which included the services of auditors, and other resources for his case.

"No, Josh, our fees were deducted before they cut your check, and our check has already been deposited. That is all yours. Congratulations!"

"Thanks! I really appreciate all that you and your team has done for me."

"Not bad for one woman office and a receptionist named Taquitha, huh?"

"I will never again judge a book by its cover---that I promise."

That afternoon Josh began thinking about the promise that he was going to do something to impact the lives of others. First he needed to make one more stop and get directions of what that was. So, he found the nearest church, walked down to the front pew, sat and asked.

"Lord, what's next? I'm waiting on You to direct the way."

Author's Notes

Special thanks go to the following individuals:

Editing - Nadine Allison McDaniels & Metra Carter

Proof Reading - Lillie Carter
　　　　　　　　　Tomeji Harris
　　　　　　　　　Martha F. Lewis
　　　　　　　　　Sharon Williams
　　　　　　　　　Micky Washington

Printing - Christine Tower (Maple-Vail Books)

Encouragement - Emma Mae (Johnson) Abney
　　　　　　　　　　Mildred Washington
　　　　　　　　　　Jessie Newton
　　　　　　　　　　Denise T. Powell
　　　　　　　　　　Cecelia Robinson
　　　　　　　　　　Torian Gooden Colon